GIN AND PANIC

Also by Maia Chance

GIN AND PANIC

Maia Chance

MINOTAUR BOOKS
New York

GIN AND PANIC. Copyright © 2017 by Maia Chance. All rights reserved. Printed in the United States of America. For information, address St. Martin's Press, 175 Fifth Avenue, New York, N.Y. 10010

www.minotaurbooks.com

The Library of Congress Cataloging-in-Publication Data is available upon request.

ISBN 978-1-250-10905-7 (hardcover)
ISBN 978-1-250-10906-4 (ebook)

Our books may be purchased in bulk for promotional, educational, or business use. Please contact your local bookseller or the Macmillan Corporate and Premium Sales Department at 1-800-221-7945, extension 5442, or by email at MacmillanSpecialMarkets@macmillan.com.

First Edition: October 2017

10 9 8 7 6 5 4 3 2 1

For my father

"I said that it was not necessary to be the foxhound, the bloodhound, the tracking dog, running to and fro upon the scent. But I will admit that for the chase a dog *is* necessary. A retriever, my friend. A good retriever."

—HERCULE POIROT IN
AGATHA CHRISTIE'S *THE CLOCKS*

GIN AND PANIC

1

November 7, 1923

I cannot believe that I, Lola Woodby, am saying this, but there is only so much ornamental ham, puff pastry, and pink fondant icing one can stomach. At least in any given day.

I leaned in for the last pillowy bite of cherry almond cake. "Mm," I said. "No." I waved for the waiter. "This one is too sweet."

"Too sweet?" Berta Lundgren said in her stern Swedish accent. She patted her lips with a napkin. "Too crumbly, I thought."

"Wasn't the first one too crumbly? And the fifth one was too lemony, I recall that much."

"We really should be taking notes—and just look at the time! We are due at the Bombay Room at four o'clock, and the subway has been terribly overcrowded and behind schedule as of late. No one wishes to walk about in this horrible cold rain. Oh, how I detest November."

"It's not so bad."

"You are cocooned in romance at the moment, Mrs. Woodby," Berta said. "You are as impervious as a duck. Trust me when I say that it is dismal outside."

Berta was small and round, with a plaited silver bun, rosy jowls, and keen, ice-blue eyes. In my former life as a flush Society Matron, she had been my cook. And oh, could she cook. Her scrummy food was to blame for my womanly curves, which I must squeeze with great ingenuity into these tube-shaped flapper fashions. At any rate, when my philandering husband kicked the bucket several months earlier and left me penniless, Berta and I went into the gumshoe trade together. And we were making a go of it . . . more or less.

The waiter appeared beside our table. Whip-thin and waistcoated, he was almost camouflaged in Delguzzo's elegant, famous, and (most important to my mother) shockingly expensive confectionery-caterer establishment in Lower Manhattan.

He eyed Cedric, the fluffy Pomeranian on my lap, with disfavor. "Yes, mesdames?"

"Do not suppose for a moment, young man, that we do not detect your rolling eyes," Berta said. "After all, we are detectives."

The waiter lifted an eyebrow. "Detectives? *Lady* detectives, who—accompanied by a rotund toy dog—spend each afternoon in the tearoom of Delguzzo's sampling every pastry, cake, cruller, chocolate truffle, and sweet biscuit under the roof? What an amusing tale."

There. You see? I was so very in love, not even this snooty human wishbone could pop my balloon. "No one served *me* chocolate truffles," I said mildly.

"Pray tell me, mesdames, what is it that you are detecting? Are you perhaps attempting to discover how much pastry cream one may consume without removing one's girdle?"

"We are researching wedding foods." I petted Cedric's ears. "Wouldn't you like Delguzzo's to cater the society wedding of the year?"

"I do not care much one way or the other. Now, what was it that you desired to ingest next? Pistachio brittle? Bluepoint oysters on the half shell? An entire honey-glazed goose?"

"We'd like the check, please," I said.

The waiter floated away.

"*Snot*," I added under my breath.

"Mrs. Woodby, I must inform you that I cannot continue with this endeavor for much longer," Berta said. "I feel as though I am going to burst, and what is more, these confectionery-caterers make unwholesome food. One must eat vegetables with one's butter."

In July, my mother had disowned me on the grounds that my going into the gumshoe trade was an embarrassment as well as a threat to our family's social standing. This would have been true had my father's immense Wall Street fortune not padded them from disgrace, and if my family were not amply capable of embarrassing themselves.

Three weeks ago, however, Mother had telephoned me out of the blue to say that Rebecca Van Dweck was no longer slated to be my sister Lillian's maid of honor, as she had eloped with her parents' chauffeur. "You shall be given this one opportunity to redeem yourself," Mother had fluted imperiously over the telephone lines. "Lillian and I are leaving for Paris soon—I expect you did not know that Worth's is making her wedding gown and trousseau?— and in our absence, you may address and mail all the wedding invitations—"

"I don't know if I'm cut out for—"

"—and select a caterer from the list I have compiled. You may save the selection of the florist for a later date."

"Wait—do you mean you wish me to choose the wedding cake?"

"Yes, but do not overindulge, Lola. You inherited that ankle concern from your father's side of the family."

Actually, I had my mother's ankles—or lack thereof. If we don't wear shoes with a three-inch-minimum heel, our ankles vanish like the dodo. To balance things out, I'd also inherited my mother's large blue eyes, full mouth, and dark, shiny hair. But while Mother coiffed, garbed, and bejeweled herself as a Society Battle-axe, my eyes were enhanced with kohl, my lips were painted with vampish Guerlain, and my hair was cut into a chic Dutch bob. And I could only afford to wear last year's fashions.

I'd agreed to be the matron of honor. A large box of addressed invitations languished, unmailed, on the floor beneath my telephone. I meant to post them, honest, but I kept forgetting. I *would* do it, however. For even if one's family is self-centered, spoiled, and prone to squawking, one cannot, sadly, return it to the store for a refund. In a way, I missed the rotters. I also adore cake.

And—I snapped back to the present—so did Cedric.

"No," I said, whisking my plate away from Cedric's stubby snout. Too late. Cake crumbs trembled on his whiskers. "Naughty, naughty peanut."

He licked his chops.

Berta was working herself up. "Simply choose a caterer for your sister's wedding and be done with it! We have eaten our way through every caterer-confectioner on your mother's list, and we have work to do—"

"Think of the money we've saved by dining in restaurants all the time at my parents' expense."

"—genuine work, for our clients. For instance, we still have not retrieved the Dove White Launderette's stolen linen carts—"

"Small fry, Berta."

"What do you expect?"

She had a point. Our business cards read,

THE DISCREET RETRIEVAL AGENCY
No job too trivial.

"We really must accept whatever job it is that Lord Sudley intends to offer us, Mrs. Woodby. When I spoke to him on the telephone this morning, he conveyed that he would pay us hand-somely."

"Dandy. Here's our check."

At a quarter past four o'clock, Berta, Cedric, and I entered the ma-hogany hush of the Bombay Room. The Bombay Room had once been a swanky place to sozzle a gin and tonic or a sidecar, but, alas, the Eighteenth Amendment had spoiled the fun and now people drank only tea, coffee, and seltzer water there.

The place was warm, crowded, and hazed with cigar smoke and costly perfumes.

"That must be Lord Sudley," Berta whispered, collapsing her um-brella. "See the large handsome fellow behind those potted palms? He is not married, according to the society column in *Tête-à-Tête* magazine. I did a bit of research at the newsstand after he telephoned this morning."

I nodded, checking my wristwatch for the hundred-and-first time in fifteen minutes.

Berta started toward Lord Sudley, realized I wasn't coming, and stopped. "Why are you dawdling, Mrs. Woodby?"

"I asked Ralph to meet me here at four thirty, and we're running late."

"Mr. Oliver will surely wait for you."

"I know. I feel ill."

Berta looked at me sharply. "What is the matter?"

"Matter? Nothing. Does my makeup look all right?"

"Yes, although when we were on the subway, I believe a small moth fluttered out of your coat."

"What? This is my favorite!" I shook my fur-collared coat. Rain-drops splattered but no moths emerged. Thank goodness. I couldn't have insects swarming at the Magical Moment. The thing was, I was

78 percent certain that my PI colleague, gentleman caller, and maddening distraction, Ralph Oliver, intended to pop the question. On the telephone, he'd said he wished to give me something, and that it was really important. What else could it be but an engagement ring? Ralph couldn't afford more than a chip of a diamond, of course, but I was so in love with him, I'd be happy with a ring from a Cracker Jack box.

"If there is nothing the matter," Berta said, "then we should not keep Lord Sudley waiting."

I hurried after Berta. We introduced ourselves to Lord Sudley and ordered seltzer waters. As soon as the waiter had delivered them, Lord Sudley asked, "Do you feel up to retrieving a rhinoceros head?" He had a resonant voice and a cultured British accent. His suit was Savile Row. That diamond tiepin was the real McCoy.

"Rhinoceros?" I coughed on seltzer. "Living or dead?"

"Stuffed, and mounted on a wall, most likely."

"Good," I said. "I don't handle guns, and certainly not safari rifles."

Berta looked smug. When push came to shove, she could wield her Colt .25 like Annie Oakley on five cups of coffee. "All we shall require is a step stool and a screwdriver," she said. "And a very large hatbox for transport."

"There is to be a pheasant-hunting party at the house where the rhinoceros trophy is currently located. I am an invited guest." Lord Sudley turned to me. "I would like to propose that you, Mrs. Woodby, attend the party under the guise of being my friend. We'll say you're an avid hunter."

"That might be a bit of a stretch," I said.

"And me?" Berta demanded. "We work as a team, you do realize."

"Ah. I see. What about this: You could pretend to be Mrs. Woodby's aunt, another avid hunter. Then you will detach the rhinoceros trophy from the wall under cover of darkness and deliver it to the boot of my motorcar. Simplicity itself."

"Hold on a tick," I said. "If it's so simple, why don't you do it yourself?"

Lord Sudley adjusted a gold cuff link. "It is a private matter."

"We require all the facts," Berta said. "We have more than once become embroiled in unpleasantness that would have been avoidable had we been given all the facts from the start."

I leaned forward, elbow on the table. "Just last month we ran into a fiasco while retrieving an emerald necklace from someone called Mademoiselle Gigi. It all would've gone much more smoothly had our client mentioned that Gigi was a Siamese cat."

"Mrs. Woodby is a fine detective," Berta said to Lord Sudley confidingly, "but from time to time she indulges in straying from the main point."

Lord Sudley smiled at me, and for the first time I noticed he was . . . rather attractive. Astonishingly fit for a man of perhaps fifty years. Strapping, really. Weathered, silver at the temples, with one of those craggy foreheads and prominent aristocratic noses that made phrases like Mr. Rochester and stormy moors and ancestral castle pop into one's head.

Not, mind you, that I cared, since I was desperately in love with someone else. This was merely a detective's detached observation of facts.

Lord Sudley's eyes twinkled. "I'm certain that when Mrs. Woodby strays from the main point, she leads one down enchanting paths and byways."

Berta made a ladylike snort.

"Is Mr. Woodby in the detective trade as well?" Lord Sudley asked casually.

"He popped off." My elbow slipped off the table. I righted myself. "I mean to say, I'm a widow."

Berta kicked me under the table.

Honestly, I felt like kicking myself. The Man of My Dreams and

Love of My Life was going to propose marriage to me in approximately—I checked my wristwatch—five minutes. Other fellows were as meaningless to me as crackers under the sofa cushions.

"Shall we return to the matter at hand?" Berta said.

Lord Sudley leaned back in his leather club chair and steepled his hands. "You won't breathe a word about this?"

"We call ourselves the Discreet Retrieval Agency for a reason," I said.

"Very well. The fact of the matter is, Rudyard Montgomery is my close chum, but he has in his possession a rhinoceros trophy that, in fact, belongs to me."

I pulled my notebook and pencil from my handbag and flicked to a fresh page. "Current location?"

"Montgomery Hall in Carvington, Connecticut. It's his family home. Lovely seaside estate. Splendid pheasant hunting and fishing, if you enjoy that sort of thing."

Not unless it's hunting for bargain-priced shoes or fishing for compliments. "Did Mr. Montgomery steal the trophy from you?" I asked.

"Not precisely. It is more that he stole the credit for having felled the beast in the first place. We were on safari together in June— Kenya, you know—and we both aimed for the same rhinoceros in the bush. We both fired. Rudy's shot went wild—he flinched just before he pulled the trigger—and my shot killed the beast. Rudy took credit. Oh, we quarreled, but I didn't wish to spoil the safari, so I dropped the issue and allowed him to take it back with him to America. However, something has arisen, and now I most urgently require the trophy. Naturally, I cannot be caught taking it. No one may know that I have it—not the servants, not Rudy's lady friend, no one. And if Rudy found out, why, it would destroy our friendship. We go on a hunting trip together twice a year, you know, and now more than ever Rudy and I must stick together because our dear old chum from the Scion Club, Winslow Bradford, who always accompanied us, he's up and kicked the bucket. Frightfully sad. Bad ticker. At any rate, my rhinoceros trophy will be missing a bit of its left ear—that's where Rudy's bullet whizzed past. The lethal shot that I fired went in, as is proper, behind its shoulder."

"Why do you require the trophy?" I asked.

"Because it is mine. Shall we discuss your fee?" Lord Sudley pulled a small leather-bound book and a gold pen from his breast pocket and jotted a figure. He showed it to us.

Berta stopped breathing.

The sum was hefty. Hefty enough to cover our rent for several months. Hefty enough to keep Berta in new chintz dresses and top-shelf baking ingredients and me in department store lipsticks and Belgian chocolates for several months, too.

"When do we begin?" Berta asked.

"Well, tomorrow, actually—"

"*Tomorrow?*" I said. "Oh. No. No, I can't take the case. Tomorrow is . . . off-limits." I planned to be with Ralph, of course, wallowing in soon-to-be-married bliss.

"Off-limits?" Lord Sudley said.

"Prior engagement."

Berta glared. Under the table, I swiveled my shins out of the reach of her kicks.

My eyes drifted past Lord Sudley. Ralph Oliver had just strolled into the Bombay Room. How is it that love makes a person look like they're always lit up by a Broadway spotlight? How did Ralph, with his shabby trench coat, tipped-down fedora, and—let's face it— empty wallet, move with such captivating self-assurance through all those tables of New York fat cats with their cigars? Every last lady in the Bombay Room was watching Ralph from over teacups or under eyelashes. And, gee whiz, who could blame them?

Ralph's bright gray eyes hit me, and a corner of his mouth twitched up. He shrugged off his trench coat and took a seat at an empty table in the corner. When he removed his hat to reveal brilliantined ginger hair and a weathered forehead marred by a shrapnel scar, I'm positive I heard a lady sigh.

"I shall perform the heist," Berta said to Lord Sudley. "Single-handedly. Mrs. Woodby and I often work separately on cases."

"It was simply peachy meeting you, Lord Sudley, and I'm terribly sorry I won't be able to assist you with this case," I said. "Berta, I'll see you back at the apart—back at the office." Better if he didn't know we worked out of a poky apartment that always smelled of Dorin of Paris face powder and cookies.

I stuffed my notebook and pencil in my handbag, scooped up Cedric, and zigzagged through the tables to Ralph.

2

"Hi," I said to Ralph breathlessly. "Hello." I sat.

"Hey there, kid." I happened to notice he had some kind of box inside his jacket—I could just make out the shape. A ring box. It had to be. "Aren't you a sight for sore eyes. How's the pooch?"

Cedric twisted and squiggled out of my arms and scampered over to Ralph, who bent to give his ears a scratch.

Ralph straightened and his eyes grew serious. "Like I said on the telephone, there's something I want to give you. Something important. I'm not sure how it's going to go over, and—" He scanned the room. "—and I'm not sure this is the best place to give it to you, but I'm going to anyway because, well, it's important to me and it just can't wait any longer. Okay?"

I could only nod. I slid my left hand onto the tabletop so it would be ready.

Ralph pulled out the box from his jacket and set it on the table.

"Goodness, that's a big box," I said with a nervous giggle.

Ralph slid it over. "Go on. Open it."

I took a big breath and lifted the box's hinged lid. I stared blankly down. "A gun?" I looked at Ralph. "You're giving me a *gun?*"

"I thought you would've already guessed what it was."

"A GUN?" The gents at the next table looked over. I snapped the box shut and shoved it back to Ralph. "There isn't room for it in my handbag."

"Tuck it in your garter like all the other ladies do."

"I don't need it."

"It's for your own safety. Do you know how much sleep I've lost since I met you, knowing you're out on cases without any protection?"

"I have Berta, and she has a gun."

"You're not always with Berta."

"I manage." I snatched up Cedric and plunked him on my lap, even though he clearly would have preferred to grovel at Ralph's feet. My eyeballs grew hot.

"Hold it." Ralph scratched his eyebrow. "Why are you—? Are you going to cry?"

"No."

"Sure looks like it."

"I hate the sight of guns."

"Don't try to fool me, kid. Were you—? Were you expecting something else in that box?"

"No."

"Yeah. Was it—?" He tipped his head. "Was it a piece of jewelry?"

"Don't be absurd."

"A ring?"

"No!"

Ralph looked around uneasily. "Say, why don't we go for a walk?"

"It's raining." Danged Prohibition! At that moment, I would've traded my soul for a highball. I summoned the waiter and he came over. "Cake, please," I said to him.

"What kind, madam?"

"The first slice you clap eyes on."

Once the waiter had left, Ralph leaned over the table and spoke softly. "I'm crazy about you, Lola, and you know it, but we can't . . . we can't get *married.*"

"Married? Us? Hah!" Why wasn't the waiter sprinting to the kitchen?

"Because us, married? That's crazy talk. Me with my work and you with yours? It would never work."

"Then what are we doing?"

Ralph looked confused. "Having fun. Dancing. Drinking." The corners of his eyes crinkled. "Other stuff."

"I thought we were headed somewhere."

"Can't we just sit back and enjoy the ride?"

"Indefinitely?"

"Nothing lasts forever."

"This isn't how it's done."

Ralph leaned back in his chair and folded his arms. "I think there's been some kind of misunderstanding," he said.

And just like that, Ralph was no longer mine. Pain clumped in my chest. "I need someone to take care of me," I blurted. Wait. Where had that come from?

"No, you don't. You can take care of yourself."

"Ralph Oliver, that is the—the most horrid thing anyone has ever said to me!"

"Really? Then you've been living pretty soft. Say, is that some kind of bug crawling around in your fur thingamajig?"

I slapped my collar. A moth flew out. "I never want to see you again, Mr. Oliver. You misled me and I—I hate you."

Ralph's jaw flexed. He shoved the gun box back across the table to me and stood. "Listen, there are a couple bullets in the bottom of the box—that's how thoughtful I am. If you care to send me a thank-you note, well, you know my address." He stalked out of the Bombay Room. I watched him go. So did all the other ladies in the room.

I was sitting there fluttering back tears and robotically petting Cedric when Berta arrived at my table. "Lord Sudley has gone," she said, sitting. "The advance check and the directions to Mr. Montgomery's house are in my handbag." She cleared her throat. "I happened to notice Mr. Oliver leaving in a huff."

"I don't wish to discuss it."

The waiter slid a slab of chocolate layer cake in front of me and arranged a fork and napkin beside it. I forked a hunk of cake into my mouth. Cedric tipped his head to watch.

"Regarding the job," Berta said, "I could easily telephone Lord Sudley and tell him you will be able to accompany me after all."

"You mean to rob the place?"

"Mrs. Woodby, we have gone over this matter a dozen times at least. When one runs a *retrieval* agency, one must at times venture into somewhat gray moral realms."

Alas, Berta was correct. Although we endeavored to take cases only from the rightful owners of whatever it was we were retrieving, we hadn't always gotten it right.

"Yes, okay." I wagged my fork. "Fine." Ralph was gone, so if I didn't have my work, that meant I had . . . zip. "We're going to Connecticut to retrieve that bally rhino's head. It's not as though I have anything better to do."

The next day—an insulting day of marble skies and intermittent splats of rain—Berta and I motored up the Connecticut coast to Carvington. We made excellent time; silently fuming about rakish ex-fellows adds ten pounds to one's gas pedal foot.

Again and again, I thought of the words that had tumbled from my lips yesterday. *I need someone to take care of me.* Why had I said that? I was thirty-one years old. I had a job (of sorts), I'd figured out how to boil an egg and how to buy postage stamps and pay the electric bill, and anyway, lots of women didn't have husbands for one reason or another. Clearly, I could fend for myself so long as, say, Al Capone was out of the picture.

Yet every time I thought about Ralph, I ran up against this brick wall: *If he truly loved me, he'd want to marry me.*

The revolting thing was, that was something my mother would say. Which simply did not bear analysis. So instead of analyzing, I went right on fuming.

Carvington was a picture-postcard Yankee seacoast town of a few thousand inhabitants. EST. 1665, a weather-beaten sign apprised us as we rolled in. The road meandered around a brown-grassed salt marsh, past the ivied brick walls of Carvington College, and through a scattering of boxy colonial houses.

Church Street was two blocks of clapboard and shingled buildings. Flintock's Groceries, the Red Rooster Café, the Old Whaler's Inn, Sewant River Bank, Wolcott Tobacco & Stationery, and Carvington Congregational Church faced a village green. Behind Church Street, a few cobbled streets sloped down to a stone seawall. In the cold afternoon light, the ocean was matte gray and the horizon was a smudge rather than a line.

After a bracing greasy lunch at the Red Rooster Café, Berta and I motored the final mile to the open gates of Montgomery Hall. We traversed a gravel drive and acres of rolling parkland. The trees opened out onto formal lawns and hedges, and then the house came into view. It sprawled on a rise overlooking the ocean, a rambling red stone Gothic mansion with arches on the porch, a slate roof, pointy stained glass windows, and one crenellated battlement.

I parked in the driveway behind several swanky motorcars and switched off the engine of my sporty Duesenberg Model A. The

Duesy used to be swanky, too, but in my reduced circumstances, its whitewall tires had gotten grimy and the spare tire on the back resembled a pretzel.

"Good heavens, a castle in Connecticut?" Berta said. "Do they expect marauders with cannons?"

"I'd bet they're more worried about the damp salt air," I said. "Piles like this cost a fortune to keep up."

No one greeted us in the drive, so Berta and I gathered up our luggage. The clasps of my hefty suitcase strained; not only had I packed clothes and toiletries for three days, but I'd also brought a hunt-themed costume for the fancy dress party Lord Sudley had warned us about. How Berta had packed all she required in one small suitcase was anyone's guess.

I had left that dratted gun Ralph gave me at home.

With Cedric sniffing around behind us, we went to the church-like oak door and buzzed the bell. Presently, a rather short, very round woman in a black dress and an iron gray bun cracked the door. The housekeeper, I supposed. She didn't seem to notice me, but instead scowled at Berta, who was the exact same height as she. In fact, Berta and the woman possessed nearly identical proportions. Face-to-face like that, they made me think of a squat set of salt and pepper shakers.

"Yes?" the housekeeper said in a humorless contralto.

"Hello," I said. "We are friends of Lord Sudley's—we're here for the hunting party. I believe we're expected."

"You're late." The housekeeper turned.

I scooped up Cedric. We followed the housekeeper inside.

"Most everyone has already gone out shooting," the housekeeper said, "so you'll just have to wait until they return." We left our suitcases, coats, and hats in the entry hall, and the housekeeper led us through dim, wood-paneled corridors to a drawing room. "Wait here. The manservant will take your luggage up later." She left us.

Berta and I went into the drawing room. With its vaulted ceiling, leaded windows, and heavy dark beams, the style was that of a rustic European hunting lodge. It was so large, binoculars might've come in handy. The walls bristled with antlers, and you could've parked a Rolls-Royce in the stone fireplace.

I didn't notice anyone else in the room. However, I did see herds of taxidermied animal heads mounted to the walls. Tiger, bear, elephant, several deer-ish things, a kangaroo, and about, oh, six or seven rhinoceros heads.

"Oh, dear," Berta murmured, eyeing the rhinoceroses. "I wonder if Lord Sudley knows about all of those?"

I spied a drinks cabinet, so I set Cedric loose and made a beeline over. A restorative tipple was what I required before inspecting rhino ears for bullet nicks.

"Drink?" I called to Berta.

"I'd adore a G and T," someone—not Berta—said.

And someone else said, "Dear me, no, I never drink. Well, perhaps you could bring me a small portion of mineral water."

I spun around. Berta had seated herself in a grouping of high-backed chairs before the fire with two other people: a young man and a middle-aged woman.

Berta said, "And I will have brandy, please. Your driving, Mrs. Woodby, has quite frazzled my nerves."

We did a quick round of introductions. Berta and I used our real names for the sake of simplicity. Fingers crossed that no one had heard of us. We claimed that Berta was my aunt, and suggested that I was Lord Sudley's newest lady friend.

The middle-aged lady introduced herself as Isobel Bradford. "You know," she said with a flare of the nostrils, "Winslow Bradford's widow."

"Oh yes," I said. "I believe Lord Sudley mentioned Mr. Bradford. One of the trio of safari-goers?"

"That's correct. Dear Winslow adored the hunt, and since he has passed on into the next world, I am attending the party in his stead. It is what he would have wished." She adjusted her half-glasses, which had long gold chains drooping from either side. In fact, quite a lot of Isobel could be described as droopy: her mouth, eye bags, and hair-style; her cardigan, ruffled blouse, and tweed skirt, which were clearly of the best quality but not designed to flatter.

The young man, lounging sideways on a chair with his legs draped over the armrest, said his name was Glenn Monroe. Then he waited expectantly, eyebrows lifted.

"Are you . . . famous?" I asked.

Glenn cleared his throat and said in a theatrical voice, "Ladies and gentlemen, without further ado—*The Filmore Vacuette Hour!*"

"Oh!" Berta chirruped, clapping her hands. "*That* Glenn Monroe! I never miss *The Filmore Vacuette Hour*. The 'Ghoulish Yarns' segment is most thrilling."

I never missed *The Filmore Vacuette Hour* either, since Berta kept the volume dial on our kitchen radio set as high as it would go.

The radio variety program, sponsored by the Filmore Vacuum Cleaner Company, featured music, radio dramas, jokes, and mono-logues, all hosted by Glenn Monroe. He looked much as I'd pictured him: twenty-five or so, bonelessly slim, with honey-brown waves swept fashionably from a high pale forehead and impeccable, costly-looking country clothes of tweed and cashmere argyle. His hand-stitched hunting boots didn't have a single fleck of dirt on them.

I made two gin and tonics, poured a brandy for Berta, a mineral water for Isobel, and another mineral water for Cedric, passed them around, and settled into a tall-backed chair by the fire. On the hearthrug, Cedric lapped messily from his glass.

"There is the hunting party," Isobel said, peering toward the win-dows. "I would have thought they would be farther afield. They've been out for half an hour at least."

"You know how it is," Glenn said with a yawn. "They must stalk those stupid birds slowly."

"Here comes dear Rudy," Isobel said.

A barrel-chested man was indeed striding across the park toward the house. It was difficult to see through the leaded windows with all their little panes, but he appeared to have a shotgun under his arm.

"Coral, too," Glenn said. He took a languid sip of his drink. "On the warpath, as usual."

Many paces behind Rudy, a woman in a hunting costume followed, swinging her arms.

Glenn turned to Berta and me. "Brace yourselves. When Coral's in a snit, everyone suffers."

I didn't give a bunny's carrot about Coral and her snits; all I desired was to retrieve Lord Sudley's rhinoceros trophy, get paid, and go back to New York City to lick my wounds. I'd slept fitfully the night before, half hoping Ralph would telephone or, better yet, knock on my door, enfold me in his arms, and murmur he'd made a mistake, that he couldn't live without me, and that of course I needed a man to take care of me forever and ever.

No call. No visit. No dice. All I'd gotten were circles under my eyes and a vague hankering for cake.

3

I gazed around at all the mournful, glass-eyed rhino heads in the Montgomery drawing room. No ear nicks detectable. "Swell trophies," I said to Glenn Monroe and Isobel Bradford. "They certainly spruce up the place. Lord Sudley told me Mr. Montgomery is a crack shot."

Berta, catching on, added, "And what a lot of rhinoceroses in particular! Why, I have only ever killed one myself, and it was an elderly one and, in the end, not very smart-looking once mounted above my fireplace."

"Ghastly things, I think." Glenn's eyelids drooped as he sipped his drink. "They're just one more way for Rudy to prove he's the manliest man around."

Isobel said, "My poor dear Winslow felled seven rhinoceroses during his lifetime. Their heads are mounted still in our library in Boston. Oh, there is Rudy passing just by the windows—and here comes Coral. Rudy appears ever so overheated."

We watched Rudy and Coral pass the drawing room windows.

Before they disappeared, I got an impression of Rudy as swarthily handsome, and Coral as tall, lithe, and redheaded.

I wheeled out a different tactic. "I wonder which of these rhinoceroses was killed most recently."

"Yes," Berta added, "for none of them look particularly fresh."

"No idea," Glenn said, yawning again.

"Why do you wish to know?" Isobel asked.

"We are thinking of going on safari in the spring," Berta said. "Ah."

It went on like that for a few minutes, with Berta and me attempting to wring out some sort of information about the rhinoceros trophies and Glenn and Isobel responding in a bored fashion.

There was a piercing *pop!* Glenn, Isobel, Berta, and I all started. Cedric's ears twitched.

"That was a gunshot," Berta whispered.

"Wasn't that *inside* the house?" Glenn said. "It sounded like a champagne cork, or—yes—like the housekeeper banging a meat mallet. That woman does everything with unnecessary violence."

"No," Isobel said, "that was a gunshot, and it came from outside, where the hunting party is loitering. Perhaps one of their guns was fired by mistake." She peered over the tops of her eyeglasses out the window. "I do hope everyone is all right. Dear Winslow once shot his own foot by mistake."

I wasn't certain where the pop had originated. "Should we go investigate?" I said.

"Surely there is nothing to investigate," Isobel said.

Arguing voices, a man's and a woman's, erupted somewhere upstairs.

"That's Coral and Rudy," Glenn said, rolling his eyes. "Quite the passionate affair. One minute they're at each other's throats, and the next they're stuffing themselves into broom closets for a quick neck."

"Mr. Monroe!" Isobel cried.

"If you're so offended by that idea, Mrs. Bradford," Glenn said, "why don't you just tootle on back to your Boston brownstone? For the life of me, I can't figure why you're hanging around in this house of sin, where the master is living with his girl without the benefit of marriage, because you're just about the wettest blanket I've ever had the pleasure of meeting."

Isobel flushed. She got up, went to the windows, and pushed one open. Cold, wet air blew in. She squinted toward the hunting party, which I could just make out. "Everyone seems to be all right," she said over her shoulder. "They're all loitering about. The dogs look quite low. Fat things. Surely they can't flush pheasants."

Now that the windows were open, we could make out snippets of Rudy and Coral's argument.

". . . and frankly you're driving me mad!" Rudy bellowed. ". . . jealous on purpose . . ."

"YOU mad? Hah!" Coral shrilled. ". . . know you'll never marry me . . . expect me to be your concubine forever . . ."

"Oh dear." Berta sipped brandy. "Perhaps we have come on the wrong day."

Glenn waved a hand. "They're always like this. It's a game they play. Rudy refuses to marry Coral, and so she gets back at him by flirting like mad with other men until he's in a towering rage, then they argue, kiss, and make up."

". . . absolutely through with this!" Coral screamed. A door slammed.

"Coral, come back!" Rudy cried. "I love you, Coral!"

Silence.

Glenn said, "I've just remembered—I've got to make a telephone call to the studio. They gave me the most preposterous lines in the script for the next show, and I've got to absolutely put my foot down. No one wishes to hear sixteen jokes about vacuum cleaners in the span of an hour. It's unendurable." He swung his legs off the chair arm and strolled, hands in pockets, out of the drawing room.

A minute or two passed and then Coral sailed in. Titian curls peeked from the brim of her brown cloche. Her green eyes were baby doll–wide, upslanted, and crisped with mascara. Her lips were as glossy red as poisonous berries, and her chic gray hunting suit hung on her in that shop mannequin way.

"Oh, hello," she said, not really looking at any of us on her way to the drinks cabinet. She set something down—a gold cigarette lighter—and poured out a tumbler of gin. When she put the stopper back on the decanter, it rattled; her hands were shaking. She tossed the gin back, patted the corners of her lips with a fingertip, and then sent a dazzling smile in our direction. "Rudy's in a rage again." Her voice was brave yet tremulous. "He's gone mad. I'm a little frightened, honestly."

"You did say you were through with him, young lady," Isobel said in a scolding tone. She trundled toward the door. "If you will excuse me, I must go to the powder room."

"You heard all that?" Coral turned back to the drinks cabinet and, seeing the gold lighter, slipped it into her jacket pocket. She poured herself another gin. "How embarrassing. I guess Rudy's bedroom is more or less above us here in the drawing room. Who are you, anyway?"

"Friends of Lord Sudley's," I said. "He said Rudy would be expecting us."

"Maybe. Who knows? Since I'm not his wife, I don't really get filled in on all the details. I'm simply expected to show up and look cute." Coral poured herself a third gin and draped herself on a giraffe-skin divan. "Men," she said. "Beasts. Now, where did I put my cigarettes?"

Berta cleared her throat. "I understand there is to be a fancy dress party this evening, Miss—?"

"Moore," Coral said. "Mm." Her tone was bored, yet she bobbed one narrow boot.

"A hunt theme, I believe?" Berta pressed.

"Yes."

"I think I shall go as a rhinoceros," Berta said.

Coral shrieked with laughter. "You must be joking!"

"No." Berta sounded hurt. "And I did happen to notice quite a lot of rhinoceros trophies in here. Do you think Mr. Montgomery would mind if I borrowed one for my costume?"

Brilliant. Berta was simply *brilliant*.

BANG!

We all jumped, and I sloshed my drink.

"Now, *that* was a gunshot," Berta said, touching the locket at her throat.

"Rudy!" Coral screamed.

"Do I smell gunpowder?" I said.

"I do," Berta said.

Coral dashed toward the door. I followed her, and so did Berta. Down the corridor, into the entry hall, up the ponderous staircase, along another corridor, and to a shut door. Coral grabbed the doorknob and twisted.

"It's locked," she cried. She rattled the doorknob, then pushed at the door with her shoulder. "Rudy?" she called. "Rudy! Open the door! This isn't funny."

No answer.

Berta and I exchanged wide-eyed glances. "I shall pop downstairs and telephone the police," Berta whispered.

"Swell idea," I whispered back.

I remained with Coral, who was getting increasingly frothed up as her cries and knocks were met with silence. Other people arrived— the grim housekeeper, Isobel and Glenn, and a handsome young man in eyeglasses and a sweater vest.

Sweater Vest: "What is the matter, Coral?"

Glenn: "Just another spat. Such a yawn."

Sweater Vest (coldly, to Glenn): "I was not speaking to you."

Coral (pounding the door open-handed): "Rudy! Rudy, I'm sorry! I'll never leave you, my love!"

From the room: tomblike silence.

Cedric: nervous panting.

Isobel: "Isn't there another door leading to this bedroom?"

Grim Housekeeper: "No."

Coral: "He's not responding! There was a gunshot!" (More door-pounding.) "Rudy! Oh, Rudy, I'm sorry. I adore you, you know that!"

Sirens yowled in the distance.

It turned out that Berta—she was always thorough—had telephoned the Carvington police station, the fire brigade, *and* the town doctor. Noisy vehicles swarmed into the drive, and about a dozen men in assorted uniforms besieged the house.

Those of us clustered around Rudy's bedroom door stood back as a brawny fireman smashed the door. Coral gasped into Glenn's shoulder.

The door splintered open. We all fell silent.

Rudy lay crumpled on the floor beside an open window, a shotgun beside him and lustrous blood leaking from his temple. The curtains wafted, and my eye fell on the too-innocent view of the side lawns and the distant line of trees.

"Rudy!" Coral screamed. She ran across the room and threw herself onto the corpse.

"Don't touch the body, miss," a policeman said. "What's this here on the floor? A key?"

Coral ignored him, sobbing, face buried in the crook of Rudy's neck.

This was not, unfortunately, my first experience with a corpse while a guest in someone else's house. It's a bit awkward. The urge to flee does battle with the requirement to stay—because who wishes to be the fink who trickles off right after a death? It's downright heartless, not to mention frowned upon by Emily Post. And then there's the milling mob wrestling with emotions ranging from heartbroken to guilty. For instance:

Eight tweedy hunters, Lord Sudley included, hogged the drawing room fireplace. They'd broken into a bottle of wine said to have once belonged to Napoléon Bonaparte. They spoke in somber tones, but their relish of the wine was obvious. (Guilty.)

The flapper mistresses of the tweedy hunters (I gathered that the wives had been left at home) whispered and giggled, got sloshed, and played Mamie Smith and Her Jazz Hounds softly on the Victrola. (Guilty.)

Cedric somehow dragged away one of the resident Labradors' large bones despite his teddy-bear size. The three Labradors, plump and wet and smelly, lazily observed from their places on the hearth. (Guilty, guilty, guilty, and guilty.)

Me, nursing an ill-advised highball. (I'd found a dusty bottle of ginger ale in the back of the drinks cabinet.) Noodling about Ralph. Trying not to noodle about Ralph. Wondering what you bally well do when your hopes and dreams are so out of step with those of the one you love. Do you adapt to his vision? Wait for him to adapt? Or move on alone? (Heartbroken. Obviously.)

Coral (also heartbroken), shut herself away in a bedroom. Despite the house's weighty construction, some of her sobs were audible all the way downstairs.

I pulled Lord Sudley aside. "I'm awfully sorry about Rudy," I said. "I know he was your dear friend."

"He was." Sadness washed over Lord Sudley's suntanned features. "I'll miss him dreadfully."

I cleared my throat. "Isn't it a little, well, unseemly the way everyone's carrying on?"

"We're hardly carrying on, my dear. And the truth is, Rudy always wanted a wake, a great, big, carousing wake to send him off to the Great Beyond in just the fashion he preferred to live. We are merely adhering to his wishes. In fact, we're just getting started."

"What do you mean?"

"That costume party I told you to pack for? It will proceed as planned. It's what Rudy would have wished."

"All right," I said doubtfully. "If you say so. And . . . what about Coral?"

"Everyone's been up to try to speak with her. She doesn't wish to be disturbed."

After that, Berta and I made an excursion up to Coral's room, with the idea that, despite her having refused the others' ministrations, we could offer some womanly comfort. Berta rapped softly on the door.

"Coral?" I said. "Coral, may we come in?"

"Go away!" came Coral's muffled scream. "I'm sick to death of all of you knocking and whispering through the keyhole. What a bunch of nosy parkers!"

Okeydokey.

Anyway, a statuesque, ebony-skinned manservant was carrying trays of tea, soup, and cocktails up to her at regular intervals. The tea and soup came back down on the trays untouched, I noticed, but the cocktail glasses were empty.

"I can't bear it any longer!" I exclaimed to Berta a bit later, as I was sipping a second highball. We were watching from the library windows as Rudy's shrouded body was loaded into an ambulance to be taken to the morgue in the nearby town of Mystic. Night had fallen like a lid.

"It is a reminder that our time on this earth is short," Berta said.

"Not that. We can't investigate the rhinoceros trophies until those hunters clear out of the drawing room, and I'm famished! We're expected to drink all this booze without any nibbles?"

"No one is forcing you to consume liquor, Mrs. Woodby."

"You do realize you're gripping a glass of sherry?"

"That is beside the point. At any rate, I would just as soon have a lie-down. I scouted out the bedrooms where the servants stowed our luggage. My room is quite delightful, overlooking the sea. Yours is . . . practical."

"Let's just take a quick peek in the kitchen. Maybe that frightening housekeeper will give us some grub."

The kitchen was located on the ground floor, after the fashion of Continental country houses, accessed by the back stairs near the conservatory. As it happened, the kitchen was unoccupied. It appeared as though dinner preparations had been called off midexecution. The cast-iron stove still radiated heat, but chopped potatoes sweated on a cutting board and bread dough ballooned out of its bowl.

"Aha—there's the pantry," I said, doubling my pace.

This was how it came to pass that I was forking up orange spice layer cake straight off its pedestal plate when Lord Sudley found us in the pantry. "Mrs. Woodby," he said. "I've been searching high and low for you."

"Mmfgh," I said, rapidly chewing and swallowing cake.

Lord Sudley stepped into the pantry and shut the door behind him. "Caught you in your native habitat, eh? Ah, Mrs. Lundgren. I did not see you there."

Berta stood at the counter ledge behind the door, holding a pickled cucumber. "Hello," she said with queenly dignity, and took a crunching bite.

"Do you still wish us to retrieve the rhinoceros trophy?" I asked.

"Yes, of course. But . . . there is something else." Lord Sudley un-folded the paper. "This is Rudy's suicide note—that is to say, his *presumed* suicide note. It was on the desk in his bedroom."

"What do you mean, 'presumed'?" I asked.

Lord Sudley passed me the paper.

Harried, manly handwriting in lead pencil read,

I cannot bear this cruel world any longer. My heart aches for the love it will never know. Good-bye.

"The police said he shot himself," Lord Sudley said, "but I don't believe that for a second. Rudy would never write this sort of drivel, and furthermore, Rudy would never kill himself. I'm dead certain of it."

"How?"

"He had the utmost contempt for suicides." Lord Sudley raked a hand through his thick hair. "I recall quite vividly a particular con-versation we had. We were on the Great Hungarian Plain—hunting red stags, you know—and in the village in which we were staying, a young man hanged himself—something about being rejected by the village beauty. Rudy had some rather harsh words to say about that, words I won't repeat in front of ladies. In short, he thought any man who killed himself over a woman wasn't a real man."

"Did you mention this to the police?" I asked.

"I did, actually, and they all but laughed in my face. As they see it, the matter is open and shut. Straightforward case of suicide: weapon beside the body, suicide note, and everyone knows Rudy's personality tended toward melancholy."

"Any money troubles?"

"No. He was his parents' sole heir when they died years ago, and I gather the Montgomerys have been well-to-do since colonial days. Still, he was one of those chronically lonely people who feel alone even when surrounded by friends. Oh, he was always jovial and a great sport, but he often drank to excess, and he always had trouble with women. Coral is merely the latest—the last—in a long line of tumultuous and, to be honest, unsuitable women whom he'd romanced."

"Perhaps it really *was* suicide," I said gently. "The policeman found a key on the floor of the bedroom. He said he must have knocked it out when breaking down the door. It appears that Rudy had locked the door—from the inside—before he . . ."

Lord Sudley rubbed his eyes with forefinger and thumb. "Oh, perhaps you're correct. But I won't rest easy unless I rule out murder." He dropped his hand from his eyes. "So. What is the Discreet Retrieval Agency's fee for solving a murder?"

Berta pepped up. "We require an upfront twenty-five percent advance, all our expenses are to be covered, and whether we pinpoint the murderer or conclude that the death was indeed suicide, the fee is four thousand dollars."

"Deal." As Lord Sudley shook my hand, he gazed deeply into my eyes. So deeply, in fact, that for a few seconds I very nearly forgot about both orange buttercream icing and Ralph. "Are you sure you are . . . quite all right? Mucking about with murder, I mean?"

"Oh yes," I said. "Do it all the time."

"When I learned your agency was headed up by two ladies, I confess I pictured two hard-boiled dames of the sort whose mug shots you see in the newspapers. You know—all squashed hats and suspiciously heavy jaws. I do not feel entirely, well, gallant, embroiling two rather genteel ladies in such a grim business."

"We are equal to the case," Berta said, glaring at my hand, which was still held by Lord Sudley.

I drew my hand away. "More than equal," I said. "If Rudy Montgomery was truly murdered, we'll find his killer. You may count on it. Oh—would you like Mrs. Lundgren and me to admit that we are private detectives, or to stay undercover?"

"No need to be secretive, I suppose," Lord Sudley said with a sigh. "Things are already complicated enough as it is, and I have every right to hire detectives, haven't I?"

4

Lord Sudley excused himself from the pantry, saying he would be missed by the hunting gents and their flapper mistresses.

Berta and I went into the kitchen to make sandwiches. Before sketching out a plan of attack in the privacy of Berta's room, we required more sustenance.

"Four thousand dollars, Berta!" I said, rummaging through the icebox. "Four thousand dollars will allow us to move into a new apartment."

"One with a proper front room for an office." Berta sliced bread. "One with two bedrooms. Seeing your bed jackets and slippers flung every which way on the sitting room carpet has grown tiresome."

"You have the one bedroom, Berta. I've been sleeping on the sofa."

"That has been impossible for me to forget. Oh, and I feel it is my duty to caution you that Lord Sudley appears to be unaccountably smitten with you—"

"Bologna!"

"Do not even attempt to deny it."

"No, I mean I've found some bologna." I pulled it from the ice-box and passed it to Berta. "Maybe it's pastrami. Either way, I'll have my sandwich with mayonnaise, extra mustard, and a pickle." I indulged in a glow of satisfaction. The likes of Ralph Oliver might not think I'm worthy of an engagement ring, but I could still win the admiration of *a British lord*. So there. "As for Lord Sudley, well, any lady with a bit of sense knows that the best way to forget one fellow is to go and get herself another."

"That is not sensible at all, Mrs. Woodby."

"I think I'll just nab another piece of that cake. Want some?"

"You will save yourself time and effort if you simply carry the entire cake upstairs."

"If you're going to twist my *arm*."

Berta finished making the sandwiches. When we were ready to go upstairs, I carried the orange spice cake; Berta followed with the sandwiches.

But the kitchen stairs were blocked by the forbidding puffinlike shape of the housekeeper.

"Oh, hello," I said breezily. "I don't believe I know your name, Miss—?"

"Murden." Her flinty gaze fell on the cake. "I see that you have located the dessert."

"Just borrowing it."

"Did you burrow into the side with a fork?"

"Um—"

"It looks like Norway rats have gotten to it." Miss Murden turned to Berta. "I hope you did not use my fresh mayonnaise to make those sandwiches."

Berta stiffened. "If that was your fresh mayonnaise, I pity you."

Miss Murden went to the stove and slung a large copper saucepan from a hook overhead. It hit the stove with a clang. "Now I'll have to make a pudding. Miss Moore ordered something sweet for the party—doesn't care a whit about whether I'd like to mourn poor Mr. Montgomery, does she? Scandalous little miss with her flimsy silky clothes and all that lipstick. They're all scandalous. Mr. Montgomery's body has not even gone cold, and they're carousing like it's Sodom and Gomorrah all over again."

Miss Murden had been in the house when Rudy died. Questioning her would be a tip-top place to begin our murder investigation. I placed the cake on the table. "Miss Murden," I said, "did Mr. Montgomery's death come as a great surprise to you?"

"No." Her head was buried in the icebox.

"Why is that?"

She emerged from the icebox with a bottle of milk and returned to the stove. "Because he was an abrasive man. Remorseless. Inflexible. Not a loyal bone in his body."

"Then there might have been, perhaps, a person or two who would not have minded murdering him?" Berta said.

"There might've been, yes." Miss Murden uncapped the milk and poured it into the saucepan.

"What sort of pudding are you making?" I asked.

"Arrowroot."

Berta sniffed. "The lowest form of pudding."

"Just for the sake of argument," I said, "if Mr. Montgomery *was* murdered, who do you suppose did it?"

"Don't go trying to make me point fingers."

Berta said, "Who else was in the house when the shot was fired?"

"Why do you two want to know all of this, anyway?"

"I am a great reader of *Lurid Tales* magazine," Berta said.

"My adolescent nephew reads that nasty pulp. Ghosts and goblins and vampires and killer robots and monster squids?" Miss Murden snorted. "Not suitable for a grown woman."

"It is most diverting," Berta said, "and it has alerted me to the fact that things are not always what they seem. What is more, we are private detectives." She pulled one of our business cards from the capacious black handbag she always carried and placed it on the counter next to Miss Murden. "We have been hired by Lord Sudley to investigate Mr. Montgomery's death."

"My." Miss Murden glanced at the card with contempt as she stirred her pudding. "You *have* been reading *Lurid Tales*. Well. I'll tell you who was in the house and could've done in poor Mr. Montgomery. In theory, that is, because the police did say it was suicide, and you're barking up the wrong tree."

"Go on," I said. I noticed for the first time that, despite her drab black dress, Miss Murden wore a saucy pair of high black T-straps with teardrop cutouts. I'd drooled over the exact pair in the window of Wright's Department Store just last week. Quite a costly pair of kicks for a servant.

"First off," Miss Murden said, "you two were in the house. What do any of us know about you? Showed up out of the blue—"

"We were with Coral in the drawing room when the shot was fired," I said.

"Humph." Miss Murden stirred the milk in the saucepan. "Weren't Mrs. Bradford and Mr. Monroe in the drawing room with you, too?"

"No, actually. Only Coral. Mrs. Bradford stepped out to use the powder room, and Mr. Monroe said he had a telephone call to make, so they were both gone."

"Aha. There are your murder suspects."

"What about servants?"

"There is only one servant living in the house besides myself, and that's Mwinyi—Lord knows if I'm saying that right."

Mwinyi was surely the manservant I had noticed carrying trays up and down the stairs for Coral.

"Only two servants for such a large house?" Berta said.

"Mr. Montgomery didn't live here most of the time. Mwinyi was hired to be Mr. Montgomery's valet, although here at the house he has been acting as valet, butler, and chauffeur. I'm more a caretaker, really—I have my own nice, snug little apartment on the third floor. This fall was the longest Mr. Montgomery ever stayed here at a stretch. Coral liked it here, he said, although I never hear the end of her whining about how dull Carvington is, and she flits down to New York City at the drop of a hat. Mwinyi drives her. Awful waste of gasoline, when she could be taking the train. The cleaning ladies come only on Mondays and Fridays, so they weren't here today. Big parties like this run me ragged, doing all the cooking myself, although Mr. Montgomery's guests always drink more than they eat."

"Was Mwinyi inside the house when the shot was fired?"

"He was out with the hunting party. Oh, I nearly forgot. That pompous college student was in the library today when it . . . happened."

"College student?" Berta said.

"His name is Theo Wainwright. Drinks endless cups of tea and never looks me in the eye, even though everyone knows who his mother was."

"Who was his mother?" I asked.

"Never you mind."

I squirreled that tidbit away for later.

"What was he doing inside the house?" Berta asked.

"Looking at moldy old books that belong to this house. He has been for a few months now—since September. Mr. Montgomery gave him permission—Theo claims he needs the books for his studies— but Mr. Montgomery didn't want him taking the books out of the house on account of them being terribly fragile. Mildew farms is what I call them. I'd burn the lot."

"Where might we find Theo Wainwright?" Berta asked.

"At the college. History department." Miss Murden stirred arrow-root powder into the bubbly milk. "Or at Mrs. Noll's boardinghouse on Scrimshaw Street."

"How do you know where he lives?" I asked.

"Carvington is a very small town." Miss Murden's tone strongly suggested she thought I had toasted corn flakes for brains.

"A few minutes before the shot was fired in Rudy's bedroom," I said, "there was another loud popping sound. Some of us in the drawing room thought it was a gunshot from the hunting party, but someone mentioned it might've been you with a meat tenderizer or some such gadget here in the kitchen."

Miss Murden shrugged. "Might've been. I was down here slaving over the hot stove during that evil hour. Oh yes—I remember that I did knock a metal bread pan from a high shelf. Metal pans on these stone floors make such a racket. Now, if it was murder—which it wasn't—but if it was, well, now that I'm thinking on it, I'd place my bets on that Mrs. Bradford."

"Isobel?" I said. "Why? She seems such a stodgy, proper type."

"Seems, yes, but she's also a snoop."

Berta and I leaned in. "Oh?" we both said.

"She's been here only since yesterday, but I keep catching her where she doesn't belong. Poking through the library in the wee hours with a flashlight. Knocking on animal-head trophies like she's trying to figure if they're hollow or not."

Well, well, well.

Miss Murden cast a narrow look toward the kitchen stairs. "Wouldn't be surprised if she's snooping right now."

"What do you suppose she's looking for?" I asked.

"Who knows? Hidden treasure? Government bonds? Maybe she's one of those mediums, looking for the ghost."

"Ghost?" Berta breathed. Every issue of *Lurid Tales* featured at least one story involving séances, ectoplasm, and mysterious cold zones.

"This house is haunted," Miss Murden said with satisfaction. "A lady in white roams the estate. She's been known to push people, so you'd best be careful on the stairs at night."

Goose bumps sprang up on my arms. "You know," I said, "there was one other person in the house when Mr. Montgomery was murdered."

"Who?" Miss Murden said.

"*You.* Any reason you'd wish to be rid of your employer?"

Miss Murden pointed at the stairs with a pudding-globbed spoon. "Out!"

I reached for the cake.

"Leave that!"

Berta managed to make a dignified exit with her plate of sandwiches, but I slunk upstairs empty-handed.

"Isobel Bradford, snooping around the estate and knocking on hunting trophies?" I said to Berta once we were shut into her bedroom with our bologna sandwiches. "That sounds suspicious."

Berta's large, well-appointed guest room overlooked the moon-burnished sea. On a point to the west, a lighthouse splashed its light out into the vast blackness. Here inside, however, a coal fire wafted delicious heat. The velvet chairs were squashy and the lamps subdued. My own chilly room, which I suspected was a renovated linen closet, wasn't large enough for a business meeting, and with its sloped ceilings, even Berta was in danger of bumping her head.

"I wonder if Isobel is searching for the same rhinoceros trophy that Lord Sudley is," Berta said. "I would not get too cozy with him if I were you, Mrs. Woodby."

"Me, cozy with a client? Never." Actually, cozy sounded aces. Cozy with *Ralph.* I gave myself a mental slap and stuffed more sandwich in my mouth. Ralph was Off-Limits.

Berta had her notebook and pencil out. "I shall position Isobel Bradford at the top of the suspect list. I did not take to her. She is one of those sour, judgmental women."

"It was awfully suspicious the way she excused herself to go to the powder room only a minute or so before the shot was fired."

"Would she have had time to reach Rudy's bedroom?"

"Easily, if she'd been brisk about it. Up the stairs and to the north side of the house. Did you notice that his bedroom is right above the drawing room, and that his window was open when his body was found? That's why we were able to hear his argument with Coral and then the gunshot so clearly, since Isobel opened the drawing room window. And remember that we smelled gunpowder?"

"I wonder why his bedroom window was open. The weather does not really recommend it."

"Perhaps the killer fled through the window—down a ladder, maybe."

"We would have seen it from the drawing room."

"True. Maybe they went through the window and up to the roof?"

"We must examine the outside of the house." Berta was writing in her notebook. "I am also including Miss Murden on the suspect list, as well as Glenn Monroe and the college student who was studying in the library."

"Oh, you mean Sweater Vest." I popped the last bit of sandwich into my mouth.

"I believe Miss Murden said his name is Theo Wainwright."

Good thing Berta had a good memory for names.

At any rate—hooray!—we had our suspect list:

Isobel Bradford
Miss Murden

Glenn Monroe
Theo Wainwright

This murder investigation would be different from the others. We'd be organized. Efficient. Superbly logical. And with only four suspects, why, we'd be clinking celebratory glasses of bootleg bubbly in record time. "Do you think Miss Murden is to be trusted about who was in the house?" I said. "There are nearly twenty other guests, to begin with."

"We must confirm all that she told us. And I must add that her supposedly fresh mayonnaise is not very nice."

"Isn't it? I hadn't noticed." I reached for a second sandwich.

5

At half past eight, Berta and I sailed down the grand staircase together, following the sounds of blaring phonograph jazz and raucous laughter. The drawing room was a mirage of cigarette smoke, cocktail glasses, and sequined dresses.

"Whew. If Rudy truly wanted a big, riotous wake, he's certainly getting it," I said to Berta in the doorway. "Let's split up. Search for Glenn Monroe, Miss Murden, and Isobel Bradford, and grill them like hot dogs." Our fourth suspect, the college student Theo Wainwright, would surely not be at the party. We'd track him down tomorrow.

Berta nodded and trooped into the party. She was dressed in a capacious green tunic with a jagged hem and a leather belt, green woolen stockings, a feathered green hat, and her usual painful-looking Edwardian boots. Robin Hood, she'd informed me, although I'd been thinking *elf*.

I thought I'd been cleverly glamorous, costuming myself as Diana the huntress in a long, gauzy, Greeky thing and a quiver of toy arrows tied to my back with gold braid. However, at least half the flapper mistresses were also attired as Diana. There was a plump Diana with a splendorous Grecian hairdo; a tall, thin Diana with scarlet-tipped fingernails and an ivory cigarette holder; and a Diana with a finger-waved bob, Cupid's bow lips, and rhinestones on her shoes. I adored the shoes.

"Ah, another Diana." Lord Sudley appeared beside me. He looked absurdly dashing in a sort of medieval tunic, boots, cloak, and a feathered headdress.

"I think I'll need a drink before taking a stab at *your* costume," I said.

"Gronw the Radiant. Chap from a Welsh myth. He falls in love with—and murders someone for, actually—a woman named Blodeu-wedd. She's beautiful. Made of flowers and whatnot." Lord Sudley lowered his voice. "I've just gotten off the telephone with Rudy's lawyer's office in New York. The firm has handled the Montgomery family's private business for decades. It seems that Mr. Eccles is on holiday in Florida, and although he is evidently boarding the first available train north, he will not arrive here at the house until the day after tomorrow."

"And you've got the jimmies about that?"

"Well, yes, actually. You see, Rudy's parents are deceased and he had no wife or children—no heirs, you understand—and his one sib-ling died years ago in a motorcar accident in Italy. I'm certain Rudy must have written out a will, but as things stand right now, I've no idea who owns this house. It'll all become clear when Mr. Eccles ar-rives, I suppose. But in the meantime—" He looked around the es-calating party. "—I do hope that whoever inherits this house won't mind stains on the carpets."

"I'd like to ask you a few questions about this afternoon," I said, "since you were out with the hunting party."

"Of course."

"To begin with, why did Rudy return to the house?"

"He realized that he'd forgotten his lucky rabbit's foot. He wouldn't hunt without it in his pocket—a silly superstition. And I gathered that Coral accompanied him to help him look for it—she said something about men being awful about finding things."

"And were all the hunting guests accounted for out there by the trees when the shot was fired?"

"Oh yes. We were standing about and trading pleasantries and so forth. Everyone was in good spirits, although jolly impatient to begin shooting."

"Why didn't you simply start without Rudy?"

"He was our host. That would've been frightfully rude."

Honestly, this bunch didn't seem to bother much about manners. One man was swinging from a chandelier in nothing but his striped underwear.

"Oh—I nearly forgot," I said. "A few minutes before the shot was fired, those of us in the drawing room heard another sound that Berta thought might've been a gunshot, although Glenn Monroe insisted it was a bottle cork or a meat mallet—"

"Ah yes. That *was* a gunshot."

"It was?"

"Mm. The manservant, Mwinyi, accidentally fired one of the shotguns while cleaning it."

Good. That was one loose thread neatly snipped away. "Isobel Bradford," I said. "Rumor has it she's been snooping around the house and—" I watched Lord Sudley closely. "—poking around the hunting trophies."

"Good heavens! Isobel?"

"Perhaps she wants the same rhinoceros trophy that you do?"

"I very much doubt that. My reasons are . . . rather personal, shall we say." Lord Sudley shook his head. "Prim, proper old Isobel snooping? I simply can't picture it."

"You know her well, then?"

"Actually, I only just met her here at the house yesterday evening, but I knew her late husband, Winslow Bradford, like a brother. We met years ago at the Scion Club in New York and, along with Rudy, he formed our little hunting trio. He always spoke a great deal about Isobel, so over the years I formed a rather vivid impression of her."

"Isobel never went on the hunting trips?"

"Oh no. She always stayed home. Winslow said she never went hunting, not even for fowl, so I'm a bit surprised she came here, but now that you say she's been snooping, well, it makes a bit more sense. She must have been looking for something that belonged to her husband."

"Why do you refer to her in the past tense?"

"Don't you know? She's gone."

"Gone!"

"Motored off as soon as the police and the ambulance left, actually."

"Where to?"

"Why, to her home, I presume. In Boston."

"Don't you see? Isobel is beginning to look like the most promising suspect on the list, and now that she's gone . . ."

"Yes, I do see. Suspicious with knobs on. Don't despair, Mrs. Woodby, or—may I call you Lola?"

"Please."

"Good—and do call me Eustace."

I bit my lip to keep myself from laughing.

"Frightful name, I realize. Makes me sound like a fat little boy in a crested blazer. Later on I'll see if I can dig up Mrs. Bradford's telephone number and address from my book, all right?"

"Peachy."

"Oh, and if you manage to procure my trophy tonight—my motorcar is the black Duesenberg in the front drive."

"*Duesenberg*," I murmured dreamily.

"And I would be most obliged if you'd tell me the moment you've succeeded. It will be such a great weight off the old bean. My bedroom is second on the right at the top of the stairs." Something indefinable glinted in Lord Sudley's—Eustace's—eye.

Why were my cheeks hot? This was strictly business.

He smiled. "But where are my manners? You look thirsty—what's your poison?"

"Highball, if you can scrounge one."

"I'll do my utmost."

As soon as Lord Sudley disappeared into the riot, I frantically scouted for Berta. Our prime suspect, Isobel Bradford, had vamoosed. We needed to give chase.

But before I could spot Berta, I was waylaid by Coral.

She had emerged from her bedroom, then. Why?

"My, Mrs. Woodby," she said, "your costume is so very *original*." She sipped her bloodred drink. Ice cubes clacked and I caught a whiff. Campari. *Shudder.* "Only joking, cutie! And don't look at my costume like that!" She wore a rust-colored silk confection of a dress with what I took to be real fox ears and foxtail attached to her skirt and headband. Strands of milky, lustrous, cylindrical beads hung around her neck. "The fox was already dead, and now that Rudy's gone I don't see why we've got to tiptoe around his bally moth-eaten collection of animal cadavers like they're holy relics." She smiled, revealing small white teeth.

Oh, what I would've given to bump Coral to the top of the murder suspect list. Too bad she'd been with Berta and me and wasn't a suspect at all.

"Are you feeling better?" I asked delicately.

Coral sniffed. "You're not going to tell me I should be tearing out my hair still, are you?"

"Well—"

"I'm done with weeping. Rudy is gone. I've got to move on with my life."

That was speedy. Although, perhaps Coral was in shock. That would explain the brittle edge to her voice, the hitch of her shoulders.

"Poor old Rudy," I said. "But I suppose he's smiling down at us from heaven, pleased that we're having a whoop-up in his honor."

"I'm sure he's tickled pink," Coral said. "He got his way, didn't he, because now here I am, left utterly in the lurch. Totally broke, with not a nickel to my name except for whatever I can squeeze out of the pawnshop for the jewelry he gave me—which won't be much. He never even gave me any diamonds! Only some rotten pearls and emeralds and heaps of these stupid things." She rattled the lustrous beads around her neck. "Cheap junk. Seven months at Rudy's side through thick and thin, playing hostess and mistress and nursemaid and mommy and psychiatrist to him, and what do I have to show for it? Nothing! I was his latest trophy, but I guess I was starting to get a little moth-eaten, too."

"I beg your pardon, but why did you stay?"

"He led me on, and I was stupid enough to keep on taking the bait. When I first met him in Antibes last spring, he gave me a song and dance about being lonely and needing a woman's touch in his life and all of that trumpery. He asked me to travel with him to Monte Carlo and I said yes—the fellow from Austria I'd been on holiday with in Antibes had suddenly remembered he had a wife and kids back home and he'd left me high and dry, so I was at loose ends. After Monte Carlo, it was Egypt, and then the safari in Kenya. It was my first outing with a bush rifle, but I bagged a zebra on my first try. Had it made into a handbag and matching shoes. A little itchy, actually. Well, flipping to the end of the book, Rudy was only leading me on the same way he always led girls on. He wanted a pretty kitten in the house, but not a wife, and anytime I dropped any hints about going down the middle aisle, he told me not to get any funny ideas."

This didn't sound at all like a man driven by tormented love to suicide. No sirree. Rudy sounded like your standard playboy. I knew the type, all right—reader, I married one. Playboys married only rich girls, and only when funds got low. And when playboys stopped having fun with a girl, why, they got rid of her and found a new one. They didn't kill themselves.

Looked like Eustace's murder theory held water.

"I'm sorry Rudy's dead." Coral slid a finger beneath her eye to catch a teardrop. "I think he was just about to agree to marry me, never mind that stupid argument we'd had before he—he . . ." She gulped. "And now it's too late! Instead of being a rich widow, now I'm several months older, and back to square one."

I scanned the crush. "Is Miss Murden serving this evening?"

"Ugh. No. Sulking up in her rooms, I'd guess—although why she's been so sulky all evening, I can't imagine, since she's one lucky duck."

"Oh?"

"Rudy was about to fire her. He meant to do it once the hunting party was done with. But now, well, she's still in a job."

"Not precisely. Her employer is dead."

"Oh. Yes. Well, she's still got a *chance* at keeping her job, anyway, once we figure out who inherits this place. Miss Murden is like some massive old light fixture that no one knows how to unscrew from the ceiling. She likes to say her family has always served the Montgomerys. She even goes so far as to claim that she's of Indian blood and that really, this land that the house stands on is hers. Can you imagine? And, well—the clever old boot—I suppose she has made certain she's here to stay."

In the kitchen earlier, Miss Murden had said Rudy was disloyal. "Did Miss Murden know that her job was in jeopardy?" I asked.

"I wouldn't doubt it. She's the good old-fashioned kind of servant who listens at keyholes."

"Why did Rudy mean to fire her?"

"He didn't tell me. 'Men's business,' he'd say, as though hearing about facts or figures would cause my head to explode." Her slanted green eyes fastened on me. "Say, what's with all the questions, anyway?"

I told her that Lord Sudley had hired Berta and me—private investigators par excellence—to look into Rudy's death.

"Look into a suicide?"

I shrugged. "Lord Sudley merely wishes to clarify the details."

"Oh, how fun. God, I need to find a cigarette. Biffo had the most scrummy Turks—where did he go?" Coral wandered off, foxtail swaying.

I found Berta pouring herself a stiff one at the drinks cabinet. I hastily told her how Isobel Bradford up and left as soon as the police had gone.

"Oh my." Berta sipped gin. "That does make her seem rather guilty."

"What are we doing here? We ought to be tracking her down."

"We have three other suspects, Mrs. Woodby, and there is also the matter of retrieving the rhinoceros trophy for Lord Sudley. That is a paying job as well. We must stay, at least until the morning, and make what progress we are able. And do attempt to relax. Your face is as rumpled as a pair of linen trousers."

The party barreled like a rudderless frigate into the night, and I did not get Lord Sudley alone again. I was eager for Isobel Bradford's Boston address, but there wasn't much I could do with the address till the morning. The Victrola boomed and keened, cigarette haze congealed, and the flapper mistresses began to shed articles of clothing. Someone tossed a rubber ball for Cedric to fetch. An archery match commenced in the dining room, couples took turns cuddling in the back stairway, and bowling with empty gin bottles and billiard balls was under way in the entry hall. Coral and Glenn were the twin eyes of the hurricane.

"It's almost as though Coral and Glenn are the host and hostess," I said to Berta as we observed the drunken bowling. The man-servant, Mwinyi, wearing elegant livery, was in charge of righting the bottles after every roll. He was sculpturally handsome, and he never spoke. "It's as though Glenn simply stepped into the role of Man of the House the minute Rudy was out of the picture."

"Glenn is not really very manly," Berta.

"Well, no."

We watched Glenn slide down the banister, crooning Van and Schenck's latest hit, "You Can Have Him, I Don't Want Him."

I shrugged a shoulder. "Modern young men. They don't wish to be like their fathers and grandfathers, with great big muttonchops and top hats and forbidding expressions."

"There was something to be said for those old-fashioned men, Mrs. Woodby. One felt there were adults in charge of things. It was, if nothing else, reassuring. Nowadays when I read the newspaper, I have the sense that enormous moody toddlers are running the show." She paused. "I notice that Glenn converses only with the prettiest girls."

"Why not? He's famous—or almost famous. He gets to be choosy."

"But he does not even pay the girls much attention, once he has them cornered. He keeps looking out of the corners of his eyes as though to see who is watching. I suspect that he is in love with Coral and he hopes to make her jealous. Now, I do not think we will make any more progress with our inquiries. The party has reached a new level of frivolity. I shall go upstairs and take a nap. With a bit of luck, the party will end before dawn so we may investigate the rhinoceros trophies."

"Good idea. I could use a nap myself."

6

I was only a little tipsy, since I had made a concerted effort to eat a great number of smoked salmon sandwiches with my four high-balls. Upstairs, first I used the—alas—shared bathroom. In my bedroom, I changed into my nightgown, cold-creamed my face, pinned back my hair, and slid into bed with Cedric beside my pillow. I read a few pages of an issue of *Lurid Tales* borrowed from Berta, and I suppose I drifted off, for I bolted upright some time later with the bedside lamp ablaze and my heart squeezing like a church organ in bad repair.

I blinked. What had woken me?

From somewhere on the other side of my bedroom door came the slow tapering *crrrrrrreeeeeeeekkkkk* of a door hinge.

My heart kept on squeezing, but I swung my legs out of bed. As I was stuffing my feet into my slippers, a woman's voice said, "*Lolaaaaaaaaaaaa.*"

Just outside my door.

Cedric was snoozing through all of this. He's a flop of a guard dog.

Dew arose on my upper lip, but I crept to the door and forced myself to open it.

The corridor was empty. Wait. No. Someone was floating through the darkness toward me in a plaid belted robe.

"Berta!" I cried, going limp with relief.

"Oh, Mrs. Woodby, I thought I heard you," she whispered. "I was just coming to fetch you. I believe the party has abated and we may attempt to procure the rhinoceros trophy."

That was it. I was quitting *Lurid Tales* before it shaved too many months off my life. Just as soon as I finished "The Lost Lass of Cairn Gorm," I would. Pinky swear.

Downstairs, everyone seemed to have gone to bed, although the place was in bacchanalian wreckage. Chairs had toppled. The suit of armor sat on a love seat. Two curtain rods were going the way of the RMS *Titanic*. Berta and I tiptoed around drifts of bottles, glasses, discarded garments, and spilled ashtrays.

"Miss Murden will be furious," I whispered.

"She will bring in the cleaning women from town."

"She'll still be furious." We stood in the center of the drawing room. I switched on my flashlight and shone the beam on the several rhinoceros heads, one by one. "Which one should we have a look at first? The depressed-looking one or the one that looks as though it's wearing three turtleneck sweaters?"

"That describes all of them, Mrs. Woodby. At any rate, here is the one with the nick out of its left ear. I identified it during the party. I am surprised you did not."

"Oh."

Berta pulled a screwdriver from the pocket of her robe. "Now, then. Would you just fetch that ottoman?"

I regarded the rhino, ten feet up. "We're going to need more than an ottoman."

"Please do not quibble."

"And . . . what if the trophy isn't really Eustace's?" I whispered. "We'll be stealing from a dead man."

"Mrs. Woodby, now is not the proper time to grapple with your conscience. Please. The ottoman."

Three minutes later, I scaled a precarious tower constructed of an armchair and two ottomans, with a screwdriver between my teeth. From down below, Berta shone the flashlight on the large wooden plaque upon which the head was mounted.

"Do you see any screws?" she whispered.

"Yes. Steady, now—shine the light to the left a smidge—that's it. Right there." I bit my tongue in concentration and twisted out a screw. "Now the one on the right." I held on to the rhino's front horn for balance, positioned myself near the second screw hole, and got to work.

"Are there more than two screws?" Berta whispered loudly. "Because otherwise—"

"I'm the one standing on this dangerous tower of furniture, Berta, so please stop interfering and let me—" The second screw gave way, and the entire rhino's head swung violently on a third and last screw. The horn hit me in the temple and I lost my balance. I spiraled my arms into space for a hideously drawn-out moment before plummeting backward—

THUMP. Onto a sofa.

There was a *clickety-clackety-clickety* sound of something showering to the floor. Lots of little things, flowing out of the cockeyed rhino trophy up there on the wall, bouncing, skittering.

"Mrs. Woodby! Are you all right?" Berta exclaimed.

"Um. I think so."

I heaved myself upright on the couch, nerves in my lower back pinging. Berta went to the floor below the rhino's head and beamed the flashlight on a pile of what looked like gravel.

I crept closer, mesmerized. The gravel shone with a low luster. "Diamonds," I breathed. "Berta! These are *diamonds*."

Berta picked one up. "Are you quite certain? They resemble bits of rock that someone has chewed upon."

"They're uncut. Raw. I'm sure of it—I saw some once in a jeweler's shop." I couldn't resist; I knelt and plunged my hands into the pile.

"I thoth I heardth voices," a woman's voice slurred behind us.

I reared back from the diamonds. The overhead light snapped on, and Berta and I turned.

Coral swayed in the doorway, barefoot but still in her sequined fox-colored party dress, white beaded necklace, fur ears, and tail. Kohl streaked below her eyes.

Drunk as a sailor.

I got to my feet, trying to block the diamonds with my legs. Which, my mother would have noted, shouldn't have been difficult given my ankle concern. "Why aren't you in bed?" I said.

Coral tipped her head to look around my legs, then staggered a little. "Wass that?" she slurred. "Rocks on the floor. Mizz Murdenz will be grouchy about that! Oldth grouch." She giggled.

I went to Coral, took her by the arm, and led her out of the drawing room. She smelled of sweat and liquor. "Let's get you tucked into bed, why don't we? You've had a trying day and you shouldn't be wandering around all by yourself like this." I sent Berta a meaningful look over my shoulder: *Pick up the diamonds and get the trophy out of there!*

Fifteen minutes later, I left Coral snoring juicily in the guest bedroom in which she'd been weeping earlier. I assumed she had bunked with Rudy, but I decided it would be too macabre to tuck her into their shared bed. Besides, the bedroom door's hinges were surely still broken after the fireman's muscular attentions earlier.

When I reached my own bedroom, Berta was waiting. The rhino's head sat on the carpet behind her, looking especially enormous in the cramped quarters.

"That was tremendously heavy," Berta whispered breathlessly.

"You're a marvel."

"The diamonds came from the separation you tore between the head and the wooden mount. I removed the mount entirely to see if there were any more diamonds inside."

"And?"

"None. Only a wire framework and a lot of cotton rags."

"Where are the diamonds now?"

Berta patted the pockets of her robe.

"All right, we must have a word with Lord Sudley."

"Indeed we must. He owes us a large check."

"He also has some explaining to do."

Lugging the rhino trophy between us, Berta and I limped along the dark upstairs corridors to Eustace's bedroom. We lowered the trophy to the floor outside his door and I knocked.

A slice of light winked on below the door and then it opened. "Great Scott," Eustace said, looking blearily handsome in paisley satin pajamas. "Is this a dream?"

"We urgently require a word with you," I whispered.

"Do you recall that I asked you to deposit the trophy in the boot of my motorcar?"

"Things have changed."

"All right. Come in." Eustace hefted the rhino trophy, staggered with it into his room, and dumped it onto the hearth rug. Berta stepped inside and shut the door.

I swung on him. "Diamond smuggling! If I had known what sort of nefarious motives you had, we wouldn't have had anything to do with this job."

"Or," Berta said, "at the least, we would have requested a far more substantial fee."

"I don't quite understand what you're suggesting," Eustace said. "Diamond smuggling? What has that to do with my hunting trophy?"

Berta went to the desk and emptied her robe pockets onto the blotter. "*This.*"

"Raw diamonds? Where did you get those? They must be worth a fortune."

"Do you mean to say you didn't know these were hidden inside your trophy?" I asked.

"Good God, no! *Inside* it, you say?" Eustace lowered himself slowly into a chair.

His amazement seemed genuine. Then again, I've come across some swell actors.

"To whom do these diamonds belong?" I asked. "Where did they come from? Who put them in that trophy, and if they were smuggled, well, why were they still inside the rhino's head?"

"I don't know, Lola. Perhaps they weren't smuggled at all. Perhaps for some mad reason, Rudy chose to keep them there."

"Does that sound like something he would have done?" I said. "Was he the hide-cash-in-your-mattress type?"

"Well, no. Even so, perhaps his finances were in danger and he wished to hide liquid assets."

"Where was this trophy manufactured?" Berta asked. "I mean to say, when was the head removed from the body, stuffed, and mounted?"

"In Kenya, a day or so after I shot the beast. The African chaps do it right out there in a carcass tent. We ate some of the meat. . . ." Eustace's voice trailed off, and it might've been the lamplight, but I thought he looked a touch chartreuse. He swallowed. "Then the head was preserved and it rode about in one of the safari trucks in our little caravan as we traveled from point to point—we were out there six weeks all told, and I bagged this old boy in the second week. When we finally sailed out of Mombasa, all the trophies we'd accumulated were shipped on our vessel, in crates. Once we'd reached Turkey—we took the Suez route—I boarded the *Orient Express* for England, and Rudy, Winslow, and Coral sailed for America by way of France. Oh—and the African manservant accompanied them, of course—Mwinyi. That was the last I saw of old Winslow, sadly. I'll miss him . . . but here I am going soft. Now, see here, I'll just write you a check for the agreed-upon amount for retrieving this trophy, we'll stash it in my motorcar, and then we've got to puzzle out a way to keep these diamonds safe until the arrival of the lawyer, at which point, I'll turn them over to him. After all, we have no reason to believe the diamonds were not rightfully Rudy's." Eustace opened one of the desk drawers, pulled out his checkbook, and wrote us a check.

Berta took it, folded it, and slid it into her robe pocket.

Eustace scooped the diamonds across the desk with the side of his hand, and they pitter-pattered like falling rain into the open drawer. He shut the drawer, locked it, and pocketed the key. "Allow me to assist you in carrying that brute to my motorcar."

Unease swilled in my stomach. Had Eustace used Berta and me as pawns in a diamond heist? No, surely not. If he had known there were diamonds hidden in the rhino trophy, he wouldn't have hired detectives to pinch it. Too risky.

Berta and I donned shoes and coats, returned to Eustace's room, and then the three of us carried the rhino out to Eustace's motorcar in the front drive. The trophy wouldn't fit in the boot, so we wedged it into the backseat and covered it up with a traveling blanket. No one saw us. Not that I knew of, at any rate. Then we went back inside and upstairs.

"I'm absolutely pooped," I said to Berta with a yawn once we'd parted ways with Eustace. "It's nearly four o'clock."

"Are you not at all concerned that Lord Sudley will make off with those diamonds?" Berta asked.

"No. Why would he? He presumably owns a palace or something in England."

"It is the usual sort of sprawling Georgian affair. Probably a nightmare to keep squeaky clean. He owns a town house in London, too—"

"How do you know all this?" I asked. A sprawling Georgian affair. I could just picture Cedric romping free on acres and acres of parkland, and I'd wear heaps of Burberry gabardine and hard-wearing woolens.

"One reads things. I see the dreamy look on your face, Mrs. Woodby, but it is *your* heart Lord Sudley is trifling with, and as such, this is none of my affair. And are you aware that in England it is customary to consume whole stewed tomatoes at breakfast?" Berta shuddered. "I am pooped as well. Let us wait until the morning to discuss our strategy."

"Drat." I stopped. "I meant to ask Eustace—I mean Lord Sudley—for Isobel Bradford's address. He said he had it in his address book."

"Surely that can wait until the morning."

"Oh, all right." I stopped at my door. "By the way, Berta, don't ever make those spooky ghost noises again."

"Whatever do you mean?"

"You know, that sort of moany '*Lolaaaaaaaa*' business. You scared me half out of my skin."

"Mrs. Woodby, I have never called you by your given name, and I would never stoop so low as to impersonate a specter. Do you take me for a starstruck ingenue?"

I swallowed. "But then who—?"

"I expect it was the highballs talking, Mrs. Woodby. Good night."

But I couldn't get back to sleep. My exhausted brain buzzed, so I switched on the lamp and continued to read "The Lost Lass of Cairn Gorm," in which occult detective Hugo Quinn stalks opium-smuggling pagan cultists in the Scottish Highlands. You know, light reading. All the while I listened for footsteps and moans in the corridor. By the time I reached the story's climactic gunfight, I could've done with another slice of that orange spice cake, but there wasn't a snowman's chance in hell that I was going down to the kitchen in the dark.

I finished the story, switched off the light, and snuggled against Cedric. I listened to raindrops tap against the windowpanes. I pondered what a sterling, gorgeous, and caring gentleman Eustace, Lord Sudley, was . . . and tried with all my might not to long for Ralph's warm, strong arms around me.

7

Berta and I slept until ten o'clock the next morning, but still we were the first guests up. Someone—Miss Murden, presumably—had set out silver chafing dishes of breakfast in the dining room, so after I took Cedric for an airing in the soggy garden, I sat down at the table across from Berta and put on the nose bag.

"Hear any ghosty moans last night?" I asked Berta.

"No. You?"

"I don't believe in ghosts, Berta."

"You sound as though you were trying to convince yourself of that."

"Do you believe in ghosts?"

"It is not that I believe or do not believe, but that I have not assembled enough facts to come to a final conclusion."

"You've been hitting *Lurid Tales* too hard."

Berta sniffed, smearing jam on a toasted muffin. She gazed out the window as she took a crunchy bite. "If I am not mistaken, that is young Theo, the history student, out there."

"Where?"

"Look out the window."

I turned. "So it is. Where's he going, I wonder?"

Theo was bicycling across the lawn in the direction of the forest, a bulging knapsack on his back.

"Funny," I said. "Miss Murden said he had permission to use the Montgomery family's books in the library, but she said nothing of him having free rein on the estate."

"We must interrogate him while we have the chance," Berta said. "He is on our suspect list."

I had hoped to motor straight to Boston once we got our hands on Isobel Bradford's address, so I sighed. "All right."

We quickly finished eating, put on coats and hats, and trudged through the chilly, misty parkland in the direction Theo had gone. Spiraling seagulls screeched overhead and salty wind whapped and sucked our umbrellas. Cedric stopped and stared up at me accusingly.

"Poor little peanut," I murmured, enfolding him in my arms. "You don't like walking through the wet grass, do you? Would you like Mommy to buy you four little boots?"

"There he is," Berta called to me.

"Where?" I peered into the dripping forest. I saw a bicycle leaning against a tree. I saw a hat bobbing around right at ground level. What in Sam Hill . . . ?

Berta and I elbowed through underbrush and found ourselves looking down into a rectangular pit the size of a motorcar, cut into the sod at a depth of about four feet. The damp mineral odor of dirt rose up. Excavated earth heaped beside it. Theo Wainwright was scraping the side of the pit with a trowel. He was utterly absorbed, his cheeks and eyeglasses rain-spattered, but suddenly he looked up and took a startled step back.

"Lord!" he cried, holding on to his battered hat. "I didn't hear you coming. Mind the edge of my pit, please. It would be a disaster if it caved in—that's it, back up another step. You two aren't exactly pixies. There. Did Miss Murden send you? I don't want another cup of tea."

"Mr. Wainwright," Berta said, "we are private detectives investigating the death of Mr. Montgomery, and we'd like to have a word with you."

"Is this some sort of joke?"

"No, it is not a joke," Berta said. "Is it really so difficult to come to grips with lady detectives? Most men cannot find anything in an icebox, let alone murderers. Shall we join you down there, or are you coming up?"

"I'm coming up." Theo stuck the trowel in the pocket of his grubby waxed-canvas coat and climbed up a crude wooden ladder to ground level.

"Female detectives," he said. "And I thought all those frumpy co-eds mucking around at the college were bad enough. Oh, it's quite obvious why no one has married them, but can't they stick to stenography courses if they must go to school?"

Ugh. I couldn't help it; I mentally nudged Theo up to second place on the murder suspect list, right beneath Isobel Bradford.

Behind his eyeglasses he was blandly handsome, like a man in a sock garter advertisement: brown hair and eyes, slight shadow on his shaved upper lip, medium sized, well-proportioned physique. He was probably only twenty-three or so, but he had all the smug ease of a seasoned professor.

"What's this about murder?" he asked. "I understand it was a suicide. There was a note and everything."

"Our client, Lord Sudley, merely wishes to be absolutely certain of things," I said. "You were in the house when Mr. Montgomery died?"

"Yes. In the library. I heard the gunshot and left the map I was studying to go upstairs, where I found everyone already congregated outside Rudy's door."

"Why are you studying in the Montgomery library?" Berta asked. "What is the matter with the library at your college?"

"It's about my thesis." Theo gestured to the dirt pit behind him. "So is this." His voice sank into a droning professorial key. "Most scholars believe that on the eve of the famous massacre of the Pequot War of 1637—I don't suppose you've heard of it—"

"Of course we have," Berta and I lied in unison.

Theo's brows lifted. "Oh. Well, most scholars believe that the English camped at the mouth of the Mystic River, approximately four miles west of here. It is my contention, however, that they camped right here in this forest, at the mouth of the Sewant River."

Sounded anaesthetizing.

"My thesis will turn Pequot War scholarship on its ear. If I am able to convincingly prove my case—and I have no doubt that I shall—my academic career will be made. I'll be able to win a professor's position at the university of my choice once I complete my doctoral degree."

"There is proof of your thesis in the Montgomerys' library?" I asked. "And out here in your mudhole?"

"It's an excavation pit," Theo said coldly. "Not a *mudhole*. And, yes. I've already found two musket balls and seventeenth-century iron nails in the correct stratigraphic layer. I'm about to break ground on another pit closer to the salt marsh, actually."

"What's in the Montgomery library?" I asked.

"Family histories and records. I'm looking for mention of the camp, or mention of artifacts having been found on the land."

"And the map you mentioned?"

Theo's lips tightened. "If you must know, it was an antique map of the estate, dating from the construction of the lighthouse on the point in 1802."

"What was your relationship with Rudy Montgomery, Mr. Wainwright?"

Theo's eyes flew wide, but he swiftly rearranged his expression to one of amusement. "You wish to determine whether or not I blipped the old coot off, is that it?"

Berta said, "You do not have an alibi, Mr. Wainwright."

"I didn't kill him. How absurd. I only met him for the first time at the beginning of the school term, after my professor told me I might find something of interest in the Montgomery library. So I went to his front door and asked for permission to look through his documents and, amazingly, he said yes."

"Why was it amazing?" I asked.

"Because he was either drunk or in a jealous rage on every subsequent occasion that I encountered him. An awful man, really. Always bellowing and posturing and trying to make certain that everyone for miles around knew that he was the alpha of the pack. Other than that, I did not know him. So sorry."

"Have you found anything of interest in the library?" I asked.

A slight pause. "Not yet. But such is the way of archival research."

"Did Mr. Montgomery give you permission to dig on his land?" Berta asked.

"Yes."

"Why?"

"Because he cared about history, quite obviously."

I said, "Miss Murden mentioned something about having known your mother—who was she?"

Theo jutted his chin and shoved his glasses up his nose. "What did she say about my mother?"

"Nothing, really, but—"

"My mother was a saint, and Miss Murden is an evil biddy."

"Where are you from?" I asked.

Another pause. "I grew up here in Carvington."

Funny. I would've never guessed he was a local. He spoke not with the coastal Yankee accent, but with the sniffier intonations of a boarding school boy.

"One last thing," I said. "If Rudy Montgomery was indeed murdered, who do you think might have done it?"

"God, I don't know. One of his hunting cronies?"

"They were all outside when he died."

"Then I suppose that skulking African valet fellow couldn't have done it either. Pity. That man looks like a criminal."

I looked at Theo closely. Was this run-of-the-mill bigotry? Perhaps. Although, something like anger snapped in his eyes. "Do you have a personal grudge against Mwinyi, Mr. Wainwright?"

"God, no. I've never even spoken to the fellow. Actually, I don't think he even speaks English." Theo stepped onto the ladder leading down into the pit. "Now, I'd like to get some work done."

Berta extracted a business card from her handbag and passed it down to Theo. "Do contact us if you think of anything useful."

Before Berta and I went back inside, we stopped to inspect Rudy's bedroom windows from the outside.

"The window on the right was the one left open when his body was discovered," I said. "It's exactly above the drawing room window that Isobel Bradford opened."

"Which is precisely why we were able to smell gunpowder," Berta said.

"Right. But as I suspected, the position of the windows means that no one could have fled through the window by way of, say, a ladder, without our having seen them from the drawing room. And—" I studied the red stone façade. "—no balconies, ledges, or vines to enable an escape to the next room over."

"Could the killer have fled through the open window by using a rope to scale up to the roof?"

I laughed, picturing Miss Murden winching herself, mountaineer-style, up the steep, rain-slicked slates. "No. Even if it could've been done, they would have been in clear view of the hunting party."

"True. I did not think of that."

When Berta and I arrived in the entry hall, Eustace was waiting for us.

"There you are," he said. "I'm afraid I've got some rotten news." He came over to me and flipped the pages of a kidskin address book. "I'd just remembered you requested Isobel Bradford's address. But look here: the page with the *B* tab, where her Boston address was written, has been ripped out. See?" One of the pages had a jagged tear near the binding.

"Goodness," Berta murmured. "It would seem that Isobel Bradford does not wish to be pursued."

"I knew she was bad news," I said. "What about Coral? She might have Isobel's address somewhere, since she's been playing Montgomery Hall's hostess."

Berta and I left Eustace and went upstairs to the bedroom where I'd tucked in Coral the night before. Coral sprawled facedown, still in her fox party dress, makeup smeared across the pillowcase. We couldn't wake her.

"Rudy's study?" I whispered.

Berta nodded.

We hurried back downstairs. After opening and shutting a lot of doors—library, billiards room, conservatory, powder room—we found a study with a big cluttered desk and a wall of wooden file cabinets. Berta snapped on the overhead light.

I hesitated. "What about our fingerprints?"

"We are private detectives, Mrs. Woodby. It is the done thing to rifle."

"Okay."

Berta began pawing through the desk drawers, so I went to the file cabinets and opened one. Bank statements, and healthy ones at that, including the most recent ones. That would seem to negate Eustace's theory that Rudy was hiding diamonds to keep a reservoir of liquid assets.

I was just opening a dossier marked OYSTER PRESERVES (Ugh. Did one smear those on Melba toast?) when Berta said, "Here it is."

I shut the file cabinet and hurried over.

Berta flipped to the Bs.

"Wowie," I murmured.

Just as with Eustace's address book, the B page that would have contained Isobel and Winslow Bradford's address had been torn out.

"What a cunning woman," Berta said. "How will we locate her now?"

"We may be able to dig up her address and telephone number in the *Social Register* of Boston, if we can locate a copy, or—" I snapped my fingers. "Remember Eustace said that Winslow Bradford belonged to the Scion Club?"

"Yes."

"Well, the club must have the Bradfords' home address on file somewhere."

"Those clubs admit only gentlemen, Mrs. Woodby, and they are guarded like King Tut's tomb."

"Sure, but the Scion Club is one of Dove White Launderette's clients, and I don't need to remind you that Dove White Launderette is still *our* client."

Confusion, then shock, then understanding washed over Berta's face. "So it is. What splendid luck."

We found Eustace in his bedroom.

"We're leaving for Manhattan," I told him. "We have a lead on Isobel Bradford's address."

"Manhattan?" he said. "That gives me an idea." He looked up and down the corridor. "Come in."

Berta, Cedric, and I stepped into Eustace's room.

He shut the door and went to his desk. He pulled something from the drawer and turned. "Here." He held up an argyle sock with something bulgy weighing down the toe.

"I hope you don't think laundry services are included in our agency's fee," I said.

Eustace burst out laughing. "Oh, my dear Lola, you *are* a pip. No, I've stashed the diamonds in this sock, but I really don't think they're safe here in my bedroom. Anyone could come in and jimmy the desk drawer open." He handed the sock to me—it was surprisingly heavy—and produced a key. "This is the key to my safe-deposit box at the East Twenty-third Street branch of Sterling National Bank in the city. The box number is engraved on the key. I keep a box there for when I'm in America—handy for storing valuable bits and bobs when I'm traveling from place to place. As long as you're going into the city, why don't you take the diamonds and lock them up there? It'll be a great weight off my mind. I didn't sleep more than an hour last night, worrying that some scoundrel was going to murder me for those diamonds. I mean to hand them over to the lawyer as soon as he shows up, of course, but that won't be till tomorrow."

Berta and I exchanged doubtful glances.

"All right," I said. "I'll telephone you here at the house as soon as we have any news about Isobel Bradford." We turned to go, but Eustace stopped the door with a large, suntanned hand.

"Wait," he said. "There is something else."

"Yes?" I widened my eyes and gave my Maybellined lashes a flick. Berta sighed heavily.

"Do be safe, Lola," Eustace said. His brown eyes pleaded like a Saint Bernard dog's. "Not only with the diamonds, but with yourself. I simply couldn't forgive myself if anything were to happen to you. It kills me a bit that I can't come along to look after you, but I must stay here at Montgomery Hall and stave off any more dreadful occurrences." He smiled and opened the door. "Off you go. I'll be waiting for you to telephone—oh, and don't mind the jewels that are already in my safe-deposit box. Those belong to my aunt Iphigenia."

8

....

Berta and I hastily packed our suitcases, and then I found Cedric wedged like an infant porpoise between two Labradors on the drawing room hearth. I extracted him. We were about to leave the house when I hesitated. Maybe I could meet Ralph in the city today. Maybe we could patch things up. Because as flattering as Eustace's attentions were, they only reminded me of how achingly I missed Ralph.

"You go ahead, Berta. I'm going to pop into Rudy's study and make a quick telephone call."

Berta regarded me shrewdly. "To Mr. Oliver?"

"Beg your pardon?"

"Because Lord Sudley's attentions are keeping the embers of romance stoked in your bosom?"

"No."

"Hmph." Berta carried Cedric, her handbag, and her small suitcase outside.

I left my suitcase by the front door, but took my handbag and the sockful of diamonds to Rudy's study. There, I found Glenn Monroe in a mustard silk robe with his slippered feet on the desk. He was speaking into the telephone receiver.

"So if you keep on throwing these rotten scripts at me, I'm gonna have to walk away, got it?" he said. He glanced up, saw me, and smiled. "Listen, I've gotta go—and I mean it, enough of this crap. I'm up to two bottles of Alkacine a day. Do you really want that on your conscience? Yeah. See you Sunday." Glenn hung up. "Morning, Lola. Looking for the blower?"

"Yes—that is, if you're finished with it."

"For the moment." Glenn drew a brown glass medicine bottle from his robe pocket, unscrewed the cap, and took a pull. "It's not what you think—it's Alkacine. The radio station doesn't give me headaches, but it sure is killing my stomach."

I gave a sympathetic nod. Alkacine was a drugstore brand of milk of magnesia. Berta used it from time to time for her own heartburn.

"I gotta drink this stuff around the clock or I feel like an active volcano," Glenn said. "But I'll leave you to it." He swung his feet off the desk and stood.

"Before you go, Mr. Monroe, I wished to ask you a question."

"O-kayo."

"Well, to begin with, Mrs. Lundgren and I are private detectives—"

"You don't say!"

"—and Lord Sudley hired us to look into Rudy's death. He has reason to believe there might've been foul play."

"Detective dames. Huh. Sounds like something out of the pictures."

I chose my words carefully. "You left the drawing room to make a telephone call shortly before the shot was fired in Rudy's bedroom."

Glenn's friendly expression slid off. He suddenly looked pinched and suspicious. "What're you getting at?"

"Did you see anything amiss during that brief period?"

"No. I was right here at the study desk, actually, with the door open. The only person I saw was Coral passing by when she came downstairs after her fight with Rudy. She didn't notice me and I was on the telephone with the station, so I didn't call out to her. She won't be able to back me up." Glenn twisted the Alkacine bottle in his hands. "A minute or two after that, there was the shot upstairs. I got off the telephone in a hurry and went to investigate." Glenn unscrewed the bottle cap and took another swig. "I think I need to go back to bed for a few hours. I couldn't sleep last night. Kept thinking I heard voices calling my name."

"Voices?"

Glenn winked. "I guess it was the Montgomery ghost. Guess she's not too happy these days." He slipped past me.

I shook off the creepy-crawlies—I do not believe in ghosts—went to the desk, picked up the telephone, and rattled off Ralph's telephone number to the exchange girl.

He picked up after five rings.

"Ralph? Hello. It's me." A pause. "Lola."

"Morning." His voice was blurred with sleepiness. Maybe a little aloof. "Where the heck are you?"

"In Connecticut on a case."

"Not the Montgomery death I read about in the extras last night?"

"That's the one."

"Sheesh. Be careful, kid."

He still calls me kid.

"Don't call me kid," I said crisply.

"You're the boss."

"I'm glad that's settled." I took a deep breath. "I telephoned because I—"

"Wanted to apologize?"

"*Apologize? For what?*"

"Telling me that you hate me comes to mind."

"Oh. That. That was because you said—"

"Listen, Lola, is this why you telephoned? To tell me all over again how we're not on the same page?"

"Not on the same page?" My voice spiraled upward. "We're not even reading the same book, Ralph Oliver!"

"Okay. I get it." A pause. "Why the telephone call?"

"You are the most impossible—"

"You don't want to compromise, Lola, but you also can't stay away."

"Oh, I can stay away, all right," I said through clenched teeth, and slammed the earpiece in its cradle. I pressed a hand to my hot forehead. That wasn't the conversation I'd imagined, full of tearful apologies and breathless promises. *That*, ladies and gentlemen, was a shipwreck.

I pushed out of the study and nearly crashed into Coral, still in last night's smeared makeup and wrinkled dress.

Had she been eavesdropping?

"Man troubles, sweetie?" she said with a yawn.

"Is there any other kind? Say, you don't happen to have Isobel Bradford's address, do you?"

"Isobel? Of course not. I used Rudy's address book when I sent out the invitations. What do you want her address for?" Coral's eyes widened, and all of a sudden, she didn't appear to be hungover in the slightest. "Something about those little gray rocks you and your Swedish pal were playing with in the wee hours?"

"Oh. Yes. More or less."

"Say, what's in the sock?"

Phooey. Why hadn't I stashed that in my handbag? "What's in the sock? More socks. Dirty ones. Got to dash!" I squeezed past Coral and made tracks for the front door.

Berta, Cedric, and I ate a substantial lunch at the Red Rooster in Carvington and then set out down the coast. I huddled at the steering wheel, peering between the rhythmically squeaking wipers. My heart ached over my telephone conversation with Ralph. The thing was, my marriage to Alfie had been as agreeable as an electric dental drill. Why was I so eager to give the institution another go? On the other hand, Ralph was infuriatingly blasé about the matter. Almost as though I meant no more to him than the girl before me.

The thought of Ralph's previous girls (he never spoke of them, but I knew with a sixth sense that there were dozens) turned my hands to chicken talons around the steering wheel. Alfie had had plenty of previous girlfriends, too—not to mention girls on the side during our marriage. Ugh. Men.

We reached Manhattan a bit before three o'clock. I made my way through the splashing, honking traffic toward the Dove White Launderette. My spirits sank lower with every block deeper into Manhattan we went. Ralph could be just around the next corner. I needed to keep away from that so-and-so. Far, far away.

I caught sight of the Empress Josephine Bakery on Ninth Street, swerved to the curb—narrowly missing a taxicab—and braked so hard, Berta grabbed the dashboard.

"What are you doing?" she cried.

"Back in a jiffy," I said, throwing the Duesy into park and opening my door.

I returned a few minutes later with a white cardboard box, nestled it in my lap, and opened the lid.

"You have buttercream on your cheek, Mrs. Woodby."

"I never buy cakes without sampling them first."

"You should tell that to Lord Sudley."

I picked up one of the petits fours from the box and stuffed it into my mouth as I eased back into the traffic.

Ten minutes and six petits fours later, I parked in front of the Dove White Launderette in the West Village. Cheery yellow light and soapy steam surged from its open door.

"Allow me to do the talking," Berta said as she climbed out of the Duesy. "Mrs. Hodges likes me."

I scooped up Cedric and followed Berta inside the launderette. Electric washing machines clunked and whined. Women in white smocks and caps folded sheets and tablecloths at a long table.

Berta was already in the back, speaking to the plump, red-lipsticked manageress, Mrs. Hodges, who had hired us last week to find and retrieve two missing laundry carts.

"We have a lead," Berta was telling her. "A rather hot lead."

"Oh, good," Mrs. Hodges said. "I thought when I hadn't heard from you—"

"We must lie low and keep our ears to the ground," Berta said. "And it has paid off. However, we do require the use of one of your laundry delivery trucks—oh, and we must borrow two uniforms."

Twenty minutes and three more petits fours after that, Berta parked the borrowed Dove White Launderette truck in the alleyway behind the swanky Scion Club on Fifty-first Street.

"Look," I whispered. "The service entrance is propped open."

"Do you intend to bring your dog along?" Berta slid the truck key into her handbag.

In my lap, Cedric swished his plume of a tail.

"I can't leave him in the truck," I said. "What if it gets towed?"

Berta heaved a sigh.

We got out of the truck, wearing our borrowed laundress smocks and caps. Berta's black handbag was slung over her forearm. With Cedric tucked under my own arm like a loaf of pumpernickel, I looked through the service door. It led to a utilitarian tiled hallway. Savory cooking smells coiled out.

"Wait," Berta said. "We must have a pretense for entering the club." She hurried back to the truck, opened the back, and returned carrying a stack of white napkins in addition to her black handbag.

I hesitated. "Laundry delivery women wouldn't carry handbags," I whispered.

"Nor would they carry toy dogs, Mrs. Woodby. Come along. We do not have much time if we wish to reach Lord Sudley's bank before it closes."

We went inside and along the tiled corridor, passing a kitchen where a man in a cook's hat was stirring something on the stove. He glanced over his shoulder when we entered.

"Linen delivery," Berta said.

"Down the hall. Linen closet's on the right."

Berta and I continued down the corridor. We found the linen closet. Berta dumped the stack of napkins on a shelf, and we kept going.

Once we reached the door at the end of the corridor, the sounds of men's bawdy laughter, clinking glasses, phonograph crooning, and a rumbling sound I couldn't identify had grown quite loud. I inched the door open.

Fellows in bespoke suits and loosened ties lounged in the large club room across the entry hall. Smoke wafted, a cocktail shaker rattled, and one fellow with pomaded hair and eyeglasses was dancing with a tiger skin rug. From beyond the staircase came more of that strange rumbling, accompanied by guffaws and hoots.

The Scion wasn't your Victorian newspaper-and-cigar sort of club.

"Golly, I hope we don't get caught," I whispered. "I *know* some of those men—look, there's Fizzy Van Hoogenband playing table tennis. They'll recognize me."

"Do not take this badly, Mrs. Woodby, but it is unlikely they would recognize you in your disguise."

I patted my starched cap. "I thought I looked all right."

"There is an office just over there, beyond the cloakroom—see?—and it appears to contain a good number of filing cabinets. Surely the members' addresses are kept in there somewhere."

"All right." We darted across the entry hall, through the cloakroom, and into the office.

No one was in there, thank goodness.

"Keep watch," Berta whispered, trundling toward the wall of filing cabinets. "This should not take long."

"Okay." I stood guard in the doorway between the office and the cloakroom.

Cedric pricked his ears; the peculiar rumbling sound was growing louder and louder, and then—*whoosh! whoosh!*—two white canvas carts sailed past the cloakroom door with men riding inside. They crashed into the club's front door. Hoots and laughter.

Wait. Those were . . . *laundry* carts.

I peered out of the cloakroom with one eye. The men were turning around inside the cart, and more men had come over to give them pushes.

The canvas sides of the carts were stenciled with the words DOVE WHITE LAUNDERETTE. The stolen carts!

I hurried back into the office. "Berta!" I whispered, "the launderette's stolen carts are here!"

Berta was jotting something into her detecting notebook. "I beg your pardon?"

"The club members stole the launderette's carts. They're using them as go-carts."

"Oh, thank heavens," Berta said, stuffing her notebook into her handbag. "I felt dreadful about lying to poor Mrs. Hodges. We shall tell her we have located the carts and come back to retrieve them later, when we are not in disguise. Oh, and I have procured Isobel Bradford's Boston address."

"Peachy. Let's skate."

The coast was clear; the laundry cart race had rumbled away for the moment. We'd almost made it to the service corridor door when a steward emerged from, evidently, the wainscoting and cleared his throat. "Laundry deliveries are to be made in the service portions of this establishment only," he said.

Berta and I froze.

"And—" The steward cast a loathing look at Cedric. "—if I find a single orange hair on the clean linens, I shall terminate all further business with Dove White Launderette."

I swallowed. "No need to do that, Mr.—?"

"My name is irrelevant."

"All right, Mr. Irrelevant. Well, you see, the thing is, this dog is actually a sort of a bloodhound—by trade, I mean to say—and he's come to sniff out two laundry carts that were stolen from the launderette's delivery truck a few weeks ago. And as you can see, he tracked them down."

On cue, the laundry cart racers rumbled past.

"I see," the steward said.

"So we'll just collect the stolen carts and be on our way."

The steward pursed his tortoiselike lips.

A few minutes later, Berta and I were pushing the laundry carts up the portable ramp and into the back of the delivery truck. Then, victorious, we were on our way.

9

Once we had returned the delivery truck and the stolen carts to the Dove White Launderette, accepted a cash payment and an invitation to tea the next week from the grateful Mrs. Hodges, changed out of our disguises, taken Cedric for an urgent promenade around the block, given him a bowl of water in the back of the launderette, used the launderette's washroom, and taken Cedric for another urgent promenade, it was half past four o'clock.

"We'll have just enough time to nip into Lord Sudley's bank before it closes, and lock the diamonds in his safe-deposit box," I said to Berta, motoring slowly on East Twenty-third in search of a parking spot. "After that, we should go directly to the train station and get ourselves to Boston. Here's the bank, but there is nowhere to park. I could double-park while you go in."

"No. You are the one who agreed to this farcical plan."

"Well, then, I'll double-park and go in while you wait—"

"The problem is, I must—" She coughed. "—*spend a penny.*"

"Again? In the bank?"

Berta drew herself up. "I do not care to discuss this matter in great detail, Mrs. Woodby."

I wedged the Duesy mostly into a spot on the other side of the block, and with Cedric leading the way with his tail and tiny chin high, we walked through the drizzle. We had not quite made it to the bank when we spotted the Automat across the street, lit up in the dreary afternoon like the gateway to Paradise.

"Do you know, I believe I shall pop into the Automat and use their powder room," Berta said, stopping. "I am certain it is much more welcoming than the bank's."

We crossed the hectic street, I scooped up Cedric, and we went in. Berta trundled off to the rear regions of the restaurant. Cedric and I loitered just inside the front door.

In the months since I'd become an impoverished gumshoe, I had discovered the ambrosial delights of Automats. New York City is teeming with them, and no one ever told me! There are no menus, no thumb-twiddling, and no waiters to pass judgment upon the number of desserts one eats, or if one skips the main course entirely and begins with pie. All you must do is go to the ornate walls with signs that read SANDWICHES, PIES, MAIN COURSES, and (yes!) CAKES and filled with little glass-doored compartments, slide your nickels in the slot, open the door of your choice, and—voilà!—time to eat.

Five minutes or so passed and Berta didn't reappear. I considered going to the bank without her, but decided against it. That might irk her. A quick bite to eat would settle my nerves.

I carried Cedric directly to the CAKES section. I did realize that my cake consumption was beginning to be a problem. I did not agree with Berta that I had a nervous condition, but I was asking a great deal of my dress seams.

However, the Automat was decidedly not the place to worry about seams. I burrowed into my handbag while still holding Cedric, by passing the sockful of diamonds, lipsticks, Milk-Bones, and chocolate bar ends, and found my coin purse.

Then for the selection. Coconut? No. That was Ralph's favorite, and it was cosmically unfair that I should have him on my mind when he had left me to navigate this cold, wet, miserable November on my own.

I swallowed the lump in my throat. Banana-pecan would do nicely. I slid in my nickel and opened the little glass door, and then my eye fell on a heretofore unnoticed slice of moist, dense-looking chocolate layer cake in another compartment. I hesitated. Then I took the slice of banana-pecan cake—it was wrapped tidily in waxed paper—and attempted to stuff it into my already bursting handbag with the intention of having the chocolate now and the banana-pecan later. I suppose I was squishing Cedric as I tried to stuff the cake, because he squirmed and paddled his paws in the air. My handbag slid off my arm, hit the floor, the cake went tumbling, Cedric took a leap, and—gadzooks!—the sock of diamonds splattered open.

I dropped to my hands and knees and gathered the diamonds up in a clammy panic. Cedric, meanwhile, snuffled into the banana-pecan cake.

Diners at nearby tables looked on with idle interest but—thank goodness I was in New York—no one came to my assistance, although a little girl picked up a rather large raw diamond that had bounced under her chair and said, "Look, Mommy! A little rock!"

"Don't touch that, dear," her mother said. "It looks dirty."

Berta's Edwardian boots appeared in my line of vision.

"Are you quite ready, Mrs. Woodby?" she whispered, glancing furtively about.

"I was waiting for you." I stashed away the last diamond and peered up at Berta. "Are you well? You look a little . . . flushed."

"Nonsense. Come along."

Outside, Berta asked softly, "Did you retrieve all the diamonds?"

"For the most part."

Then I happened to look through the Automat windows to see a bandy fellow in a fedora and a swanky little suit looking right back out at us—or, rather, at Berta.

"Is that Jimmy the Ant?" I cried. "Berta! You were talking to Mr. Ant in there! *That's* what took you so long."

"He does so dislike that name." Berta hastened to the crosswalk.

"You arranged a meeting?"

"Yes, if you must know. I telephoned him from the launderette, just to say hello, and he insisted upon a brief rendezvous when I told him we planned to stop at the East Twenty-third Street branch of Sterling National. He is, as you know, lying low, so I have not seen him for at least two weeks."

"A bona fide drought. Did you kiss?"

"Mrs. *Wood*by!"

I trotted after Berta, shaking my head. Jimmy the Ant—no idea what his real surname is, if he even has one—was Berta's low-life, on-again, off-again gangster beau. He was Bad News, and frankly, with his petite physique and lolling glass eye, I couldn't for the life of me figure why Berta even gave him the time of day. He was a dapper dresser, though. I'd never seen him without spats.

We reached Sterling National Bank. Fancy iron grilles had already been fastened over the glass doors, and a man inside the lobby was locking up.

"Stop!" Berta cried. "We must come in!"

The man shrugged theatrically.

I checked my wristwatch. "We've still got one minute!"

Sorry, he mouthed, and walked deeper into the bank. A moment later, the light snapped off.

"Rats," I muttered. Rain dribbled off my hat brim, and my hand-bag with the sockful of diamonds suddenly felt as heavy as an anvil.

After that, we didn't motor down to our poky little Washington Square apartment; there was no time. We went directly to the vicinity of Grand Central Terminal and left the Duesy parked high inside one of those alarming new car elevators. I convinced Cedric to pay his taxes on the sidewalk, cleaned it up with a newspaper and disposed of it—Berta looked on smugly—and then we plunged into the echoing chaos of the station.

At the ticket window, I purchased two one-way fares to Boston's South Station on the *Merchants Limited*. Twenty minutes later, we boarded the train.

This was an all-parlor car, a splurge since we'd been unexpect-edly paid cash by Mrs. Hodges and because we were both bone-tired. Instead of blah rows of seats and no-frills compartments, the *Merchants Limited* boasted red velveteen seats with tasseled pil-lows, arched ceilings edged in gold, and thick carpets. The first time I rode in an all-parlor train, I felt like I was rattling down the track inside a Fabergé egg.

Berta and I settled into squashy seats, made our dinner reserva-tions with a conductor, and a few minutes later, the train groaned and lurched through the long tunnels of Grand Central Terminal and, presently, out into the cold wet night.

"Seven fifteen for dinner?" I said with a sigh. "That's nearly an hour away."

"You will survive." Berta took an issue of *Lurid Tales* from her handbag and passed me a second magazine, the cover of which de-picted a beleaguered girl with a waved bob surrounded by a gray phantom swirl. "Here is the new *Spectral Stories*. I have not even read it yet."

"Thanks." I stared moodily out at the lights flicking past, petting Cedric, the magazine resting unopened on my knee.

At 7:13, Berta and I migrated to the dining car, where we were led to a small, beautifully laid table near the front end. Outside the velvet curtains, the dark night whizzed past. Raindrops streaked sideways across the window.

We were enjoying after-dinner coffees with slices of orange-chocolate torte when two men in suits and hats stood up at the back end of the dining car and made their swaying way down the aisle. Our waiter leaned over our table to refill Berta's coffee cup just as the men were attempting to pass. The shorter of the two men, a sallow fellow with thick, owlish eyeglasses, stumbled heavily against the waiter. The waiter toppled to the aisle, and the owlish fellow thumped on top of him. The well-bred diners in the car murmured and exclaimed at decorous volumes. I scooted back my chair and lent the owlish fellow a hand. The waiter was on his hands and knees, mopping up spilled coffee.

"Gee, thanks, miss," the owlish fellow said. "It's these new eyeglasses. I'd bet you anything the doc gave me the wrong strength 'cause the whole world's been bucking like a wild pony."

The other man, tall and gangly with a long, scholarly looking face, was helping set to rights the cups and saucers and plates on our table. "There you go, ladies," he said in a rich baritone. "Right as rain. Beg your pardon." He lifted his fedora, and he and the other fellow turned and exited the dining car through the rear door.

The waiter was now on his feet. He finished refilling our coffee cups and went on his way.

"Such gentlemen," Berta said.

"Something isn't right," I said. "I can't put my finger on it."

"I know what it is. You have not finished your cake."

"It's not cake. It's torte."

Berta and I returned to our seats in the parlor car. It wasn't long before Berta was snoring softly beside me with *Lurid Tales* lolling open on her lap. I read *Spectral Stories* for perhaps an hour, and it reminded me distressingly of that moaning *Lolaaaaaaa* business in the hallway of Montgomery Hall the night before. Even so, I found myself quite unable to keep my eyes open. I swirled down into a dizzy black pit with the endless, rhythmical chugging of the train rebounding inside my skull.

"Madam?" a man's voice said, muffled as if through layers of gauze. Someone shook my shoulder, setting off rolling breakers of nausea. The voice grew more distinct. "Madam, wake up. We have arrived in Boston."

With great effort I opened my eyes to see a blurry blue blob. "Whuh?" I managed. Cedric bounced up, paws on my shoulder, and licked my face.

"Madam, we have arrived at South Station. This is the end of the line. You must disembark the train."

"Thrain?" I said.

"Is this woman beside you your traveling companion?" the blurry blue blob asked.

"Thtop talking tho loud," I mumbled. I turned my head. Berta was still snoring beside me, head thrown back, molars exposed.

"Clearly you two ladies have had too much to drink," the blue blob said. "Please leave now or I shall be forced to summon the station police."

"All right, all right," I muttered. I shook Berta until she snorted awake. "C'mon, Berta, we muss go. We're here." I wobbled to my feet, hugging Cedric so tightly that he wriggled until I loosened my hold. Berta struggled to her feet, clutching her handbag and *Lurid Tales*. She practically fell down the steps onto the nearly deserted, lamplit platform, where our two suitcases sat waiting for us. I went shakily down the steps, tripped at the bottom, and Cedric boinged neatly from my arms just before I splatted onto my hands and knees, knocking both suitcases sideways.

"Enjoy your stay in Boston," the blue blob said coldly, withdrawing into the car.

I got to my feet. My knees throbbed.

"I am ever so dizzy," Berta said, her Swedish accent twice as thick as usual.

"Me, thoo. Leth find a bensh and siddown for a minute before we try to find a hothell."

We picked up our suitcases and weaved along the platform and into the echoing bright station. Travelers crisscrossed. Luggage carts rumbled. Enormous clocks whirred and clicked.

"I fear I am going to be sick," Berta said, and staggered to a garbage bin, where she was indeed sick.

Call me a bozo, but it wasn't until then that it dawned on me: something was terribly wrong with Berta and me. We hadn't drunk any alcohol, not even a drop. Had we contracted some horrible plague? I wobbled over to Berta, still bent over the garbage bin, and patted her back. "I see thome benshes over there," I said. "Nice and quiet thpot. Leth go rest and then find a doctor."

I stretched out on one of the benches with my head on my handbag, Cedric on my belly, and my suitcase under the seat. Berta curled up on the other bench. The ceiling did the foxtrot for a moment and then everything went black.

When I woke again, I had a headache like a pulsating hatchet blade. My mouth was tacky, my legs felt rickety, but my thoughts were stark and clear.

"Knockout drops," I muttered. I sat up on the bench. "Berta!"

Berta sat up gingerly. Her gray bun sagged one way, her hat another, and her cheeks were ashen.

"Berta, those men in the dining car gave us knockout drops. Crashing into the waiter was just a distraction. How could we have been so stupid? They turned around and walked out of the dining car *the way they'd come*."

Berta clucked her tongue. "Mickey Finns. How dare they? Oh! Check your handbag!"

Oh golly golly golly. I opened my handbag.

The diamonds were gone, sock and all.

"Phooey!" I screamed up to the lofty ceiling. My voice echoed back. None of the other travelers even glanced in my direction.

10

....

We made a plan. In a nutshell, it was: (1) Change into clean clothes and brush teeth. (2) Drink coffee. (3) Make another plan.

I clipped on Cedric's leash and we walked woozily out into a clear, cold Boston morning. Poor little Cedric had been a perfect gentleman in the train station. I led him to the nearest lamppost.

Then we crossed noisy Atlantic Avenue, passing beneath the elevated train tracks, found a small, respectable-looking hotel, and booked two rooms. Berta and I both washed, changed, and then, leaving our suitcases in our hotel rooms, wandered a few blocks until we found a dinette. The hostess eyed Cedric doubtfully, so I slipped her a fiver. She stuffed it into her apron pocket. "Keep him outa sight under the table," she said, and led us to a window booth.

Berta and I did not speak until we both had drunk a full cup of coffee and eaten several bites of steak and eggs.

"How's your head?" I asked her.

"Aching. Yours?"

"The same. And I'm breaking into a cold sweat about those missing diamonds. Once I lost several hundred dollars on a bad colt at Saratoga Springs, and I felt just awful. But this . . . oh golly, Berta, what're we going to do?"

"First, we will not panic. It is a waste, and it is terribly aging. Second, we do not yet know whom Rudy Montgomery named as his heir, and thus, we do not yet know whom those diamonds belong to. We are here in Boston to locate Isobel Bradford and we must focus all our energies upon that. Not only is she one of our murder suspects, but if she was seen knocking on hunting trophies, she likely knows about those diamonds."

"Okay, okay." I shook tomato catsup on my steak and eggs. "Berta, I hate to bring this up, but you didn't happen to mention the diamonds to Jimmy the Ant when you spoke to him at the Automat, did you?"

A pause. "It is possible."

"Berta! Jimmy works for *Lem Fitzpatrick*. He might've squealed about the diamonds."

"Jimmy would never do such a thing."

Lem Fitzpatrick is one of New York City's most notorious gangsters. He's got his fingers in all sorts of criminal pies, but convictions stick to him like oil sticks to butter.

I brought my voice down to a murmur. "If we've gotten ourselves mixed up with Fitzpatrick, things could get—"

"It was not necessarily Fitzpatrick who sent those thugs on the train, Mrs. Woodby. It could have been Coral, for instance—"

"Coral?"

"She did see the diamonds last night."

"Sure—in double. She was blotto." But she had seen me holding the sock in Rudy's study . . .

"Why, the thugs could even have been sent after us by Lord Sudley—"

"Hooey!"

"—as a way to keep the diamonds for himself without letting on to us that he was the thief."

"That's a stretch."

"Did it not seem odd to you that he asked us to lock up the diamonds when the lawyer was already on his way?"

"No, I thought he was being conscientious. And I think you're biased against poor Eustace. He's our *client*, for goodness' sake, and he's also the most gentlemanlike fellow I've ever met."

"You are blinded by his good looks. And by the notion of his estate in England."

Ignoring that (because I suspected it was a teensy bit true), I slipped a nibble of steak under the table for Cedric. "You're right about one thing: We have no proof that those were Fitzpatrick's thugs. You must telephone Jimmy and ask him about it, okay?"

Berta nodded. Her pale blue eyes shone wetly.

Uh-oh. Was she crying? Over Jimmy the Ant, who resembled an inexpertly taxidermied lizard?

"I'm sorry," I said. "Men really are hangnails."

"Not all men." Berta touched the locket she always wore at her throat. I had never asked her about it before; I'm a chicken. Berta is familiar with my extended menu of flaws, embarrassments, foibles, and anxieties, but she keeps her own cards close.

I took a deep breath. "All right. Tell me about him."

"Whom?"

"The fellow in the locket."

"Locket?" Berta slid it out of sight between two dress buttons.

"Is it Mr. Lundgren?"

Berta buttered toast. "There is no Mr. Lundgren."

"You mean you're a widow?"

"No, I mean I was never married."

"How can that be? You're *Mrs.* Lundgren."

"Lundgren is in fact my maiden name. I assumed the title of

Mrs. to lend myself an air of respectability when I came to the United States to pursue work in domestic service. Ladies of the house prefer to hire married women. They worry about their husbands and sons, you know, and in my youth, I was considered very pretty."

"You never told me you're not really a Mrs."

"Because I lied to you, in essence, when you hired me as your cook."

I waved my fork. "Water under the bridge. But, say—who's in the locket, then?"

Berta smeared marmalade on her toast, meticulously avoiding the edges. "Lars."

I raised my eyebrows.

"He was a young fisherman in my village in Sweden. He quite turned my head—I was only seventeen years old, of course, so a bit impressionable."

But you still have his picture in your locket and you're over sixty. "What became of him?"

I braced myself for one of those sad tales of deadly influenza, or disappearance in a war, or of Lars marrying the village harpy and proceeding to father ten kids. But Berta said, "I do not know. He simply vanished one day. He left all his things behind in his cottage. And no one in the village ever heard from him again. I do not wish to discuss this further. It tends to rile my heartburn."

"Okay," I mumbled. "Sorry." A long-lost love for Berta! I never would have guessed.

After breakfast, we purchased a city map at a newsstand on Boston Common and studied it carefully. We discovered that Marlborough Street, where Isobel Bradford's house was, began just on the other side of the park. I'd been to Boston before, of course, although on those occasions, I had been either a spoiled debutante or a pampered

Society Matron, and thus I had zipped about in fancy motorcars thinking of little besides how much I loathed my mother and/or my husband. But one really knows a city only if one walks around in it.

Berta and I agreed that our headaches and lumbars would benefit from fresh air and exercise, and set off on foot with Cedric gamboling along at the end of his leash.

The Bradford house was one of a long block of tall, regal brownstones with bow windows, postage stamp–sized front gardens, and spiked iron gates. The door was painted shiny black, and the brass kickplate reflected my battered T-strap pumps. I rang the bell. After a moment, a butler, squat, pin-striped, and sporting a fussy little clipped mustache, answered.

"Yes?" he said with a disapproving eye-flick down and up the three of us crowded on his threshold.

I passed him one of our cards. "My name is Mrs. Woodby, and this is Mrs. Lundgren. We are private detectives investigating the death of Rudolph Montgomery in Carvington, Connecticut. We would like to speak with Mrs. Bradford. She left so soon after Mr. Montgomery's death, we didn't have a chance to ask her if she had seen or heard anything amiss." I'd had enough doors slammed in my face not to let on that Isobel was our uppermost murder suspect.

"I am sorry, but there must be some mistake. Mrs. Bradford has not been in Connecticut since Easter."

Berta and I exchanged frowns. Had Isobel somehow sneaked off to Connecticut without her butler knowing?

Berta smiled. "Oh dear, how confusing. Do you suppose we might speak with Mrs. Bradford all the same?"

"I do not think—"

"I myself have become a detective only recently, after more than forty years in domestic service," Berta said, "so I am only too aware of how busy you must be, Mr.—"

"Adams." His mustache relaxed a notch.

"Mr. Adams. We would very much appreciate you telling Mrs. Bradford we are here."

"Very well. Come in." Adams let us into a narrow entry foyer and left us there.

"Swanky pad," I whispered, taking in the marble floor, carved staircase, and gilt-framed portraits of sour Puritans.

After a minute, Adams returned. "Mrs. Bradford says she will see you, as she is most dismayed about Mr. Montgomery's death." He led us upstairs and into a parlor with tall windows overlooking the street. Velvet furniture mingled with potted orchids and ivory bric-a-brac, and at first I didn't see the woman in the armchair in front of the fireplace.

"Thank you, Adams," she said in plummy, Boston Brahmin tones.

Adams left, shutting the double doors.

Berta and I stared in disbelief at the woman by the fire. We had never laid eyes on her before.

"Oh dear, I see you have brought a dog," the woman said. She was about sixty years of age and reminiscent of a greyhound, with a long face, protuberant and clever brown eyes, an old-fashioned silver chignon, and yardstick posture. A book lay in her lap. "Nasty, pushy things, dogs. Never mind, come and sit down. Adams will bring coffee. Why are you two standing there like lost ewes? Goodness. I was expecting hard-boiled dames, but you look as though you should be selling ice creams at a carnival—" This was directed at Berta. "—and you look like you'd be running the kissing booth." That was directed at me.

"Thanks for seeing us, Mrs. Bradford," I said brightly. "The funny thing is, we were expecting someone else, too." Berta and I settled in chairs opposite Isobel. I kept a firm hold on Cedric in my lap, because Isobel looked as though she'd enjoy kicking him.

"Why would you expect someone else? I have lived here for decades." The book on Isobel's lap was *The Pilgrim's Progress*. The literary equivalent of having one's mouth washed out with Ivory soap.

Berta and I explained how another woman calling herself Isobel Bradford had attended Rudy Montgomery's fateful hunting party and scarpered just after the death.

"Do you have a sister?" I asked Isobel.

"A sister who is also named Isobel? Don't be ridiculous. It sounds as though someone was pretending to be me."

"But who?" I asked.

"How would I know? Some sort of foul charlatan or actress, I suppose. The world is crawling with desperate women on the make." Isobel gave Berta and me pointed looks. "I read of Rudy Montgomery's death in the newspaper this morning. There was no mention of foul play, so why are you investigating? And who hired you?"

"Our client has reason to believe that Rudy was murdered," Berta said.

"Goodness." Isobel did not appear fazed.

"Did you know him?" I asked.

"Actually, no. My late husband, Winslow, was great friends with him, but they always met out in Africa or India or the Poconos. I do not hunt, so I never went along. However, although I did not know Rudy, I cannot say I would be terribly surprised if someone did murder him."

Berta and I leaned forward. "Why is that?" I asked.

"He was a cad. Winslow would tell me the most shocking stories. A woman in every port, as they say. So if it was murder, well, I'd blame it on a girlfriend, or a jilted girlfriend, or perhaps an enraged husband."

"Do you really have no idea who might have been impersonating you at Montgomery Hall this weekend?" Berta asked.

"No."

"Whoever the impostor was," I said, "she was someone who was aware that you had been invited to the hunting party in the first place."

"I wasn't invited."

"But everyone there seemed to have been expecting you. Coral—Rudy's girlfriend, who was acting as hostess—behaved as though it were natural that the woman impersonating you should be there."

"I never received an invitation. When would it have arrived?"

"Sometime in early October."

"I see. Well, Rudy always invited Winslow down to Connecticut for those sorts of things, but not only were wives not welcome—I can see you know precisely what I mean—but I wouldn't dream of going. Winslow would come home from Montgomery Hall with the most appalling reports of debauchery. Chorus girls, gin and cards, jazz, and all the rest."

"Didn't you mind your husband going?" I asked.

"Although I did not approve of Rudy's style of living, it was my duty to permit dear Winslow some pleasure in life. Men's clubs and hunting parties and so forth. At any rate, Winslow did not approve of Rudy's style of living, either. It was more that he overlooked it for the sake of the hunt." Isobel paused. "I do think Rudy might have been mixed up in something rather horrid, something worse than the run-of-the-mill girls, liquor, and cards."

Aha. Here it was. "Go on," I said.

"My poor Winslow seemed greatly troubled at the end of his days. His conscience was troubling him. He rambled vaguely about the nature of guilt, and in a roundabout way I pieced together that he was in particular troubled by something that had occurred on the latest safari in Kenya. One night, only a week or so before he died, I was at his bedside reading to him one of his favorite novels, Collins's *The Moonstone*—do you know it?"

"No."

"Well, I had barely begun reading when Winslow suddenly cried out, 'It's not right, Isobel! Something must be done!' I had no idea what he was speaking of, and he would tell me no more."

Adams glided in with a coffee service and placed it on the low table before the fire.

"Adams," Isobel said, "did you see an invitation arrive from Montgomery Hall in early October?"

"Why, yes, madam. I do recall accepting an envelope from the postman with Montgomery Hall as the return address—although I must mention that the handwriting was appalling, like that of a shopgirl."

Coral must've addressed the envelope.

"But I never saw the invitation," Isobel said. "What became of it?"

Adams moistened his lips. "I cannot say, madam."

Isobel finally lost her composure. Her voice became shrill. "You cannot say what became of my private correspondence?"

"It must have been the kitchen maid whom we let go in early October. A poor decision on my part to have ever hired that girl in the first place." Adams cleared his throat. "German."

"The woman who was impersonating Mrs. Bradford in Connecticut was at least fifty-five years of age," Berta said. "A somewhat dowdy person with an abundance of unruly gray hair—"

"Ah!" Adams exclaimed. "I knew that woman was up to no good."

"What woman, Adams?" Isobel asked.

"In the first or second week of October, a woman matching that description came to the door and insisted upon being given entry into the house. She said she had some business with Mrs. Bradford related to her charitable work at the Museum of Fine Arts. I left her in the entry hall—it was raining that day and I could not in good conscience allow her to wait outside, particularly if she was indeed associated with the museum—and went to ask if Mrs. Bradford would see her in the parlor. However, as Mrs. Bradford did not feel inclined to do so, I returned to the entry hall and sent the woman away."

"This woman would have had access to Rudy's invitation?" I asked.

"Yes. The mail sits on a side table in the entry foyer after the postman delivers it."

"Did she give you a name?" I asked.

"I cannot recall. And she did not pass me a visiting card."

"Well, then," Isobel said with a superior little smile. "There you have it. Some woman off the street stole the invitation, and Rudy's death has nothing to do with me. So if there is nothing else . . ."

Berta and I stood. "Thank you for your time, Mrs. Bradford," I said.

Berta left one of our cards on Mrs. Bradford's coffee table, and Adams ushered us, with corgi-like urgency, out of the house.

11

It sounds as though this woman is a con artist," I said to Berta. We walked slowly down Marlborough Street so Cedric could sniff every shrub and iron fence. "It sounds as though she came to the Bradford house, saw the invitation to Montgomery Hall, and seized a chance opportunity. For all we know, she's escaped from a women's prison or a loony bin. She could be more than capable of murder." I thought of the woman who'd been posing as Isobel. She'd seemed so composed, so sure of herself. "We must find her."

"She could be halfway to Texas by now, Mrs. Woodby."

"We'll go back to Carvington and ask around the town. Someone must have seen something."

"Why would this impostor have wished to go to Montgomery Hall at all?" Berta said.

"To steal something, of course. She could've easily guessed from the invitation that it would be a wealthy household, and don't you remember that Miss Murden said the impostor was snooping around the house, knocking on trophies and so forth?"

"That sounds like a lot of bother when she could have simply stolen the silverware."

"Maybe she knew something we don't."

"That there were diamonds in one rhinoceros trophy, you mean."

Right. The diamonds. "Well, yes." I gulped. It was time to face the music. "Which reminds me—we must telephone Lord Sudley and break the bad news that we lost track of the diamonds."

"You never should have agreed to lock them up for him."

"The silver lining is that if the diamonds were Rudy's, he'll never know the difference six feet underground. And with any luck, his only heirs are his Labrador retrievers."

We meandered through the Back Bay neighborhood, and inside the lobby of a Copley Square hotel I found a coin-operated telephone and asked the exchange girl to put me through to Montgomery Hall in Carvington, Connecticut.

After a lot of clicks and crackles, the phone rang and someone picked up. "This is Miss Murden," the familiar doomsday contralto said, sounding very far away.

"Oh, hello, Miss Murden, this is Lola Woodby, the private detective."

Tomblike silence.

"Would you be an absolute doll and fetch Lord Sudley to the telephone for me?"

"I suppose I could try."

I waited for a few minutes, tapping my toes, rolling my eyes at Berta, and inspecting my woefully unkempt fingernails. Would Berta consider a beauty salon manicure to be a business expense? I was afraid to ask.

"Hello? Lola?" This was Eustace's smooth, reassuring voice on the line.

"Hello, Eustace. I'm afraid I have a bit of bad news. I'm awfully sorry about this, but some—ah—" I swallowed. "The diamonds have been stolen."

A pause. "Is this a joke?"

"Afraid not. We didn't make it to the bank in time to lock them up, you see, and on our train to Boston a couple of goons slipped us Mickey Finns and made off with the goods."

"Well, dash it all, isn't that a hideous bother. Are you quite all right? Do you require me to wire funds?"

Berta, who was bent close to the telephone receiver, nodded vigorously.

"No, no," I said. "Our pocketbooks were left untouched."

"All right. Now, you ought to return to Montgomery Hall at once. I don't wish to speak of it over the telephone—an operator girl could be listening in. I'm told that's a bit of a problem here in America—"

I was fairly certain I heard an indignant sniff on the line.

"—but there has been a rather stunning development."

"Not another murder?"

"It'd be best if we spoke in person."

"All right, we'll come as soon as we're able." I rang off. "I'm surprised he wasn't angry about the stolen diamonds," I said to Berta.

"You can do no wrong in his eyes, Mrs. Woodby."

I wished Ralph had been present to hear Berta say that. And, phooey. Between being wrecked by that Mickey Finn, feeling lousy about the stolen diamonds, and meeting the real Isobel Bradford, I hadn't really thought of Ralph all day. Nice while it lasted.

We walked to South Station and purchased tickets for a New York, New Haven, and Hartford Railroad train that stopped in New London, Connecticut, about fifteen miles from Carvington. It wouldn't depart for two hours.

"I confess I am glad about that," Berta said to me, "for I must have a lie-down. That Mickey Finn made me feel quite old."

Berta returned to her room at the hotel across from the train station for a nap. Cedric and I found the nearest beauty salon and I had my nails filed, buffed, and varnished in a fashionable scarlet with white half moons. Then I was ready to take on the world. Or at least a well-sealed envelope.

After we'd settled our handbags and luggage plus one Pomeranian in our train compartment a while later, Berta said to me, "I telephoned Mr. Ant from the hotel."

"Oh, you mean Jimmy the *snitch*?"

"He is not a snitch. He said that he indeed saw you spill diamonds beside the Automat cakes dispenser, but that he did not breathe a word of it to anyone."

"And you *believe* that—"

"It seems that his colleagues—the two thugs we encountered on the train—were dining at the Automat as well, and *they* witnessed you spilling the diamonds."

"Oh."

"Mr. Ant would not betray me, Mrs. Woodby."

"He's a gangster," I said darkly. "Do you really wish to get serious with a gangster?"

"Goodness. No one said anything about 'serious'—although Mr. Ant has proposed marriage on two occasions, come to think of it."

"What?" Even *Jimmy the Ant*, wielder of tommy guns and wearer of white wing tips, was more capable of domestication than was Ralph Oliver?

"I am not a young woman with marriage and babies on the brain, Mrs. Woodby. I have my own income, a roof over my head, and every intention of enjoying my freedom."

That gave me pause. Should I simply follow Berta's lead and become a fancy-free gal about town?

"Well," I said, "here's one thing we know with certainty: Lem Fitzpatrick has those diamonds. They might as well be locked up in the Tower of London, for all the chance we have of getting them back."

"We will think of something, Mrs. Woodby. We always do." Berta pulled out the glossy new issue of *Dime Dramas* she'd purchased in the station.

Frowning—how could Berta be so dratted complacent?—I pulled out *Spectral Stories* and a Hershey's bar. With Cedric curled up in my lap, I began to read. The train shuddered out of South Station, past the endless, depressing, wooden triple-decker houses that ring Boston, and into the dusk.

It was nearly midnight when we stepped onto the platform at the New London station. There had been some sort of trouble on the track near Providence, and we'd wound up stalled for hours. We had eaten dinner in the dining car, however, read our pulp magazines cover to cover, and fortified ourselves with chocolate and nips of gin from Berta's handbag flask. Altogether it was a nicer way to spend the evening than fessing up to losing a sockful of diamonds.

We entered the empty station. As Berta used the coin-operated telephone to call a taxi service, I studied the posters and flyers tacked to the walls. Chesterfield cigarettes. Women's Temperance League meeting. And taking top prize for shuddersome, a large poster advertising the Wednesday performance of something called Menchen's Manikins on Carvington's village green. Garish illustrations depicted grinning marionettes: ballerina, kid in baseball cap, wigged judge, Big Bad Wolf. What is so very unnerving about puppets? Is it their almost-humanness, or is it their proclivity for violence?

At last, a battered taxi rolled up, and the driver agreed to motor us to Carvington.

As we rolled up Montgomery Hall's drive, rain bucketed down. Beyond silhouetted trees, the sky glowed a weird metallic indigo. Every window in Montgomery Hall's main floor was lit up, and only two motorcars remained in the front drive—Eustace's black Duesenberg and a disreputable, saggy-topped Chalmers that looked . . . familiar.

"No paddy wagons, ambulances, or hearses," Berta said. "And it appears that the hunting-party guests have gone."

"Things are looking up," I said with forced jauntiness.

I leaned forward to pay the driver. The windshield wipers squeaked back and forth.

"Better you than me staying here tonight," he said as he counted the change. "Folks say this place is haunted, and on a night like this, I just might start to believe it." He got out, dragged our suitcases from the back, and rumbled away into the night.

No one answered the door when we rang the bell, so Berta and I let ourselves in. We heard voices and, leaving our luggage in the foyer, made our way toward the drawing room. Cedric bounded ahead joyfully, but I peered hard at every shadowy corner.

We stopped just outside the drawing room's open doors and attempted to grasp the tableau within:

Redheaded vixen Coral perched on the edge of a sofa in a gold velvet dress, thin bare arms hugging her elbows, shoulders hitched, eyes wide. Radio star Glenn Monroe lounged beside her, one ankle on his knee to expose a checked sock, bobbing his foot up and down, nursing both a cigarette and a G and T. History student Theo Wainwright paced in front of a roaring log fire with a glass of brandy in hand and a forelock of dark hair loose across his forehead. He spoke in animated undertones to a man with an open briefcase on his knees. The fat Labradors loafed on the hearth, and Cedric joined them. No one seemed to notice Cedric's arrival.

Eustace appeared beside us in the corridor. "So you've made it," he said softly. His eyes were warm with concern as he looked me up and down. "I'd instruct Miss Murden to send hot-water bottles up to your rooms, but I'm afraid she's cashed in her chips."

"She's gone?" I asked. After seeing that Chalmers parked in the drive, I felt like I needed a bottle, all right. A bottle of Scotch.

"No, merely holed up in her quarters and refusing to lift a finger until her position is clarified."

"Is the family lawyer in there?"

"Yes, Mr. Eccles. He arrived earlier this afternoon. Rudy was buried in the family plot in Carvington Cemetery, and then Mr. Eccles read the will. Therein lay the stunning news that I alluded to on the telephone: Theo Wainwright is Rudy's sole heir."

My jaw dropped. "Theo? Why Theo?"

"Well, it seems that Theo is Rudy's son. Illegitimate, of course, but his son all the same. Theo's mother—she is deceased—worked here at Montgomery Hall over twenty years ago as a maid in Rudy's father Teddy's household. And, well, you know how these things go. Rudy supported the woman and her child in secret, encouraged the woman to educate her son, and even paid for his boarding schools and college."

No wonder Theo had been defensive about his upbringing when we'd questioned him earlier. No wonder he hadn't picked up the coastal Yankee accent. No wonder Rudy had given him the run of his library and estate.

Eustace continued, "Theo is rather put out because he had believed himself to have won scholarships to these institutions based upon his intellectual merits. More than anything, I fancy he is dismayed to learn that he isn't half so clever as he believed himself to be."

"Before today, did Theo know Rudy was his father?" Berta asked.

"He claims to be completely astounded by the news. Of course, he's a very rich young man now, with a heap of things to sort out with the lawyer. There are stocks and bonds, the house and all its contents, and of course robust bank accounts." Eustace smiled wryly. "So if Theo had any inkling that he was Rudy's heir, then . . ."

"That's a rather deluxe motive for murder," I finished.

"Yes."

"What about Coral and Glenn?" Berta asked. "Why are they still here?"

"Coral is dumbstruck—Rudy didn't bequeath a penny to her—and she's also a bit drunk at the moment. I fancy she's frightened about where she's going to go, now that her home has been pulled out from under her. Glenn is comforting her. Making snide remarks, drinking a great deal of alcohol *and* Alkacine, smoking like a factory, but comforting her nonetheless. It is a rather peculiar little group in there, isn't it? Now. How was your excursion to Boston, aside from the dreadful business on the train? Did you catch up with Isobel Bradford?"

"Yes and no," I said. I explained how the Isobel Bradford we'd all met at Montgomery Hall was an impostor.

"Good heavens. An impostor! Oh, and I did not intend to mention those diamonds to anyone—mucks everything up, you know," Eustace said, "but I understand that Coral saw them that night? And she happened to mention them to Theo."

I heard air squeaking out of Berta's lungs. Wait. Were those my lungs?

"You'd better come in and say your piece about how the diamonds were stolen," Eustace said. "It's ruffled a few feathers, I'm afraid, and Theo has even gone so far as to—well, you'll hear it for yourself."

I didn't like the sound of that.

"I've told them that you were attempting to retrieve the rhinoceros trophy for me when you came upon the diamonds," Eustace said, "although no one seems to care much about that bit."

12

·····································

Berta and I trudged into the drawing room like two schoolgirls sent to the headmistress's office. Everyone stopped talking and stared at us—Coral blankly; Glenn with a smirk; Theo accusingly; and Mr. Eccles, the lawyer, with his eyes latched on Berta with a keen and not altogether professional interest.

For a lady who looked like she ought to be on a box of pancake flour, Berta certainly could reel in the fellows.

"Well?" Theo demanded. "What's this I hear about stolen diamonds?"

Standing side by side, Berta and I took turns stammering out the tale of the gangsters on the train and the Mickey Finns. Naturally, we didn't mention how Berta blabbed about the diamonds to her underworld beau, Jimmy the Ant.

"We're honestly expected to believe that rubbish?" Theo asked when we'd finished.

Glenn burst out laughing and clapped his hands. "This is one swell two-lady act you have here. I wish I could get you on my radio show."

"Truly?" Berta breathed.

Oh boy.

At that moment, Mwinyi glided into the drawing room carrying a tray of coffee things. He noiselessly set it on a low table and reached for the coffeepot.

"Leave it," Coral said to him, waving a hand. "I can do all that."

Mwinyi made a silent bow and retreated toward the door, but it wasn't in that melt-into-the-woodwork way of most good butlers. No, Mwinyi, though silent, had an electric effect upon the room. We all watched his broad shoulders, his graceful gait, the gleam of his black curls. Theo was looking daggers at Mwinyi, and I still couldn't decide if this was base bigotry or a personal grudge. And I was convinced that Mwinyi gave both Coral and Glenn the jumps.

Neglecting to interview Mwinyi had been a slipup, hadn't it? We knew very little about him, and yet any reader of detective fiction will tell you that one overlooks butlers at their own peril. I bumped *Question Mwinyi* to the top of my mental to-do list.

After Mwinyi was gone, Glenn piped up first. "Say, I'm not kidding about having you two lady detectives on *The Filmore Vacuette Hour.* I'm telephoning the producer at first cock's crow."

"Oh, shut up, Glenn," Coral snarled.

"Why should I?" Glenn slitted his eyes. "As far as I'm concerned, I am free to do whatever I wish. This isn't even your house anymore, Cor. Oh, wait—*it never was.*"

"Hold your tongue, Glennie-wennie," Coral said in a precise, steely voice that made me wonder if she truly had been drinking. "Or else I just might be forced to give your producer a jingle and tell him exactly why you dropped Jillie Harris."

Another mental note: *Find out who Jillie Harris is.*

Glenn went blotchy, pulled out his Alkacine, unscrewed the cap, and took a gulp.

Theo said to Berta and me, "This house is mine now, along with all its contents. Those diamonds belonged to my father, which means they now belong to me."

Coral and Glenn watched Berta and me. They wore the viciously alert expressions of children burning ants under a magnifying glass.

"I want my diamonds back," Theo said. "Do I make myself clear?"

Berta turned red. I nodded. What else could I do?

"I suppose I am also obliged to inform you that I have hired a private detective to make certain nothing else of mine goes missing," Theo said.

"What?" I said in a choked voice.

"Since I could not convince Lord Sudley to drop you two," Theo said—

"And because I have every right to look into my friend Rudy's death as I see fit," Eustace put in mildly.

"   I decided that the only course of action was to enlist the services of a real detective to keep an eye on you."

Eustace said, "Theo has very graciously allowed me to stay on at Montgomery Hall until I make further arrangements. Even though we do not agree about the best way to tie up the loose ends regarding Rudy's death, he understands how close I was to his father."

"And who is this 'real detective' whom you hired, if you please?" Berta asked.

I already knew the answer. I'd seen his junky Chalmers motorcar outside.

"A Mr. Oliver," Theo said. "The Discreet Retrieval Agency seems to crash around like the proverbial bull in the china shop, so somebody must clean up the mess. Oh, I read of your few successes, so don't bother to tell me about those. Dumb luck."

My knuckles clenched hard around my handbag straps. "I gather that Mr. Oliver is here now? I saw a disreputable-looking motorcar in the drive." I wouldn't mention that Berta and I were acquainted with Ralph. I needed to keep as much control over this fiasco as I could.

"Yes, he is here. He said he wished to stay here in order to reduce his expenses."

That didn't sound like something Ralph would worry about. No, he was staying here at Montgomery Hall just to bug me.

"I suggest that unless you plan to wind up marching in lockstep at Auburn Prison," Theo said, "your so-called detecting should concern finding those diamonds rather than inventing convoluted theories about how my poor father didn't commit suicide. You don't look convinced. Well, then, try this on for size: I want my diamonds back by midnight on Tuesday, or I'm having you arrested for theft."

Berta gasped. All I could think of was those awful striped pants they make women prisoners wear. Horizontally striped pants, you understand.

"Don't you think you're being a bit injudicious, Mr. Wainwright?" Mr. Eccles, the lawyer, said in a coaxing, adenoidal voice. His baggy eyes were fixed unblinkingly upon Berta.

"Is it injudicious to desire the return of unspecified thousands'—perhaps millions'—worth of diamonds? No, I don't think so. Now, you absurd pair, get out of my house."

"Theo, be reasonable!" Eustace exclaimed. "These ladies have had a most trying time of it. You can't cast them out into the night."

"Oh yes, I can."

Normally, I would've taken a direct and speedy route out of there. But it was raining cats and dogs, I didn't have a motorcar to get to the station—where the last train of the night had already been and gone—and I doubted Berta and I could find a place to stay in Carvington at this hour.

"You're a man of property now, Mr. Wainwright," Mr. Eccles said.

"A man of power. Please do not consider it forward of me to suggest that you must now exercise benevolence—noblesse oblige, if you will. Besides—" He beamed at Berta. "—such lovely ladies should be treated like the porcelain swans that they are."

Berta touched her cheek in an absent, girlish gesture.

Mr. Eccles's smile broadened still more, and his eyes glittered with mischief.

Good grief.

"Don't be a little fink, Theo," Coral said. "Give the old birds a nesting box for the night. It's pushing one o'clock."

"Oh, all right," Theo said sulkily. He threw himself in a chair. "But I want them out first thing in the morning."

My heart was heavy with fatigue and humiliation as Berta and I lugged our suitcases up the stairs. Cedric trailed behind. He would have remained in the drawing room with the Labradors if it weren't for the Milk-Bones with which I'd bribed him. My eyes slid left and right, expecting Ralph Oliver to stroll out of the shadows. Which would be awful, of course. Particularly if he were in shirtsleeves and suspenders . . .

"First thing in the morning, we skidoo," I whispered.

"I could not agree more," Berta whispered back. "If I were not so weary from our recent exploits, I would not consent to staying here another minute."

"How on earth are we going to get those diamonds back from Lem Fitzpatrick? And the nerve of Theo, hiring Mr. Oliver to—to baby-mind us!"

"I would have thought you would be pleased, Mrs. Woodby, for now Mr. Oliver has been *employed* to look after you."

Jeepers. This wasn't precisely what I'd had in mind when I'd said I needed someone to take care of me. "I must keep well clear of him—

we must. He'll cramp our style. Say, I don't suppose you could flirt madly with Mr. Eccles so he'll convince Theo to soften up about the diamonds and that deadline?"

"Mrs. *Woodby!*"

"I'm not blind."

"Neither am I."

We reached the top of the stairs and turned in the direction of the bedrooms we had used on our previous stay. The corridor was lit by a few feeble electric sconces.

"It was dumb of us not to have questioned Mwinyi yet," I said softly. "He isn't a suspect, of course, since he was out with the hunting party at the crucial juncture, but as Rudy's valet, he may be an absolute font of facts."

"I was thinking along the very same lines, Mrs. Woodby. In addition, something about him causes Theo to grow nervous in his presence, which is decidedly curious, since Theo also suggested that Mwinyi does not even speak English."

"Oh—and did you hear what Coral said to Glenn, about someone named—what was it?—Jillie Harris? Something about telling his producer why he'd dropped her? Glenn went quite ashen."

"Jillie Harris is a radio actress—this was all in the papers this summer. I do wish you would stay abreast of the news."

"Show business gossip is hardly news, Berta." We stopped outside Berta's bedroom.

"Jillie Harris is one of the stars of *The High-Jinx Club* radio program. Glenn and Jillie were, as they say, an item for several months. They were photographed together frequently—they made such a lovely couple, you see—but a few months ago they broke things off."

"Then Coral was threatening to expose something about Glenn's private life."

"Yes. I expect Jillie Harris knows some unflattering details about

Glenn as a result of their months of—" Berta coughed delicately. "—familiarity."

"Maybe we ought to look her up."

"Indeed."

We bade each other good night and I continued along the corridor to my own room.

My hatbox-size room had not been cleaned since I left it yesterday. Miss Murden must have failed to recruit cleaning ladies after the murder. I suppose no one relishes the notion of scrubbing borax into bloodstained carpets.

I changed into my nightgown, robe, and slippers, and then ventured out to the shared bathroom, which was blessedly unoccupied. I cold-creamed off my makeup, rinsed my face, and I was brushing my teeth when the door swung open. I yelled through a mouthful of dental cream, "Occupied! This bathroom is *occupied!*"

Cedric merrily squiggled to the door. Why wasn't he barking? And why hadn't I locked the door? Dumb, dumb, dumb.

"Lola."

"Ralph?" I spluttered on dental cream. "I mean, Mr. Oliver? How dare you?"

"People keep asking me that." Ralph lounged on the doorframe, arms folded, wearing his baggy suit trousers and—oh no—shirtsleeves and suspenders.

My knees went wonky. I tried to discreetly spit dental cream into the sink. This is impossible to do. "Why the heck did you take on a job to follow me? It's—it's an outrage."

"Easy money, kid. I know your habits."

"Shh! I can't have anyone know that we are acquainted." I peered into the dark hallway behind Ralph. "Shut the door, for Pete's sake."

"I thought you'd never ask." Smiling a little, Ralph stepped inside the bathroom, shut the door, and crouched to scratch Cedric's ears. Cedric braced his forepaws on Ralph's knee and wagged so hard, his hind legs rotated back and forth.

"Okay." I pointed my toothbrush at Ralph. "How is it that every time I have a big job, you show up?"

"Guess you're just lucky." Ralph stood. "How about you join me in my room for a nightcap?"

"Not on your—"

"I've got highball fixings."

The devil. "Oh, all right—but this is a professional meeting. Between colleagues."

"Sure. I'm down the hall, around the corner, up three stairs, and on the left. There's a stuffed grizzly bear next to my door. You can't miss it."

After Ralph left, I returned to my room and reapplied mascara and a dab of lip rouge. I was absolutely fuming, of course, and it isn't entirely professional to meet one's colleague while in a pink dressing gown and marabou slippers. I was just too tired to change; unlike Berta, I had never slept off last night's Mickey Finn.

I ventured forth. I found the three stairs, the grizzly bear—poor fella—and Ralph's door.

"Come in," he replied to my knock.

Cedric and I went in and I shut the door.

Ralph stood at a writing desk, pouring fizzing ginger ale over whiskey. He passed me a glass and lifted his own. "To colleagues."

"To colleagues sharing information."

We clinked and sipped. I sat primly on the desk chair and noted Ralph's bulging arm muscles.

Look away, look away.

"All right," I said after a few fortifying sips of highball. "Tell me exactly what Theo Wainwright said to you when he hired you."

"Can't."

"How did he happen to hire you, out of all the gumshoes in the world?"

"Not at liberty to say."

"Argh!"

"We've been over this a million times, Lola. I can't compromise my jobs."

"I tell you all about mine."

"That's your call, kid. How's the murder investigation going?" He half sat, half leaned on the desk right next to me. Oh, rats. I could smell his shaving soap and the warm, wild scent of his skin. I could've counted the lines fanning from his bright gray eyes and the freckles across his weathered cheekbones. I could've traced the vulnerable white scar on his forehead, the cords of his neck. . . .

I meant to get up and move away, truly I did. But some sort of paralysis had gripped me. "I'm not going to tell you anything about my investigation, except to ask you for a bit of professional advice."

"Yeah? I love giving professional advice." Ralph set down his highball, leaned in, and nuzzled my ear with his dry, soft lips.

"Stop distracting me," I murmured. "We're through, Ralph."

"Got it."

Nuzzle.

I forced myself to focus, despite all the distractions on my ear. And my throat. And the back of my knee. "Now, what would you do—this is strictly a hypothetical question, mind you—if two thugs working for a gangster boss such as, oh, such as Lem Fitzpatrick—"

"*Fitzpatrick?*" Ralph growled.

"—happened to slip one a Mickey Finn and steal a large quantity of diamonds from one's handbag—"

"WHAT?"

"—how would one go about getting the diamonds back?"

Ralph pulled away. "Someone slipped you a Mickey Finn?"

"And Berta, too. On a train to Boston." I filled him in on the rest of the sorry tale.

"You're all right?"

"Now I am."

"Drop it."

"I can't. Theo wants his diamonds back, and he hinted at having Berta and me arrested for theft. In fact, starting tomorrow we're banned from Montgomery Hall. Berta had to wheel out her feminine wiles just so we'd have a roof over our heads tonight."

"How do you two get yourselves in these messes? Listen. I'll go to see Fitzpatrick. I know where to catch up with him."

"Where?"

"I hear he's been at the Moody Elephant a lot lately. You know, that speakeasy below Caffè Agostini on Macdougal Street—oh no. I shouldn't have told you that. Don't go there alone."

"I'll go with Berta."

"Go with me."

I couldn't be a baby and rely on Ralph for muscle. I ran my own detective agency, for crying out loud. Besides, Ralph had callously told me I could look after myself.

"I'll think about it," I lied.

"Don't do anything rash. Now, where were we?" Ralph's big warm hand slid down the back of my dressing gown.

I shivered with pleasure. Summoning up my very last drop of self-control, I wriggled away. "Hold it. We can't—we've got a few things to square away, Ralph."

"Things?"

"You know, the same-page problem?"

"Seems to me we're on the same page right now. Exact same sentence, seems like."

"I mean it, Ralph."

He sighed. "What's the matter with just enjoying the present?"

"That's childish."

"It's sane."

"Are you suggesting that I'm not sane?"

"Kid. Please." Ralph got up, went to the bed, sat on its edge. He ran a hand through his hair and it tufted up like a guinea pig's. "Here's the thing. I can't . . . No, let me rephrase that; I don't know *how* to, you know, settle down."

"Maybe because you've never tried it." Oh, golly. This would be when he'd tell me he had a former wife or two on the books and no interest in repeating the experiment.

But he said, "I told you a little about how it was for my brother and me growing up, right? How our mother took off to live with another man when we were little, how our dad was pretty rough on the two of us? I don't know what a nice home looks like. I don't know what a good marriage looks like—and frankly, in my line of work, all I see are *bad* marriages, every day. So I've gotta break it to you, kid, no matter how much I love you, there isn't a chance in hell that I'd subject me or you to that. All I can offer you is more of how it's been all along—separate places, no wedding bells, but, I promise you, I'll be there for you." He tried a lopsided smile. "And we'll keep having fun."

"Oh." My heart wrung itself. Here I was, hitting that brick wall again. *If he truly loved me, he'd want to marry me.* "I see." I picked up Cedric, stood, and polished off my highball, keeping my eyes on the floor so Ralph wouldn't see how wet they'd become. "Then we really are through." I went to the door.

"Suit yourself, kid."

I didn't stick around to hear more.

13

I brushed my teeth again, because of the highball, and to get rid of the tragic taste in my mouth. Turns out that peppermint Colgate is no match for heartbreak.

The vague, sunlit hopes I'd had for a future with Ralph, well, those were all just gorgeous dreams. It was time to wake up and smell the coffee. There was a reason that these hopes had been vague. It was because part of me knew all along that Ralph standing at the altar, Ralph making me scrambled eggs in the morning, or—yes, I know I'm an idiot—Ralph burping a baby, were impossibilities. Whether the impossibility of it all was entirely *his* fault, I was in no mood to ponder.

And love? Somehow, contrary to the punch line of every fairy tale I'd ever read, love didn't even factor in.

Despite the scent of Ralph on my skin, the doom of the stolen diamonds, zero progress on our murder investigation, and a hollow feeling where my heart went, I fell heavily to sleep.

Not for long. I woke with a start to Cedric's warbling little growls.

There is nothing quite so chilling as being woken by your dog growling in the night. You know they mean business.

I strained my ears over the sound of my own thudding pulse and the rattle of the windowpanes. Cedric's ears were pricked in the direction of the door, and all I could think of was that voice that had not been Berta calling my name two nights ago. . . .

Then I saw a faint light flashing through the gauzy curtains.

Something outside the house, I could manage. A ghost in the corridor, I could not.

I got out of bed and went to the window.

Rain flogged down and bare tree branches thrashed, but I made out a yellow light at the edge of the woods. I squinted. It was a lantern, yes, a lantern held by someone moving amid the trees with—could it be?—a shovel in hand.

Theo, perhaps? But why would he be out digging on a night like this? Why would anyone, for that matter?

My visibility was compromised by the darkness and lashing rain. I was almost sure that the person wore a fisherman's raincoat and hat when the lantern suddenly extinguished and I lost track of the figure.

I was crawling back into bed when, from out in the corridor came the dreaded "Lolaaaaaaaaaaaa. Lolaaaaaaaaaaaaaaaaaaaaa."

I waited, gripping the blanket under my chin. Maybe it would simply stop.

Cedric growled again.

"Lolaaaaaaaaaaaaaaaaaaaaaaaa."

I forced myself to go to the door. I cracked it.

"Lolaaaa. LOLAAAAAAA."

The voice was a flimsy alto with an impatient edge.

"Come on, peanut," I whispered to Cedric. The corridor was as black as pitch, so I felt my way by patting along the wall.

"Lolaaaaaaaaaaaaaa!"

I kept going with leaden feet, skittering heart, and Cedric's fluff brushing against my ankles.

I gauged that I'd reached the top of the stairs, although it was so dark, I may as well have been blindfolded. I reached out and wrapped my fingers around the bannister finial—

I heard soft breathing close at hand, I felt a hand at my back, and . . . someone pushed me. Hard.

I cried out and grabbed the finial. My feet bicycled for traction on the steps. Cedric yapped ferociously, footsteps padded—

The lights flicked on.

"Good heavens, Lola, are you all right?" This was Eustace, swooping to my aid and helping me off the stairs.

I blinked in the electric light. "Someone pushed me."

Ralph appeared, hair tousled, face strained, with Cedric boinging around his ankles.

The sight of him made my belly wad up like old chewing gum.

"What happened?" he asked.

"She fell on the stairs," Eustace said to Ralph.

"I was *pushed*," I said.

"Are you certain?" Eustace said. "You must be very tired."

Ralph lifted an eyebrow, taking in for the first time, it seemed, that I was in a filmy nightgown, marabou slippers, and pressed against Eustace's chest like a baby koala to its mother. "Evening," he said to Eustace. "Ralph Oliver."

"Lord Sudley. You must be Theo's detective."

"That's right."

Eustace gazed down at me, his brown eyes soft with concern. "Go back to bed, Lola. I'll fetch you some warm milk, and then you must tell me precisely what occurred."

"If I hadn't managed to grab the finial, I could have broken my neck—"

"Poor little duck," Eustace murmured. "Now, run along. I'll be back up in a tick."

"Careful, I think your nursemaid's apron is showing," Ralph said to Eustace.

Eustace stiffened. "Precisely what are you implying, old chap?"

"Lola is a grown woman. You don't need to coddle her. Quite frankly, she ought to find it insulting."

"I'll find it however I please," I said.

"You've already met Lola, then?" Eustace asked Ralph. Both men's chests seemed to inflate as they sized each other up.

"Course. We're colleagues. Besides that, she's my mark." Ralph winked at me; I narrowed my eyes.

"I see," Eustace said. "Well, then, perhaps you ought to take a stab at being a gentleman and move aside so that she may return to her room."

The two men looked each other square in the eyes without blinking. Eustace glanced away first, and started down the stairs, muttering, "Deuced upstart."

Ralph watched him go and then said softly to me, "I wouldn't recommend drinking any milk that goofus brings you."

"What do you mean?"

"Maybe *he* pushed you."

"You're jealous."

"Of him? He talks like he swallowed a tureen of turtle soup."

"You can't have it both ways, Mr. Oliver. If you don't want me—"

"I want you."

"—then you simply must let me go. I'm off to bed." I scooped up Cedric and sailed away, though my shaky legs listed leeward.

Eustace did bring me a mug of warm milk, which I accepted at my bedroom door and firmly said good night, although not before he'd warned me to "steer well clear of that Mr. Oliver, because he has an uppity look in his eye. Irishman, I take it."

I locked and relocked my door, and braced a chair under the doorknob as I'd read about in *Spectral Stories*.

I didn't drink the milk. Not because I thought Eustace would poison me, of course. I simply don't enjoy warm milk.

I woke to rapping on my door. I cracked my eyes. Pale morning light leaked through the curtains, and a drizzle smeared the windowpanes. Bed won, hands down. I rolled over and closed my eyes again.

More knocking. "Mrs. Woodby?" came Berta's muffled voice.

Sigh.

"Come in," I called, and struggled upright in bed. Beside me, Cedric yawned, curling his pink tongue.

"It is locked."

I got up, moved the chair, unlocked the door, and stumped back to bed.

Berta, scrubbed and tidy in a mauve wool dress, said, "Oh dear me. Difficult night? I did see Mr. Oliver—"

"Urgh. I don't wish to hear his name spoken ever ever *ever* again."

"I notice that Mr. Oliver always contrives to get hired on cases in close proximity to ours."

"I said I don't wish to talk about that blister!"

"It is almost as though he cannot stay away from you, as though you exert the gravitational pull of a large, round, pale moon—"

"Go 'way. I'm not done sleeping."

"Miss Murden woke me an hour ago to inform me that Theo wishes us to vacate his house—he has quite taken to the role of lord of the manor—at once. Do get up. I do not wish to fan his anger, and what is more, we have much sleuthing to accomplish today. We must ask the townspeople of Carvington if anyone sighted Isobel Bradford's presumed impostor after she fled Montgomery Hall, attempt to discover if Theo knew in advance that he stood to inherit the estate—oh—and we must find some way to contact Lem Fitzpatrick about the stolen diamonds."

I floundered upright. "I have a lead on Fitzpatrick. But I need coffee."

"There is a little leftover coffee in my room."

"Miss Murden brought you coffee?"

Pink blotched Berta's neck. "Mr. Eccles, the lawyer, kindly brought it to me—"

"Berta!"

"—along with some toast, because he correctly guessed that, otherwise, I would go without breakfast."

"Stop." I massaged my eye sockets as everything came oozing back. The man with the fisherman's hat and the lantern in the trees. The impatient ghost voice. The push. I told it all to Berta in a rush.

"And . . . Lord Sudley was the first on the scene after the push?" she asked.

"You need not lift your eyebrows so high. You'll give yourself a headache. Whoever pushed me must've been the same person who made the fake ghost moans—I suspect she lured me out there for the express purpose of pushing me. And that was a woman. An alto."

"The only other women in the house are Miss Murden and Coral."

"Miss Murden has the voice of an executioner, and Coral's voice is so chirpy—"

"But still, the person you saw moments after the push was Lord Sudley."

"Oh, I give up. Let's get out of this horrible house."

"Before we leave the estate, we really should go to the trees and look for clues about what the person in the fisherman's hat was doing."

"All right, but we can't let Theo see us. He'll telephone the cops.

We can't let Ralph see us, either. I'll be darned if I allow him to rain on our parade. We'll give him the slip—where is he now?"

"Mr. Eccles told me that Mr. Oliver was dining heartily in the breakfast room."

I threw off the covers and swung my legs out of bed. "Then we'll simply evaporate before he finishes his second round of sausages."

Berta went away and came back with a half pot of cold coffee and some cold buttered toast on a tray. There was a rosebud in a little vase, too. "Wowie. You certainly made an impression on Mr. Eccles," I said.

"Mrs. Woodby, I do wish you would not jump to conclusions."

"Can't help it. I'm a detective."

"I will leave you to get dressed and pack, and then we really must be on our way."

"Fine. I suppose we'll have to wait to tell Eustace what we're up to, because I don't want Theo to catch us wandering the house. Wait. If we're going to poke around in the trees before we scuttle off, what are we going to do with our suitcases? We rode a taxi from the train station last night."

"I have taken care of it, Mrs. Woodby." Berta's voice was calming, but she did not meet my eye. "After you pack your suitcase, leave it in your room."

"I suppose Mr. Eccles is going to transport our luggage to Manhattan on a golden chariot? I don't know how you do it."

Berta waved an impatient hand. "Hurry up and drink your coffee, and do dress warmly. Flat shoes if you have them—"

"I've sworn off the things."

"—and at least two layers of wool."

Ten minutes later, Berta and I tiptoed downstairs in coats, wool dresses and sweaters, hats, handbags, and armed with umbrellas against the spitting rain. Cedric looked handsome in a Fair Isle sweater. He didn't normally consent to wearing doggie attire, but he was making an exception because of the sodden weather.

"Someone's in the front driveway," I whispered, stopping on the stairs. "I see a motorcar." I prayed it wasn't Ralph. I couldn't bear to face him, nor could I bear to be outfoxed by him. "It's Theo. He's getting out of dear old Dad's Rolls-Royce."

We hurried back up the stairs and wandered around until we found the back stairs. We headed down again. The stairs took us to the hallway near Rudy's study, the billiards room, and the conservatory.

Why was an alarm bell jingling in my head?

"We could exit the house by way of the conservatory," Berta whispered. "I recall there is a door that leads to the garden."

"When were you in the conservatory, Berta?"

"During the costume party. That cheeky old gent with the muttonchops claimed he wished to show me some figs. I do not know why I gave him the time of day—"

Berta and I stopped short, having come face-to-face with Mwinyi. He had come from Rudy's study, holding an empty tray. He didn't appear surprised to see us, and inclined his head as he passed.

"Wait," I said. "Mwinyi. May I ask you a few questions?"

"Yes, madam." He stopped, and tucked the tray under his arm.

From inside the study came Coral's voice. I couldn't make out her words, but it sounded as though she was speaking on the telephone.

I asked Mwinyi, "How long had you been working for Mr. Montgomery when he, um—"

"Died?" Mwinyi gave a fleeting smile. "I would have thought detectives would be more comfortable speaking of death." A rich African accent burnished his perfect English. Why had Theo suggested Mwinyi did not speak English? Was it because Mwinyi took care to keep silent while working? Or had Theo been attempting to discourage Berta and me from speaking to Mwinyi?

"Well," I said, "our agency doesn't specialize in murder—we usually find lost items and—*ow.*" Berta had stepped on my toe.

"Then you are amateurs," Mwinyi said. "Just as Miss Coral suggested."

Berta scowled. "Would you please answer the question?"

"Of course. Mr. Montgomery hired me as his valet last spring."

"I understood Mr. Montgomery was in Europe last spring," I said. "Coral mentioned something about having met him in Antibes."

"That is correct," Mwinyi said. "I was fortunate enough to make the acquaintance of Mr. Montgomery in Monte Carlo just after I was abruptly dismissed by my previous employer, who had ruined himself in the casino and who was thus no longer able to pay my wages. Mr. Montgomery, who frequently traveled to the country of my birth, Kenya, was happy to engage a manservant who could also work as a translator."

That added up neatly.

"Who was your previous employer?" Berta asked.

"The Baron Von Lynden of the Netherlands. He, like Mr. Montgomery, enjoyed big game hunting in Kenya, which is where I first made his acquaintance many years ago."

There was the clang of the telephone being hung up in the study, and then Coral's voice carried out the open door. "Well, well, if it isn't Punch and Judy, grilling the servants."

Mwinyi took the opportunity to slip away.

Berta and I went to the study door.

"I thought Theo banished you forever." Coral sat at the desk in a silky floral robe. "He told me *I'd* be banished unless I confined my smoking to the study."

"We are just on our way out," I said.

"Why so sneaky?"

"I do so hate good-byes," Berta said.

"Sure you do." Coral's chest rose and fell swiftly, as though she were short of breath. Yet her attitude—feet tucked under, leaning one elbow on the chair arm, lips closed—was relaxed. She reminded me of a ballerina, the way they pretend to be ethereal even when they're sweating buckets and panting like bulls. A cup of black coffee sat on the desktop, wafting steam. Mwinyi must have brought it to her. She looked at Cedric. "You know, in that sweater, your dog looks just like a fellow I used to go steady with."

Aha. I'd finally realized why that alarm bell had jingled a few moments ago. "Coral," I said, "I've just remembered something Glenn Monroe told us." I hated to lose time since we were dodging Ralph and Theo, but this was important.

"Glenn?" Coral tossed her head. "I wouldn't put a lot of stock into what he says. He's been an actor since he was a kid, you know. His mommy never taught him the difference between truth and fiction. What did he tell you?"

"That he was on the telephone in Rudy's study when the fatal shot was fired. That he saw you pass by this open door—"

"Little Glennie-wennie suggested I'm a killer?"

"Actually, no. He saw you pass by the door before the shot was fired—on your way to the drawing room, where you saw Mrs. Lundgren and me. It's only that, well, if you passed by the study door, then you had come down the back stairs. Wouldn't the shortest route from Rudy's room to the drawing room have been the main stairs?"

"I was in such a tizzy after that awful argument, not thinking straight. I can barely remember any details about that afternoon, actually."

Was it possible Coral already had been squiffy with alcohol by the time Rudy was shot?

"Sometimes I use the back stairs because I feel like Miss Murden is always—always watching me," Coral said. "I don't trust her. And Glenn is a little viper. I thought he was my friend, but really he's trying to wreck my life. I never should have invited him up here. I thought it would be fun to have him around when all those dull hunters and their cheeky little girlfriends came. I thought we could laugh at everyone the way we used to. But ever since he landed that radio host gig, why, he isn't the same Glenn he used to be. He's calculating. Sneaky. I don't even know him anymore."

"You've known Glenn for a long time, then?" I asked.

"Yonks. We met in New York at the Unicorn Theater. I was working in the chorus line and he was doing a slapstick act—that was before I went off to Europe to seek my fortune. I was gone for years. When I came back in August, he was the very first person I rang up. Naturally he was delighted to come and enjoy the estate and all of Rudy's motorcars and wine cellar and so forth. But when it gets down to the nitty-gritty, he's no longer my friend, is he?"

"What was it you meant last night," I said, "when you mentioned something about telling his producer why he'd dropped Jillie Harris?"

Coral glanced away. "I really shouldn't say. It's personal. Why don't you ask him?" She stood. "If I were a detective, I'd be wondering what he's still doing here in Connecticut."

"We thought he was here to comfort you," I said.

"Hah! All he does is make mean little remarks."

"Wait," Berta said. "Before you go, could I ask you another question?"

"Oh, all right—but make it snappy."

"We understand that on his deathbed, Winslow Bradford was troubled about something to do with the Kenyan safari. You were on that safari, Coral. What do you suppose might have been troubling him?"

Coral gave a tinkling laugh. "Oh, that."

"Was it to do with the diamonds in the rhinoceros trophy?" I asked.

"No. I never knew a thing about those until you old girls busted them out that night. Poor widdle Theo's just about to blow a gasket, thinking he might miss out on a treasure like that. I guess Rudy was deeper than I thought."

"You believe that Rudy hid the diamonds in the trophy?" I asked.

"Well, sure. Who else? Thinking back on things, I recall how funny Rudy was acting in Mombasa, when we were getting all our things onto the ship sailing for Turkey. He was so anxious about the crates of trophies. He even yelled at some native porters who were carrying them, and once we had cleared customs there at the port, I distinctly recall him heaving a sigh of relief."

"Why would Mr. Montgomery smuggle diamonds if he was already so very wealthy?" Berta asked.

Coral swept a hand around the richly appointed study. "We don't know where Rudy's wealth came from, do we? Maybe all this was paid for with smuggled diamonds. After all, he traveled to Africa on safari once or twice a year for decades, as far as I could make out."

"If those diamonds were smuggled," I said, "then they may not rightfully belong to Theo, you know."

Coral's face went blank for a moment. Then she shrugged. "That's his problem. Don't think for a second he's going to let you off the hook about getting them back, if that's what you're—"

"Back to Winslow Bradford," Berta cut in. "Troubled on his deathbed."

"Winslow? The thing about Winslow was, the poor old duffer was simply goofy about me. I thought it was rather sweet, sort of like when you sit on Santa's knee at Wright's Department Store and he gives you a squeeze, but Rudy was fit to be tied. Jealous, you know. One night, I allowed Winslow to feed me roast crocodile with his fingers, which sent Rudy into a rage, and no sooner had I placated him with a bit of a neck than Winslow went into a snit. He stormed into his tent and refused to come out, and played Wagner really loudly on his crank-up phonograph. All just a bit of fun, girls—I know you, Lola Woodby, don't mind having a couple fellows tussling over you, now, do you? Toodles!" Coral swayed past us.

Berta and I proceeded to the conservatory.

"I suspect that Coral made a hobby out of making Rudy jealous," Berta said to me, pulling open one of the glass conservatory doors.

"And Winslow felt guilty about his flirtation with Coral on safari but he didn't mention it to his wife because, well, who would?"

We stepped out into the marrow-chilling morning. A formal garden of boxwood hedges and gravel paths gave way to a lawn. I hadn't taken two steps when a tiny scrap of golden paper fluttered on the path in front of my shoes. I picked it up. "What's this?" The scrap of paper was curled and torn. "It looks like a bit of the wrapper from a stick of greasepaint."

Berta inspected the paper. "Greasepaint, perhaps, or one of those oil pastel sticks that artists use. I wonder what it is doing out here. It could not possibly have blown all the way from town."

"Perhaps it was shed by one of those flapper mistresses the other day. Maybe one of them came out to the garden to patch up her Cupid's bow during the party." I could not think what the little curl of gold paper meant, but I tucked it into my coin purse for safekeeping all the same. You just never know.

14

The plan was to investigate the trees where I'd seen the man with the lantern, and then wend our way into town. It was a mile, which seemed awfully far in this weather, but we couldn't bally well telephone a taxi from the house.

"We will have a proper breakfast at the Red Rooster and feed Cedric there," Berta said, "after which we will pump the townspeople for clues."

"Super."

We set off across the side lawn toward the trees. Berta took mincing steps through the mud, and Cedric flat-out refused to walk at all. I stole many glances over my shoulder. No one was following us, but anyone could have been watching from the house's shiny, blank windows.

"The man with the shovel was just over here," I said as we reached the far edge of the massive wet lawn.

"What makes you think it was a man?"

"Well, nothing, actually. I mean, the person wore a fisherman's raincoat and hat, but I suppose it could've been a woman. I couldn't see exactly what they were doing, but that was almost certainly a shovel they were holding."

"If they had a shovel, then they were digging. This is nowhere near Theo's pit, however."

We stepped beneath the shivering trees. Mushy brown leaves carpeted the ground. Three pheasants strutted past. "Look," I said. "Fresh dirt." Berta and I went to the base of a tree. "Someone dug a small hole and then filled it back in." I glanced over my shoulder toward the house. We were still in plain view. Oh well. We could always make a break for it. I found a stick.

"Mrs. Woodby, what are you doing with that stick?"

"I want to see what that person buried." I poked around in the hole with the stick, but did not feel or see anything. "Maybe it's something small, like a piece of jewelry."

"I have a different idea," Berta said. "I suspect that the person was not hiding something in this hole, but searching for something."

"For what?"

"Do you require more coffee, Mrs. Woodby?"

"Well, yes, actually—"

"Diamonds."

"You think Rudy Montgomery buried diamonds on his estate?"

"Whyever not? It appears that he hid diamonds in a rhinoceros trophy hanging in his drawing room. *Aha.*" Berta pointed. "Another hole at the base of that tree—and that one, too."

As we wandered deeper into the woods, we noted thirteen holes. Some were at the roots of trees, others at the base of an old, tumbledown stone wall.

"Do you see how all the holes were dug beside some sort of marker, such as a tree or a stone?" Berta said. "One always buries treasure beside a landmark."

"I suppose you learned that nifty tidbit from *Lurid Tales?*"

"That is of no consequence."

"Well, if there are buried diamonds on the estate," I said, "then that could create motives for murder we weren't even aware of."

Hearing the crunch of twigs, we turned.

"Buried diamonds?" Glenn Monroe said, striding out of the mist with a walking stick, belted hunting jacket, and tall boots. "I just knew you pair were the life of the party—everyone else is still sawing logs and here you are, digging up booty." He stopped a few paces away, grinning under his dripping hat brim. His teeth were spectacular. His eyes were a bit shifty.

"We haven't dug up anything," I said. "As you can see, we don't have a shovel, Mr. Monroe. I don't suppose you do?"

"Shovel? Me? The closest thing to a shovel you'll see in my hand is a caviar spoon."

"Why are you out so early on this dreadful morning?" Berta asked.

"Getting a spot of exercise before I head back to the city. Healthful country walks and all that. That was the entire point of this stay in the country—healthful relaxation. Too bad it all turned to murder and mayhem, because now my nerves are simply sautéed to a crisp and I've got the radio program this evening. I'll tell you, there's no rest in show business. Maybe I oughta become a dentist."

"Speaking of show business," I said, "what did Coral mean last night when she said she'd tell your producer why you dropped Jillie Harris?"

Glenn started patting his jacket pockets. "What has Cor been saying about me this time?"

"She said you were lying about seeing her pass by the study door before Rudy was shot," Berta said.

"Called *me* a liar, did she?" Glenn found what he was looking for in his pocket—a bottle of Alkacine—and unscrewed the cap. "That's a laugh. You know, Cor and I used to be as thick as thieves, but something's happened to her. She's gone hard. I'm beginning to wonder if . . ." He sipped Alkacine.

"What?" I asked.

"It's nothing." Glenn's voice abruptly shifted to a chipper radio-broadcast drawl. "Say, I wasn't joking last night when I said you two would be marvelous on the program."

"Us?" Berta said, preening. "On a radio program? Goodness, Mr. Monroe, what a flight of fancy!"

Berta is absolutely dotty for radio programs. If it isn't Yankees baseball broadcasts or Ed Wynn, it's jazz orchestras or one of the new drama programs.

"I could do sort of an interview of you two," Glenn said, "just a couple questions about this gumshoe business of yours—folks will go nuts about a couple of lady gumshoes—and you'd do your two-lady bit, kinda like you did last night with the quick back-and-forth—say, you could even tell that story about the gangsters and the Mickey Finns and the stolen diamonds—!"

"We cannot discuss active cases," I said, my hairline perspiring under my hat. The only time I'd ever performed in public was at age six in a Sunday school nativity play in Scragg Springs, Indiana. I played the donkey, and it was not a success.

"Thank you for the offer, Mr. Monroe," Berta said, "and as the head detective of the Discreet Retrieval Agency, I accept."

I said, " 'Head detective' isn't really—"

Berta jabbed me with her elbow.

"Swell," Glenn said. "Could you get to the WPAF studio this evening by five thirty? The show broadcasts at six. We're at 195 Broadway, in the AT & T building. Fourth floor. Tell 'em Glenn Monroe's expecting you."

Glenn set off toward the house. As he went, he took another swig of Alkacine.

As soon as he was out of earshot, I said, "What about consulting with me before signing us up for publicly broadcasted humiliation? And who made you the head detective?"

"Mrs. Woodby, think of the publicity! It is free advertising for our agency. It would be foolish to squander such an opportunity. Any humiliation will be strictly up to you."

I sank into myself. Pouting, I suppose you could say, although I felt I deserved a little sulk. At least we'd managed to evade Ralph.

We followed the path out of the trees and emerged on a grassy bluff overlooking the whitecapped ocean. Salty wind gusted up. It was the sort of weather that was exhilarating if one was in love, but absolute purgatory if one was heartbroken.

"I'd kill for a steaming cup of coffee," I said with a shiver.

"I as well. Come on—there is the town." A path curved down to silver-shingled fishermen's cottages strung along a seawall, terminating at a pier and warehouse.

"Whoever was digging those holes could have easily come from town, then," I said, wiping ocean spray from my forehead. All right, sweat. Nervous sweat about speaking into a microphone on a citywide radio program in approximately eight hours.

We set off down the path. The bottom widened to a sandy road leading behind the row of fishermen's cottages. Smoke puffed from chimneys, and saggy motorcars and trucks were parked along the road. Fishing nets hung from porch rafters, and what I guessed were crab or lobster pots cluttered others. A smug cat sat in one of the windows watching Cedric.

Two anchored fishing boats bobbed near the pier. At the rear of the warehouse were stacks of crates, and two parked delivery trucks whose sides read CARVINGTON FISH CO. in crisp blue lettering. As we passed the warehouse, a burly white-haired man in a cable-knit sweater emerged from one of the cottages, nodded to us in greeting, and proceeded into the warehouse.

Berta said softly, "We are looking for someone who was wearing fisherman's clothing in the woods, are we not?"

I nodded, and we went to the half-open warehouse doors.

"Hello?" Berta called, her voice echoing.

"Hello," a gruff male voice called from the interior.

We went in. The warehouse was lit only from the open door. The man was stacking crates. He turned. He had a brown, weather-beaten complexion, small suspicious eyes, and although he had a Santa Claus belly, he appeared powerful and spry.

"Good morning," I said. "My name is Mrs. Woodby and this is Mrs. Lundgren. We are private detectives who have been hired to look into Rudy Montgomery's death."

"Bad business," the man said, and shook first Berta's hand and then mine. "Woman detectives? What'll they think of next? Abe." His hand was very large, and snaggy with calluses. "The police ruled it suicide, didn't they?" He strode deeper into the warehouse, to a powerboat balanced on blocks, and grabbed a huge canvas tarp.

"Yes," I said, "but there are some loose ends we'd like to tie up. For instance, there was a woman who called herself Isobel Bradford at the house on the day of Mr. Montgomery's death, but who left shortly after."

The man flung the tarp over the boat, covering only a third of it. Wet strands of seaweed clung to the bottom.

"We would like to ask this woman some questions," I said, "but I'm afraid we can't find her. Can you tell me if there is a taxi service in the village?"

"No taxi service, but young Nat who works at Flintock's Groceries will motor folks about for a fee." The man came back toward us, stopping a pace away. "Nat makes a lot of runs to the train stations in Mystic and New London."

"Thank you," I said. "Oh, and on our walk down here from

Montgomery Hall, we noticed bunches of freshly dug holes in the forest. Do you know who might have made those?"

"Sure they weren't dug by animals, now?"

Berta said in a testy voice, "It would be a terrifyingly large badger to have made those holes, and a very mathematical one as well, judging by their circular precision, Mr.—?"

"Murden."

Berta and I exchanged surprised looks.

"I reckon you've met my sister Esther," Abe said with a chuckle.

"We have," I said.

"She get up your snout? Don't be afraid to admit it. Even when Esther was a baby, she was all gloom and doom."

Berta said, "And you, Mr. Murden, are a fisherman? I noticed the delivery trucks outside."

"Yup. Cod. Lobsters now and then. Used to be oysters, but they all got farmed out along this coast, sad to say. The whole town depended on those oysters, and they just dwindled away to nothing." Abe's eyes flashed with anger.

"But aren't the fishermen themselves responsible to make sure their stock isn't depleted?" I asked. I felt impolite asking this, but I was curious to know what was at the bottom of Abe's anger.

"Not if we've got damned rules and regulations tying our hands." Abe scratched his neck, which looked a little rashy from his sweater. "That's all in the past, though. Carvington oysters are ancient history as far as I'm concerned. Now it's cod, morning, noon, and night. We're doing all right. Anything else I can help you with?"

"What was your sister's—Miss Murden's—relationship with Mr. Montgomery like?" I asked.

Abe's eyes squinched. "What're you getting at? Trying to pin that man's death on Esther, eh?"

"No, no," Berta said in a placating tone. "We only worry that he did not leave her with sufficiently excellent references in order for her to find a new domestic position."

"She told me the new master, Theo Wainwright, might keep her on."

"Oh, good for her," Berta said. "Thank you for your time, Mr. Murden." She gave him one of our cards, and we left.

15

Berta, Cedric, and I walked on through the drizzle to Church Street.

"Look, here's the grocer's," I said. "Let's look for Nat."

Flintock's Groceries was cool inside, fragrant with vinegary and yeasty scents. The bald man sitting at the counter peered over the top of his newspaper at us. "Help you?" he said.

"We would like to speak with Nat, please," Berta said.

"What about?"

"His taxi service. We may require his services in getting to the train station."

Actually, this was true, so we'd be bopping two birds with one stone.

"Nat!" the man shouted.

We heard footsteps in the back, and a chubby young man in denim overalls emerged. "Yes, Mr. Flintock?" Then he noticed us. "Oh. Hello."

Berta recited our spiel about being detectives looking into

Rudy Montgomery's death. Nat's guileless blue eyes widened, but Mr. Flintock rattled his newspaper with scorn.

"Did you happen to take anyone from Montgomery Hall to the train station on Thursday afternoon?" I asked Nat. "Perhaps a somewhat stout woman of middle years, with gray hair?"

"Nope."

Rats.

"I took her to Carter's Menswear in Mystic."

Berta released a small whinny. I leaned forward. "Really?"

"Yep. Around, oh, around four o'clock on Thursday, when all the police cars and ambulances were parked out front. She was as cool as could be, though, not worried one bit by all that business. She rattled off the address for Carter's—though I already knew where it was, since that's where I buy my overalls—and I left her there, with her suitcase. Seemed like a funny place for a hoity-toity-looking lady like her to go shopping for her mister, but she paid me double."

"Good boy," Mr. Flintock put in. "Always make outsiders pay double."

"We heard you might be able to drive us to the train station," I said to Nat.

"Sure thing. What time?"

"Actually," Berta interrupted, "we do not yet know what time, so if we require a ride, we shall return after we have eaten."

"Okay," Nat said.

"Why the subterfuge?" I asked Berta as we walked across the street to the Red Rooster. "We must get to New York, which means we must have a ride to the train station. Why not have Nat motor us? Is it because he'll charge us double?"

Berta opened her mouth, but before she could speak, my answer rolled up beside us in a junky Chalmers motorcar whose engine projected a molar-vibrating *thugga-thugga-thugga-thugga*.

"Morning, ladies," Ralph said, leaning an elbow out the window. "I've got your suitcases here, and as per my agreement with Mrs. Lundgren, I'm giving you two a ride to the city. But first, how about some breakfast?"

I looked agape at Berta. Then, struck utterly speechless with fury at her and at Ralph, I stiffly carried Cedric inside.

On the baked-goods display case at the front of the restaurant sat a pile of doughnuts under a glass dome. I put Cedric down, grabbed a doughnut, and marched over to an empty table. Cedric trailed after me, causing a stir in his Fair Isle sweater.

A few minutes later, Berta and Ralph slid into the chairs across the table from me. The doughnut was long gone. I kept my face buried in my greasy paper menu, which, I regret to say, shook.

Someone—Ralph—lowered the menu with a gentle hand. "Look, kid, I'm sorry it's gotta be this way. But you and Mrs. Lundgren have your job and I have mine, so why not collaborate?" Under the table, Cedric whined and bounced for Ralph.

I slapped the menu on the table. "I've had just about all I can take of you two!" I stabbed a finger at Berta. Her pale blue eyes were round, her lips pursed. "You, lying to me—we're supposed to be partners! How can I trust you if you set up clandestine arrangements with—with people I can't bear to be around? Not to mention all that 'head detective' hogwash!" I pointed at Ralph. "And you—why won't you just leave me alone? Don't give me that line about needing easy money, because this job looks to me like an enormous waste of your time."

Ralph held my gaze. Presently, I found it necessary to drop my pointing finger onto my lap. Only then did he say, "All right, I'll be honest. Theo Wainwright called me up about this job, and sure, it's easy money, but more than that, I'm worried about you. How come you keep taking on these murder investigations, anyway? You're supposed to be finding lost necklaces and puppies. I mean, isn't it a *retrieval* agency you're running?"

"Why should we leave all the good cases for other detectives?" I said.

"Listen, I'm here to help. And I'm sorry we don't see eye to eye about all the other, uh—" Ralph scratched his eyebrow. "—the other stuff."

"What about spying on us?" I demanded. "Is that still on your agenda?"

"Sure."

I clapped a hand to my forehead.

"Your client Theo is one of our murder suspects," Berta said to Ralph. "I very much hope you will not disclose any delicate information to him."

Ralph sighed. "Okay, okay. I'm not one to jigger up my own investigations, but I see what you're saying. I'll think twice about what I tell him."

"Before we motor to the city," Berta said to Ralph, "we must make a stop at Carter's Menswear in Mystic. We have a hot lead on a lady con artist."

Incredibly, this was as good as it was going to get: Berta not apologizing for being sneaky and bossy, and Ralph still planning on baby-minding us.

I unclenched my teeth and waved for the waitress.

I waited until I had drunk two cups of coffee and the waitress was sliding pancakes and sausages in front of me to ask her, "Excuse me, but do you know why someone would secretly dig holes on the Montgomery estate?"

She tipped her blond head. "Well, sure! Probably because of the treasure."

My fork clattered on my plate. Berta choked on coffee. Ralph leaned back in his chair.

"Treasure?" I said. "What is it? Who buried it—and when?"

"Well, no one knows when it was buried. Nobody really knows what it is, either, except that it's some kind of money. Here in Carvington, everyone has always known about the treasure. Why, Miss Murden just made mention of it the other day at the women's chorale rehearsal."

Coffee threatened to shoot out of my nose. Miss Murden singing in a women's chorale? I supposed she did resemble a church bell in those long black dresses.

"What did Miss Murden say about the treasure?" Berta asked.

"Oh, that some of the guests up there this week were snooping around, looking for it. Course, *she's* not hurting for money."

"On her housekeeper's salary?" I thought of Miss Murden's costly shoes.

"I guess not, because only a few weeks back, she started driving a brand-spanking-new Cole Touring Car around. Those things cost a mint! I think she was blackmailing Mr. Montgomery is what I think, just like in that radio play they aired last week about the Spanish prince who met the American heiress in the Scottish castle."

"Did anyone here in town ever suspect that Theo Wainwright was Mr. Montgomery's heir?" I asked. This waitress was a gold mine of gossip.

"Oh no." She fidgeted with her apron ties. "Never an inkling. His mother—she died of pneumonia a few years back—she always led us to believe Theo's dad died in the Great War. Kept to herself, mostly, anyway, and Theo went away to school in Massachusetts starting when he was only five or six. No wonder he turned out so rude."

"About the treasure," I said, "no one knows anything about what sort of money it is?"

"No. That's what makes it so thrilling! Some say it's Indian treasure from before the colonists arrived, and some say it's something the colonists buried, maybe to hide from the Indians or maybe to hide from the Redcoats during the revolution. Or maybe it's something left by Captain Hook—they say he stopped here, you know—and others say it's treasure from the South Seas brought over by Captain Montgomery on his whaling ship—"

"Judith!" an aproned man behind the lunch counter barked. "Customers!"

"Sorry," Judith whispered, and scurried away.

"Now we've got one more elusive thing to investigate," I said to Berta, glugging maple syrup on my pancakes. For lack of any alternative, I was ignoring Ralph. "I don't feel like we're making much headway in this case. It seems like everyone is lying, and the stolen diamonds are about the world's worst monkey wrench." I shot Ralph a dirty look. "Or, one of the world's worst monkey wrenches."

Carter's Menswear stood on Mystic's Main Street, which was a stretch of tight-packed storefronts—Rexall Drugs, a variety store, laundries, bakeries, a grocer's—with a clattering trolley and muddy motorcars traveling its length. Carter's grimy front windows displayed overalls, boots, and stacks of plaid wool shirts, and a large sign read EVERY-THING UNION MADE.

Here went nothing. Our one slim thread of a lead for tracking down the lady con artist and Isobel Bradford impostor.

Ralph waited in his motorcar with Cedric while Berta and I went inside.

Stacks of folded clothing towered on tables and shelves, and the air smelled bitterly of indigo dye and mothballs. We approached the counter, where a thickset shop lady in chintz, wire glasses, and a crimped bob was studying us grimly.

"May I help you?" she asked in a flat voice.

"Yes, actually," I said. "We're attempting to track down an

acquaintance of ours who was last seen being dropped off here at your shop on Thursday afternoon. Were you working then?"

"Yes. This is my store. Well, mine and my husband's, but he takes care of the books in back since I'm the one who's good with folks." She stared at us unblinkingly.

"Right," I said. I described the Isobel Bradford impostor, and before I had even finished, the shop lady was nodding.

"I remember her. Dressed to the nines in a fur coat and pearls."

My heart sped. "Did she purchase anything?"

"A fisherman's rain slicker and hat and a pair of men's woolen trousers. Said something about a costume party in New York City."

Holy moley. "Thanks ever so much," I said.

Berta and I went back outside and climbed into Ralph's Chalmers, Berta in front and me in back. Ralph was slouched low in the driver's seat and writing in a notebook.

"I'd bet a million bucks it was that lady con artist last night digging those holes!" I said to Berta. "She left Montgomery Hall, went straight to this menswear shop to purchase a disguise, and, well, she must be hiding out somewhere nearby in order to dig for treasure in the woods at night."

"Sounds far-fetched," Ralph said, putting his notebook away.

"First of all," I said to him, "I know precisely what you're recording in that little notebook of yours."

He gave his fedora brim a tug.

"And second of all," I continued, "this is *our* investigation, and *we* will judge whether or not something sounds far-fetched." I turned to Berta. "I want to go straight back to Carvington and track down our Isobel Bradford impostor. Now that we know she's probably digging for that treasure, well, she may have a splendid motive for murdering Rudy."

"I do agree that this con artist sounds terribly suspicious," Berta said, "but it is important that we go to the city today. It will be a boon to our agency to advertise on *The Filmore Vacuette Hour*."

"On the what?" Ralph said.

"Mind your own beeswax," I said.

We also had plans to visit Lem Fitzpatrick at the Moody Elephant that evening, although I wasn't about to mention it in front of Ralph. I sighed, gathered Cedric onto my lap, and settled in for the long drive.

If you ever have endured three hours in a motorcar driven with masculine competence by the fellow who has broken your heart—forced to watch his large rugged hands on the steering wheel, the stubbly contour of his jaw, forced to endure his half smile each time he catches you looking—then you know what I went through. In the end, I managed to soothe myself by making a mental tally of Ralph versus Eustace, Lord Sudley. According to my arithmetic, Eustace was a sparkling diamond to Ralph Oliver's five-and-dime glass.

Once we reached Manhattan, the first stop was to rescue the Duesy from the elevator parking garage near Grand Central Terminal. After that, Berta and I would have just enough time to motor to our apartment and wash, change, and look over our mail before heading to—gulp—the radio station.

"I guess this is good-bye," I said to Ralph as I unpeeled myself from his backseat with Cedric in my arms.

"Sure," he said with a wink. "See you round."

I grabbed my suitcase and slammed the door. He had every intention of following us. Of course he did.

Berta and I had to wait in a sort of open-air garage area while the attendant set the machinery in motion to bring the Duesy down from its perch. Ralph sat in his motorcar across the street, reading a newspaper. It was enough to make one scream.

When Berta, Cedric, and I had piled into the Duesy and were rumbling out of the garage, Ralph set aside his newspaper and angled his motorcar into the traffic. Lucky for me, a slow-moving bus blocked his path and his view of us. Instead of driving down the street so he could follow us all the way home, I nipped into the first alleyway.

"Heavens to Betsy! What are you doing?" Berta cried, embracing the dashboard.

"Come on, Berta. We can't have him slinking after us. Who knows what he'll tell Theo? Besides, lady to lady, don't you care that he's broken my heart?"

"He told me that he loves you."

I dinged a garbage can, knocking it over. "Love? Hah! If he loved me, he wouldn't refuse to try."

"Try what?"

"I don't know. Try to forget the pain of his past. Try to change his way of thinking. Try to adapt. Shouldn't he do that for me?" I reached the end of the alley and veered left, narrowly missing a Model T. Its horn beeped.

"You must adapt as well. And you must be patient with Mr. Oliver. He is a man who has seen terrible things. When I heard of the horrors of the Great War, I began to understand the haunted looks in the eyes of all these poor young men."

"What am I supposed to do? Twiddle my thumbs till I'm old and gray just because he's a chicken? Do you know what he told me? That there isn't a chance in hell that he'd even think of getting married!"

"Oh dear. Things are worse than I feared."

There was nothing left to say. I gassed it toward home.

Amid the snowdrift of mail waiting for us on our foyer floor was a telegram from Paris. From Mother.

CHECKING ON PROGRESS OF CATERER SELECTION.
LILLIAN FEARS YOU ARE BUNGLING JOB. APPRISE
AT ONCE. WE ARE AT RITZ PARIS.

Somehow I'd forgotten all about selecting a caterer for my sister's wedding. I'd choose Delguzzo's. I mean, they were all more or less alike, weren't they? All that remained, then, was to stop by and pay the deposit with a blank check my father had signed for me, weeks ago, for the purpose.

16

································

WPAF was housed in the towering granite American Telephone and Telegraph building at 195 Broadway. Berta and I rode the elevator to the fourth floor, and stepped into a carpeted corridor in which men and women dashed about.

"Berta," I said, "that radio program in which Jillie Harris, Glenn Monroe's former lady friend, stars—"

"*The High-Jinx Club.*"

"That's the one—is it produced in this station?"

"Yes. But why?"

"You'll see."

We located the reception room, as Glenn had instructed, and no sooner had we entered than a woman with a clipboard approached us.

"You must be from the Discreet Retrieval Agency," she said.

Berta and I nodded.

"You're almost too late, you know." She eyed Cedric, who was panting in my large handbag. "What about the pooch?"

"Oh, he might wish to say a few words," I said. "You don't suppose you could give me Jillie Harris's telephone number, do you?"

Suspicion clouded the secretary's face.

I added quickly, "Jillie and I are great friends, and she was at a party at my family's Park Avenue place, you see, and she said she'd give me the name of her hairdresser, but she forgot."

The secretary thawed. With certain people, the words *Park Avenue* work like sunbeams on cream cheese. She ruffled through her clipboard and then read aloud, "KL5-1711."

"Thanks!" I beamed, committing the telephone number to memory.

The secretary stashed our coats and hats, and led us into what she called the main studio. Chairs were arranged on the nearer side of the room, occupied by a few people. The other half of the room was taken up by a grand piano, a felt-covered table holding several unidentifiable items, and a cluster of people looking over papers—scripts, I guessed—and murmuring amongst themselves. At the center of it all stood a microphone on a brass stand. A cord snaked away from the microphone to a large wooden box on wheels. I hadn't the foggiest how radio transmission worked, so this wheeled box may as well have been Ali Baba's cave.

Windows overlooked the tall buildings opposite, and thick curtains hung on all the other walls—presumably for sopping up extra sound like bread for gravy.

I took out my notebook, jotted down Jillie Harris's telephone number, and stuffed it back inside my handbag beside Cedric. "There's Glenn," I whispered to Berta. "In a tuxedo. Why is everyone wearing formal attire if the audience can't see them?"

"According to *Radio News* magazine, it is to help the performers get in the proper mood," Berta said. "Many of them are or were stage performers as well."

"Girls!" Glenn said, striding our way. "Boy am I glad you showed!

I was starting to get worried you were blowing me off, and after I had to beg my producer to let you on. Riled up my heartburn something awful." He thumped a fist on his chest.

"Sorry," I said.

"We're putting you on the front end of the show, right after the opening song and my introductory remarks—which, no surprise, is a shtick about Vacuette cleaners. Sound good? Okay, great." Glenn herded us over to some chairs off to the side.

My hairline grew damp as we waited. I couldn't do this! How could I *do* this? Even Cedric, panting in my handbag, appeared more serene than I.

"*Berta,*" I whispered. "*I can't—*"

"You're on the air!" a main in pleated pants and suspenders said.

The woman at the piano kicked off a jazzy little tune, and three women gathered around the microphone and burst into cheery-sweet harmonization ending with "*Welcome to the Vacuette Houuuuuuuuuuuuuur.*"

Then Glenn was at the microphone with that chipper drawl. "Good evening, ladies and gentlemen. Those were the divine voices of the Vacuette Sisters, and this is *The Filmore Vacuette Hour*! Say, are you weary of drudgery? Fed up with a dirty house? Does sweeping your floors never end and beating your rugs out of doors make you weep? Yes, you say? Then why not ask your fellow to purchase you a Filmore Vacuette today?" Glenn changed his tone to a conspiratorial aside. "Oh, and fellows—ladies just can't say no to a Filmore Vacuette. With its smoothly turning wheels, presto-zip bag, and gleaming chrome trim, the Filmore Vacuette is guaranteed to dazzle, certain to cause swoons, and don't forget: The Filmore Vacuette has cleaning . . . in the bag!"

The pianist tore into a swooping, romantic melody with lots of crashing chords while Glenn stepped back to take a sip of water from a glass on a table. His face was a little pinched as he swallowed. Stomach acid, I guessed.

Then Glenn was beckoning us with a finger, and I found myself at the microphone between Berta and Glenn, hugging Cedric in my handbag and contemplating a break for the door.

The piano music ended and Glenn said, "And now, ladies and gentlemen, it is my profound pleasure to introduce two astonishing ladies for our question-and-answer segment.'" Glenn looked down at his script. "Mrs. Lundgren, head detective, and Mrs. Woodby, assistant detective, are New York City's only lady gumshoes. Some of you may have heard how the Discreet Retrieval Agency cracked a couple murder cases that stumped the police, but you're hearing them on radio broadcast for the first time here, on *The Filmore Vacuette Hour*."

A brief tinkle of theme song from the pianist.

Glenn turned to Berta. "Tell me, Mrs. Lundgren, what's the best part of being a lady gumshoe?"

Berta leaned over the microphone. "Thank you, Mr. Monroe. The best part is the adventure. The chases, the clues, the danger, subterfuge, and disguise! Why, there are times when I must pinch myself, for it is all so very thrilling—oh, and by the way, our telephone number is KL5-1919 and our motto is 'No job too trivial.' Please do ring us up today. We specialize in retrieving items thought to be lost forever, and we will stop at nothing to get the job done. If we—"

"Thank you, Mrs. Lundgren," Glenn said, edging in front of Berta. He turned to me. "Mrs. Woodby, as the assistant detective, have you learned a great deal from Mrs. Lundgren?"

I tried to say something, but my throat was stuck. Honestly, I don't mind having my photograph snapped, provided I've had time to fix my hair and makeup and bathing suits aren't involved, but having my voice shot out into the airwaves? Paralyzing.

Glenn bugged his eyes at me.

My throat unstuck and I opened my mouth, hoping something eloquent would pour out, but nothing came but "Uck."

Glenn turned to Berta. "Mrs. Lundgren, how did you learn to detect?"

"I have read a goodly number of detective novels, including every volume by the great Frank B. Jones, Jr. In addition, both Mrs. Woodby and I rely upon our feminine intuitions and our sharp wits. Do not forget, our telephone number is KL5-1919 and we will work day and night to crack your case, large or small, and if you should ever—"

"Thank you!" Glenn cried, pushing Berta gently out of the way to get to the microphone.

"KL5-1919!" Berta cried, lunging for the microphone.

Glenn cut her off at the pass. "Ladies and gentlemen, the Discreet Retrieval Agency!" He cued the pianist, who launched a sappy ballad.

Berta and I returned to our chairs.

"I'm not so sure how discreet our agency is going to be after this," I muttered to Berta.

"Then we shall change the name," Berta whispered. "Perhaps the Extremely Successful Retrieval Agency will do nicely, because mark my words, our telephone will be ringing off the hook."

I had my doubts.

The pianist finished and Glenn was joined at the microphone by four men and women holding scripts. They began a radio drama about an innocent girl named Libby who receives a letter saying she's inherited a pile of dough from a long-lost uncle, and goes to his eerie mansion to collect. Berta sat on the edge of her seat, handbag clasped on her knees, engrossed.

I attempted to pay attention—but honestly, I was still recuperating from my humiliating bout of stage fright, and anyway, the drama's plot was a bit hackneyed. There was the ghoulish butler, the handsome young gardener, and things going bump in the night. Oh, and since this was *The Filmore Vacuette Hour,* at intervals we heard the mansion's maid vacuuming the rugs in the background. The vacuuming sound, along with assorted thuds, knocks, rings, and clicks, was produced by a man at the sound effects table. He also simulated quite perfectly the sounds of a popping cork and whistling wind.

I could understand why Glenn had been chosen to host the show. He read the parts of the narrator, the ghoulish butler, a newspaper reporter, and even a lady opera star, making each character's voice utterly unique. Heartburn or no, the guy had an amazing knack for voices.

I bolted upright in my chair. Voices! Geewhillikins. *Voices.*

I nudged Berta and whispered, "We need to talk."

"Not now, Mrs. Woodby," she whispered, and turned back to the radio actors.

I twiddled my foot. I petted Cedric's ears. My brain spun.

What if—just for the sake of argument—what if *Glenn* was the one who'd been making that creepy ghost voice at Montgomery Hall? He had just demonstrated that he could easily simulate a female voice. What if *he* had tried to push me down the stairs last night?

Glenn had a mysterious, intimate-yet-strained relationship with Coral; clearly the two were more than casual friends. Perhaps there was a murder motive buried in that relationship. Perhaps Glenn had been torn up with jealousy and bumped off Rudy or maybe Glenn had done it as a favor for Coral. Had their plan backfired? Is that why they seemed so fizzed with each other now?

I wasn't sure. But my feminine intuition, as Berta had phrased it, insisted that these radio-show sound effects were a piece of the puzzle.

The radio play wrapped up (Libby got her millions and the handsome gardener to boot), the man in the pleated trousers announced we were off the air, and there was a general migration toward the studio door.

"Thanks, girls," Glenn said. "You did a real good job. I'd invite you to dinner, but the truth is, my heartburn's boiling like a pot of bouillabaisse. All I want to do is down a bottle of Alkacine and go to bed. Thanks again."

"Wait," I called after him, but he didn't hear. I wished to look him straight in the eye and ask him if he was Montgomery Hall's ghost.

"Let us hurry back to the apartment," Berta said to me, breathless with excitement. "People could be telephoning us with job offers this very moment. Now, where did that secretary put our coats and hats?"

"Wait," I said. "I must speak with Glenn." Where had he gone? I craned my neck.

"I have just had an idea," Berta said. "We could ask Mrs. Snyder from across the hall to answer our telephone for us." Mrs. Snyder was the young mother of a fat, imperious baby, and she was home alone much of the time while her husband, a sulky poet, hunted for his muse. "We could pay her for her time. I am certain she would be keen on the extra household income."

"Sure, why not?" I said. "Mrs. Snyder is intelligent and she's—"

A shrill scream cut me off. The crowd around us collectively gasped and murmured.

Berta said, "Oh my. I do not like the sound of that."

More screams.

I didn't say anything, but followed the screams along with everyone else. I found myself amid a cluster of people looking through an open doorway into a sort of lounge. The secretary with the clipboard was standing in the middle of the room, screaming away, and at her feet was the frozen, contorted body of Glenn Monroe. Milky fluid trickled from his mouth. His blue eyes were peeled wide.

The sound effects man pushed through, knelt beside Glenn, touched his neck, and then looked up at all of us standing aghast in the doorway. "Somebody telephone for an ambulance. And the police. He's dead."

The blabbering secretary was led away, and the sound effects man shepherded everyone from the lounge door. I stood on tippy-toe, and before I was pushed along with the others, I saw that Glenn clutched a brown glass bottle in one dead hand. Of course. That milky fluid trickling from his mouth . . .

Someone had poisoned Glenn's Alkacine.

17

Berta nearly exploded with impatience while we waited to give our statements to the police. There were dozens of people at the WPAF studios and all of us were required to be interviewed, so the evening dragged on and on.

"Think of all the telephone calls we could be missing!" Berta wailed, pacing back and forth in a corner of the crowded reception room.

"If anyone is truly keen to hire us on the grounds of one embarrassing radio bit," I said, "they'll telephone again." I started on yet another one of the turkey, bacon, and mayonnaise sandwiches that someone had brought up from a delicatessen. Murder makes me ravenous, I guess. I fed Cedric a bit of bacon.

At last I was called into the station's smaller studio, which the police had taken over for their questioning. To a tired-looking policeman, I gave my account of hearing the screams and seeing Glenn's body with the Alkacine bottle in one hand. "What was the cause of death?" I asked.

The policeman didn't even glance up from his notepad. "Cyanide poisoning."

My guts twisted. "Golly."

"It was in that bottle of milk of magnesia he was holding. Seems he suffered from heartburn and drank that stuff like water. Everyone in the studio knew it, too."

"Do you suppose someone here at the studio poisoned him?"

"Course." The policeman snorted. "Not likely to be some crazy man off the street, now, is it?"

"No, but, well, the thing is, I'm a private detective—"

"You? Haw-haw!"

"—and Glenn Monroe happened to be present in the house when Rudy Montgomery was killed."

"Read about that in the papers. Rich guy in Connecticut, right? It was suicide. Say, you aren't one of those detectives who try to drum up business for yourself by blowing things all out of proportion, are you?"

I swear that when the policeman said *proportion,* he leered at my hips. "No," I said, smoothing my skirt, "I am not. I suspect there could be a link between the two deaths, but you are not, of course, obliged to take that into consideration."

"Nope, I sure ain't."

"Glenn Monroe was at Rudy Montgomery's estate in Connecticut just this morning, I happen to know. Someone there could have poisoned his Alkacine—"

"That'll be all." The policeman waved chubby, dismissive fingers.

Deflated, I went back to the reception room, and shortly after that, Berta disappeared to use the powder room. She was gone for an eternity. When she at last returned, her eyes shone and she told me she'd given her statement to the police. "We are free to go," she said.

"Why do you have that mad gleam in your eye?" I knew that gleam. Berta had detected a hot lead.

"Suffice it to say that our investigation has taken a ninety-degree turn."

"What did you discover?"

Berta tapped her nose. "Not until we are home."

"Home? What about the Moody Elephant?"

"It is too early still, Mrs. Woodby, and I am most eager to go home and put forth our business proposition to Mrs. Snyder."

I checked my wristwatch. It was a little after nine o'clock. Berta was correct: Far too early for a speakeasy. Besides, if we meant to put the screws to a big-cheese gangster about some diamonds, a spot of gussying up was in order.

We rode the elevator to the lobby and ventured out into the evening. Broadway and Dey Street were a wilderness of careening headlamps, roaring engines, and exhaust fumes, and a damp north wind whipped in the crevasses between buildings. I beat back the desolate feeling that was twining itself around my spirit. This was a night for snuggling with one's sweetie before a crackling fire. Not tracking down villains.

But the splendid news was that Ralph Oliver hadn't caught up with us again. Ten points for me.

After Cedric paid a call on a fire hydrant, I flagged down a taxi. "I really must telephone Eustace and tell him what's happened to Glenn," I said. Though I had barely given Eustace a thought all day, now I found myself hankering for a dose of his coddling. I'd been thinking of his attentions as a sort of hot-water bottle for the soul, but . . . could it be that I had a genuine pash for him? And if so, what was wrong with me, that I could develop a crush on Eustace while still reeling from Ralph-induced heartbreak?

....

A taxi screeched to a stop at the curb. Once we were squashed in the backseat, I said to Berta, "All right, spill it: What is our investigation's ninety-degree turn?"

"*Shh,*" Berta whispered with a meaningful look at the back of the cabbie's head. "*Not here.*"

Oh, for Pete's sake.

Several minutes later, we arrived home at Longfellow Street, Number 9. Mrs. Snyder opened her apartment door with her baby on her hip. Stinging smoke unfurled from behind her. "Mrs. Lundgren! Mrs. Woodby! What a nice surprise. Would you come in? Alistair won't sleep, so I've made some biscuits—I only scorched a few."

"No, thank you," Berta said quickly. She disapproved of Mrs. Snyder's use of the new boxed baking mixes. "We are here to enlist your help."

The baby was looking at us narrowly, as though he knew his mother's attention was about to be diverted and he was not amused.

Mrs. Snyder, a sandy blonde rarely seen in anything but a dressing gown and house slippers, happily agreed to answer our telephone and take down names and numbers of any potential clients, in exchange for a healthy daily sum. She said from inside her own apartment she could always hear our telephone ringing. Berta said she'd bring over the extra door key shortly.

"This'll give me something to do while Quentin is gone, and since Alistair can't talk yet, I'll enjoy speaking to grown-up people from time to time." Mrs. Snyder tenderly kissed Alistair's squishy, orblike cheek. "That's why I'm always burning everything I cook."

That settled, Berta and I crossed the hall to our own apartment and let ourselves in. Berta went straight to the kitchen and switched on the oven.

"What are you making?" I asked, lingering in the doorway.

"Gingersnaps."

"To help us get over the shock of Glenn's death?"

"Do not be silly. We must take something to bribe the speakeasy doorman."

"Oh." Rats. "*Now* are you going to tell me about our investigation's ninety-degree turn?"

"Make a pot of coffee. I shall reveal all as soon as the gingersnaps are in the oven."

Berta mixed the dough, spooned it out onto her cookie pan, and slid it into the hot oven. Meanwhile, I made a pot of coffee in the stovetop percolator and set out cups, cream, and sugar.

At last, Berta sat down and sipped her coffee. "Now, then," she said. "Do you recall when I excused myself to go to the powder room at the radio station?"

"I worried you'd been kidnapped."

"I was conducting an investigation of the crime scene."

"Weren't there police in that room?"

"Indeed there were, but they left to pursue a rumor of coffee and crullers."

"Did you start that rumor?"

Berta ignored the question. I don't believe even the Bolshevik secret police could make her crack. "I took the opportunity to slip into the room. Glenn's body had already been removed, as well as the bottle of Alkacine. But his valise remained. I took the liberty of looking inside—putting on my gloves to avoid leaving fingerprints. In addition to radio scripts, the valise contained a book titled *Lost Treasures of the United States*."

My pulse thrummed. "Treasures?"

"I flipped to the index, and had just enough time to see that there was an entry on Montgomery Hall when I heard footsteps approaching and was forced to cut my inspection short. That book was some sort of treasure hunter's guide, Mrs. Woodby. Perhaps Glenn planned to return to Connecticut and search for the treasure. In fact, recall how we encountered him in the woods this morning? Perhaps he had already been searching for the treasure. What is more, we may be entirely incorrect about the reason for Rudy's death. Perhaps he was not killed as the result of a petty personal feud or sordid romantic jealousy. Perhaps he was killed because of the treasure. And perhaps, so was Glenn."

I allowed that to sink in. "It must be the same murderer, right?" I said. "Because two murders so closely tied together would be awfully coincidental."

"As occult detective Hugo Quinn observed in 'The Case of the Broken Scarab,' an apparent coincidence only means that one is still missing a piece of the puzzle. Glenn knew too much about the treasure, perhaps, or saw something he should not have."

"You know, I think it's high time I telephoned Eustace. I'd nearly forgotten, and this is all on his dime."

"Indeed. The original investigation for which he hired us has suddenly grown a good deal more complicated."

More complicated and, quite possibly, more dangerous, because while a single murder was one thing, a second murder smacked of a desperate killer.

I went to the telephone in the little hallway off our kitchen, nudging aside the box of Lillian's unmailed wedding invitations with my toe. Were those—oh dear—were those dust bunnies gathering inside the box? I really must get cracking on that.

I dialed 0 and asked the operator to put me through to Montgomery Hall. The manservant, Mwinyi, answered "Hello?" in his richly accented baritone.

"Hello, this is Mrs. Woodby. Could I please speak with Lord Sudley? It's urgent."

"Yes, madam."

I waited, wondering if Theo planned to give Mwinyi his walking papers. Servants as decorous and discreet as Mwinyi were difficult to come by. I knew this well from my former days as a Society Matron.

"Lola?" This was Eustace on the line. "Mwinyi said you had an urgent message. Are you quite all right? I've been worried sick ever since you disappeared this morning."

"I'm all right, but I'm afraid the news is pretty grim." I told him all about Glenn's death by cyanide poisoning at the radio station, ending with Berta's discovery of *Lost Treasures of the United States* in his valise. "Have you heard of the Montgomery treasure?"

"Oh yes. Rudy enjoyed boasting about his legendary treasure and his ghost whenever he got really drunk. I fancy he felt it lent his estate an aura of history and mystique."

"Mrs. Lundgren and I feel that Glenn's death and the treasure must be bound up somehow in Rudy's death, so we'd like to pursue these new angles as part of our ongoing murder investigation."

A slight pause. Then, "Yes, of course. It'd be foolish to ignore any of the angles."

"We'll be motoring back up to Carvington tomorrow to follow up on a few leads, although naturally we won't be staying at Montgomery Hall—"

"Try the Old Whaler's Inn on Church Street. The locals speak well of it. Smashing fried oysters there, I'm told. And—" Eustace cleared his throat. "—the missing diamonds?"

"We're working on it."

"You really are superlative, my dear girl. Now, do ring me up the moment you've booked into the inn." Eustace *ahem*ed again. "The truth is, Lola . . . well, forgive me for my absolutely wretched timing, but, well, the thing is I . . . You see, it didn't quite sink in until after you'd left this morning without saying good-bye and I was suddenly overcome by the bleakness of your absence and . . . my dear girl, I've quite fallen in love with you and I'm simply perishing to see you again. Is that horribly improper of me?"

For some reason, I sounded like a breathless stage ingenue as I replied, "Of course it isn't inappropriate, you silly boy. I'll see you tomorrow." I hung up the earpiece with fumbling fingers.

Well. Imagine that. Lord Sudley was in love with me. Tall, manly, handsome, smartly dressed, and country-estate-owning Lord Sudley.

This was a real crush, wasn't it? This dazzled, smug sort of feeling? Wasn't this a tender green sprout of True Love?

I went in a fog to the kitchen and sank into a chair.

"Mrs. Woodby, you look as though you have been struck on the head with a skillet," Berta said.

"Lord Sudley said he's in love with me."

Okay, I hadn't expected Berta to squeal with delight and beg to be my matron of honor. But I thought some form of congratulations were in order.

Berta only placed her coffee cup carefully in its saucer and said, "Such fascinating timing."

"I beg your pardon?"

"You telephoned Lord Sudley to inform him of Glenn Monroe's demise, and he chose that moment to profess his love?"

"I think he was too jittery to tell me in person."

"You do not wonder if he is attempting to distract you?"

"Distract me from what? You seem to require a lot of reminders that Eustace isn't one of our suspects. He's our client."

"I do not trust that man, Mrs. Woodby."

"You trust his bank checks."

"Oh, but we have not attempted to cash them yet. I wonder how Coral will react to Glenn's death."

Changing the subject, was she? Swell. "She seemed to be equally peeved by and fond of him."

"I think we have been remiss not to have looked into either Coral's or Glenn's backgrounds."

"Hold on a tick—you've just reminded me of something." I got my detecting notebook from my handbag and dashed back to the telephone. I flipped to the page upon which I'd jotted Jillie Harris's number, picked up the earpiece, and dialed 0. "KL5-1711," I told the operator.

After three rings, a woman said, "Hello?"

"Miss Harris?"

"Yes." Her voice was guarded.

"Miss Harris, my name is Lola Woodby. I'm a private detective investigating the death of Rudy Montgomery—"

"Who gave you my telephone number? Someone at the studio?"

"Yes, and I'm afraid, as of this evening I'm also looking into the death of Glenn Monroe."

That silenced her.

"Were you aware of his death?" I asked gently.

"Yes—Betsy from the studio telephoned me about an hour ago— and it's a crying shame! Poor little Glenn never did anyone any harm. Sure, he could be a pill and he always was the very first to criticize what a girl was wearing, but—say. How come you're calling?"

"I'd like to ask you a few questions, but it would probably be best to speak in person." Inspiration struck. "I don't suppose you'd like to join my detecting partner and me for a drink at the Moody Elephant this evening?"

"Would I? My latest feller's up and left me for some tootsie he met at a soda fountain, and what with Glenn dying, I don't feel like being alone tonight. Meet you there in, say, about an hour?"

"Peachy." I rang off.

Fueled by too much coffee, I set about dolling myself up for the Moody Elephant. By the time I'd finished my makeup, wriggled into a midnight blue velvet Lanvin, slipped on my highest Pinet pumps, and emerged from the bathroom, Berta was waiting grimly in the sitting room with her coat buttoned and her handbag on her knees.

"It sounded as though you were competing for the gold medal in the pole vault," she said.

"Not every lady has the ability to bake her way into men's hearts." I patted my perfectly waved bob. "The rest of us must resort to lipstick and high heels."

"Mr. Eccles, the lawyer, has yet to taste my baked goods, Mrs. Woodby."

I shrugged on my fur-collared coat. "I'll bet he hasn't," I said. As a sort of punishment, I suppose, a tiny moth fluttered out of my fur collar. I shooed it away.

18

Macdougal Street was only a few blocks from our apartment, which goes a long way to illustrate the sort of neighborhood Washington Square was. It wasn't dangerous—or at least, I always slept like a log there—but things weren't precisely respectable, and miles from swanky. Artists, immigrants, show business types, and the more enterprising sort of criminals bumped shoulders there, and you could buy the nicest French pastries and Italian cured meats.

Caffè Agostini buzzed with late-night customers and coffee vapors. Light shone from the green-painted storefront, and inside, the spectacular espresso machine imported from Italy, Caffè Agostini's claim to fame, gleamed and hissed.

Berta and I approached the woman wrangling the espresso-machine levers. "Would you kindly direct us to the powder room?" I said.

She looked us up and down through the steam. "Sorry."

Berta leaned in conspiratorially and said, "I understand it is a very *moody* powder room. One frequented by, strange to say, *elephants*."

Incredulity slackened the woman's face. "You pair?"

"We're thirsty," I said.

The woman shrugged, and tipped her head toward a rear door.

The door led to a dim little hallway, which terminated at yet another door. We knocked, and a round peephole slid open.

"Whatcha lookin for?" a gravelly voice said through the hole.

"I would think that is obvious," Berta said, unbuckling her handbag and drawing out a waxed paper packet of gingersnaps. Spicy, buttery scents blossomed into the air. "Open the door, and these cookies are yours."

And we were in. Magic.

A freight elevator took us underground, and we found ourselves in a brick-walled cavern filled with jazz, smoke, and raucous voices. Musicians strummed and wailed onstage at one end of the room, and scantily dressed girls twirled and kicked their legs. Some of the tables were occupied by men and women playing cards—poker, I deduced by the hand gestures.

I craned my neck, searching for Lem Fitzpatrick as we squeezed through to an empty table and gave our drink orders to a waiter.

"Ah," Berta said. "There is Jillie Harris." She twiddled her fingers, trying to capture the attention of a beautiful, laughing blonde a few tables over who was surrounded by rapt men.

"How do you know that's Jillie?" I asked.

"Because her likeness has appeared on the cover of *Radio News* on more than one occasion. Oh good, she is coming our way."

Jillie Harris slunk over in a gold dress with a martini in hand. She leaned over our table to be heard through the hubbub. "You're the detectives who telephoned?"

"Please, Miss Harris," Berta said, glancing around, "we do not wish to call attention to our vocation in such an establishment."

"Oh, of course." Jillie slid into the empty chair beside me. "Hi. You must be—was it Lucy?"

"Lola," I said. "Lola Woodby. And this is my partner, Mrs. Lundgren. Thank you for agreeing to speak with us."

"Well, it's just awful what happened to Glenn, and I'd like to do whatever I can to help lock up the killer. I mean, gee whiz, a murderer lurking around the WPAF studios?" She shivered her powdered bare shoulders. "That's where I work." Jillie had dangling diamond earrings; a neat little head of bleached finger waves; eyebrows painted to be long, tapered, and wistful; heavy kohl; and a glistening crimson Cupid's bow as symmetrical as a real lip line. Oh, Jillie was lovely, but while men see a woman like that and go gaga for *her*, a woman—at least one who knows her way around a vanity table—goes gaga over her paintbrush technique.

I said, "Miss Harris, do you have any idea who might have poisoned Glenn?"

"He was, well, he wasn't well liked in general, because he was always a bit too snide, but he wasn't ever truly unkind to anyone. He'd make comments, little pinpricks, stinging a nerve, you know, but never going deep enough to really wound . . . No, I can't imagine who could've poisoned him. It must've been someone really off their rocker, don't you think?"

"One must be insane to commit a murder," Berta said, "although at times it is a temporary insanity, born of desperation."

"Golly, you're giving me the creeps." Jillie gulped her martini.

I decided not to let on that Berta was quoting, verbatim, "The Lost Lass of Cairn Gorm."

"Have you ever met Glenn's friend Coral Moore?" I asked. "She lives up in Connecticut on the Montgomery estate."

"No, but Glenn told me all about her. They were friends for ages—since they were kids, I figured, though I never heard all the details. Maybe they were next-door neighbors?"

"That's funny," I said, "because Coral told me they met in New York as adults when they were both working onstage."

"Maybe I got it wrong. My memory's got more holes than a doily. Anyway, I never could make it up to Connecticut on the occasions Glenn invited me along—seems there were wonderfully wild parties up there."

"Do you know why Glenn would've been upset if . . ." I searched for the most delicate phrasing. "Why would Glenn have been nervy if Coral threatened to tell the radio station producer why he dropped you?"

Jillie blinked her mascara-laden eyes like a fawn in the headlights. "Don't you know?"

"Know what?" I asked.

"That Glenn was *otherwise inclined.*"

"Oh." *Oh.*

"Glenn didn't want his producer to know—he didn't want the public to know. It would've ruined his career."

"But I saw you on his arm with some frequency," Berta said. "In the gossip columns and radio magazines, I mean to say."

"Well, sure. We were friends, and it was good for his career to be seen with a pretty girl on his arm. Listen, you can't believe a thing you read in the magazines. It's all made up."

The waiter arrived with Berta's brandy alexander and my highball, and we dipped in. When Berta came up for air, she asked Jillie, "Did Glenn ever mention a treasure to you? At the Montgomery estate?"

"Treasure? Gosh, no—but that could explain why he was spending so much time up there. And I thought it was because he'd met a cute fellow or something. Come to think of it . . ." Jillie tipped her head. "There was the fellow we ran into one day at City Hall."

"Go on," I said.

"Well, Glenn and I were walking along just in front of City Hall—headed to the Forham Grill, I guess—and a scrummy dark-haired fellow was hurrying up the steps. Glenn called out to him—gee, I wish I could remember his name—and they exchanged a few pleasantries about Connecticut and the people up there, so I figured the fellow was from that neck of the woods. It was all really rushed and awkward, though. I had the feeling the fellow was just itching to get away, and he did as soon as he could without even looking my way once."

Jillie wasn't used to being overlooked by men; her brown eyes flashed.

Berta said, "Was his name Theo?"

"That's it! Theo. All brooding and nervous. Wearing eyeglasses."

What could Theo have been doing at City Hall in New York? He lived in Connecticut.

"When was this?" I asked Jillie.

"Oh, sometime last month."

"Do you know the address of Glenn's home in the city?" Berta asked.

"Of course. Four-twelve at the Branson Building on Central Park West. Why?"

"No reason," Berta said in the dotty-maiden-aunt voice she wheeled out when she wished to evade questions.

I took a sip of highball and saw, over the edge of my glass, Ralph walk in. The jazz trumpets suddenly sounded like they were underwater. Eustace, Lord Sudley, might be worldly and powerful, but he simply didn't have Ralph's style and grace. No one did. But I'd learned the hard way that style and grace aren't sturdy foundations for a life together.

"Lola?" Jillie said. "You all right? Need a glass of water?"

Ralph spotted me and didn't take his eyes from mine as he snaked through the tables.

"Evening, kid," he said. "Mrs. Lundgren."

"Now I'm getting why you couldn't breathe," Jillie said to me.

"Well, well, what a surprise," I said to Ralph.

He sank into a chair. "Evening, ladies. Thought I'd find you here. Say, I saw Fitzpatrick over there at the gambling tables. I'd like to help you two sort out your little, ah, situation with him. Why not strike while the iron's hot? Maybe Lola and I oughta approach him first—that all right, Mrs. Lundgren?"

"Fine," Berta said.

Jillie leaned over the table toward Ralph, forcing me to tilt back. "Are you a private detective, too? Because if you are, I've got an urgent case for you."

Ralph treated her to one of his heart-stopping smiles. "Oliver. Ralph Oliver."

"Jillie Harris—call me Poopsie."

Was this a joke?

"All right, Poopsie. What's your poison?"

"Whatever you're having."

"What I'm having is fun."

"Okay!" I yelped, scraping my chair back and standing. "Time to go and speak with Fitzpatrick."

Ralph lifted an eyebrow. "Okay, Mrs. Woodby." He stood. "Poopsie, Mrs. Lundgren, please excuse us."

Jillie pouted. "Don't take too long."

I stormed toward Lem Fitzpatrick's table, Ralph right behind me. "What do you mean by flirting in front of me?" I whispered hotly over my shoulder.

"You've let me know loud and clear that you hate me, how you don't want anything more to do with me if I'm not game for wedding bells, so as far as I'm concerned, I'm free as a bird." Ralph said all this in an easy, calm tone, and I got the heart-crumpling feeling that he wasn't simply attempting to make me jealous. No, he really believed we were through.

Which is what I wished for. Of course it was. And Eustace, Lord

Sudley, was in love with me. It was all this dratted cigarette smoke that was making my eyes water.

I had met Lem Fitzpatrick before, and he isn't the sort of fellow you bring to tea with Granny. Oh, he's good-looking, all right, in that tall, dark, and hungover sort of way. He is also rumored to have sunk his own brother to the bottom of the East River with a couple of cement shoes, thereby crowning himself the uncontested kingpin of New York City crime.

So—I want to make this perfectly clear—when I clung to Ralph's arm as we approached Lem's table, it was merely because I felt a smidge skittish.

"Take it easy, kid," Ralph whispered in my ear. "You're wound as tight as a ukulele string."

His breath on my ear sent one hundred watts flashing straight through my belly and down to my toes, causing me to totter. "Take it easy?" I whispered, steadying myself on his arm. "This is *Lem Fitzpatrick.* I heard that at the movies, he eats nails instead of Cracker Jack."

Ralph chuckled. "Just a rumor."

Lem looked up from his cards when we stopped beside him. The green-shaded lamp threw his eye sockets into shadow, but I saw his jaw tense.

"Howzit?" he said. He eyed me up and down like a rack of lamb in a butcher shop window. "Say, we've met, haven't we?"

"We may have crossed paths."

Fitzpatrick squinted up at Ralph. "I've seen your mug before, too, haven't I?"

"Sure," Ralph said. "This mug was once on a Coca-Cola advertisement."

"Mr. Fitzpatrick," I said, "I have a small business matter I'd like to sort out with you." I looked around at the motley gang of slicks, thugs, and molls stooped over their cards. "Alone."

"How about next month?"

"What about right now?"

"All right," Lem said. "But you can't bring your strong-arm man."

Fear shot through me. "Allow me to at least bring my, um, business partner, Berta Lundgren."

"Another dame? Fine. Meet me in my office in a coupla minutes."

"Where is your office?" I asked.

"Up on the roof." Lem lit a cigarette, eyes pinched against the smoke, and turned back to his cards.

As we walked away, Ralph whispered to me, "Sure hope you've got that gun I gave you in your garter."

"What good would that do me?" I said. "I wouldn't even know how to shoot it, and I already have a difficult enough time keeping my seams straight."

19

<hr />

I joined Berta at our table and broke the news. As a result, she had to visit the powder room. Twice. Then we said good-bye to an oddly pale Ralph and returned to the freight elevator. It clanked all the way to the roof. The door moaned open, and freezing wind gusted in.

"Good thing we brought our coats," I said, hugging myself.

Berta did not answer. I couldn't see her well in the dim light, but I knew her silence was less about being afraid of Lem Fitzpatrick than about her phobia of heights.

We stepped off the elevator. The glittering city expanded around us, and the sky glowed a deep plum. Water tank, fire escape . . . and Lem Fitzpatrick, lounging on the ledge, looking out at the city, smoking.

Berta and I approached him.

"Hello, Mr. Fitzpatrick," I called.

Lem half turned. "Why d'ya look so scared? I ain't gonna hurt you."

We stopped a pace away.

"We're not afraid," I said. Unconvincing.

Berta was eyeing the ledge with wide eyes. "But we *are* cold. I have no desire to contract whooping cough, so shall we get down to brass tacks?"

"Sure."

"You tell him," Berta whispered to me, taking a step back.

I cleared my throat. "It's like this, Mr. Fitzpatrick. It seems that your, um, underlings—"

"Henchpersons," Berta corrected.

"—your henchpersons stole some items that were contained in an argyle sock on a New York–Boston train two evenings ago."

Lem tossed back his head and barked with laughter. "That was you two? Haw-haw! My boys said it was a coupla rough customers! Haw-haw-haw!"

"You must return the items," I said.

"Those items are worth some heavy sugar," Lem said. "So's the sock, for that matter. Felt like genuine cashmere."

"Those items didn't belong to us," I said, "and we'll be arrested for theft if they aren't restored to their rightful owner by Tuesday at midnight."

"Not my problem, dollface. Unless . . ." Lem took a crackling draw on his cigarette. "Know what else my boys told me? They overheard something about you two sleuthing up in Carvington, Connecticut."

Berta and I didn't answer.

"Here's the deal. I'll give you back your *items* if you do something for me."

"Oh?" I said. Would he ask us to become contract killers, or perhaps burlesque dancers in one of his speakeasies? I could just picture Berta agreeing to such terms.

"It's that fish company up in Carvington," Lem said.

"Fish?" I said. "What could possibly interest you about fish?"

"None of your business, but I'll tell you anyway. In case you hadn't noticed, oysters are one hot commodity in the restaurants here in New York."

"I had noted the craze," Berta said, "although why anyone would wish to consume them quite escapes me."

"I hear you loud and clear, lady, but my chefs douse the little buggers with lemon and butter and all sorts of cream sauces, and people slurp 'em down. If you ask me, it's like swallowing snot."

"Pardon me," I said, "but it's a fish company in Carvington. Not an oyster company."

"Huh. You sure about that?"

Actually, I wasn't. At the warehouse on the Carvington waterfront just that morning, Abe Murden had certainly covered up his powerboat in a hurry. And then—yes!—there was that file in Rudy Montgomery's study, marked OYSTER PRESERVES.

"Also," I said, "you mentioned your . . . chefs?"

"At my restaurants," Lem said. "Ambrose's—heard of 'em? Got three and I'm thinking of opening up a fourth. Bought up the chain last year after the founder, Leopold, had a kinda scary accident."

Eek.

"I got my own oyster suppliers, and don't much care for the way these boys in Carvington are underselling me. Delguzzo's? The Golden Grill? Cheaper oysters! My profit margin has shrunk to the width of a cat hair." Lem tossed his cigarette end over the side of the building. "I wanna know exactly what's going on up there in Carvington. So here's what I want you girls to do. You're gonna get a camera and go and photograph that so-called fish company's operation. The pier. The warehouse. The fishermen. The boats. Hell, I want you to get your roly-poly rumps on a dinghy and go photograph their goddamn bay. They're doing something real funny up there to cut costs the way they do, and I wanna see exactly what so I can—" Lem clucked his tongue, slicing a hand across his throat.

"—take 'em down. Bring me photographs. If you do that, you can have your sockful of *items* back."

I licked my dry lips. "Are your restaurants' oyster profits really worth more than those items? And what do you intend to do with the photographs?"

"Just get 'em!" Lem shouted.

Berta and I shrank back.

"Unless, course, you don't want your items back."

"Um," I said, "we—"

"We shall do it," Berta said loudly. "We will deliver an assortment of photographs to you by Tuesday at noon."

Lem broke into a lazy smile. "Swell. Mail 'em to Caffè Agostino when you've got 'em. Address 'em to Felix the Cat. If I like what I see, I'll have one of my boys deliver your sock to you."

I swallowed the panic rising in my throat. This was no good. No good at all.

Once Berta and I were chugging downward in the freight elevator, I swung on her. "Why did you agree to take those photographs? You must consult with me about these things! It's—it's underhanded and unpartnerlike."

"Why did I agree? So that we may retrieve those diamonds and avoid Theo Wainwright's having us arrested."

"Don't you see, Berta? Lem has no intention of returning the diamonds. They have got to be worth a fortune! It's simply impossible that oyster sales at his restaurants are worth more. Now, thanks to us, he's going to have his cake and eat it, too. Who knows what he means to do with those photographs? He might be planning to fog the fishermen or blow up their warehouse—"

"Oh dear." Berta touched her locket. "Such possibilities did not occur to me."

The elevator thunked to a stop at the level of Caffè Agostini.

"Yes, well," I said, "now we're in a jam."

As usual.

"Let us go home," Berta said. "We have no further business at the Moody Elephant, have we?"

I thought of Ralph, who was probably at that moment goggling at Jillie Harris's exquisitely painted face. "No," I said. "No further business."

We were trudging upstairs to our apartment when Mrs. Snyder popped out of her door in a dressing gown and a headful of curling pins.

"You're here!" she whispered, waving a memorandum pad. "I took down two names and numbers of people who said they heard you on *The Filmore Vacuette Hour* and might have a case for you."

"Splendid," Berta said. "Excellent work, Mrs. Snyder."

Mrs. Snyder ripped the sheet from the pad, passed it to Berta, and bade us good night.

The telephone was ringing when we stepped into our foyer. Berta hurried to answer it, and returned, disappointed, to say that it was for me.

"Hello?" I said into the receiver.

"Glad you got home safe." It was Ralph. "G'night." He hung up.

I slept till nearly noon—the first solid night's sleep I'd had in days—and then staggered into the kitchen, where fresh coffee steamed in the percolator but no breakfast awaited me. Rectangular cookies were cooling on the baking rack, however, so I put a few on a plate, poured myself some coffee, and sat down.

"There you are," Berta said, sailing in. "I have just been across the hallway speaking with Mrs. Snyder. She will have her work cut out for her. How did you ever sleep through all that ringing?"

"Ringing?" I bit into one of the cookies. "Golly, Berta, these cookies are hard as rocks."

"Those are teething biscuits for Baby Alistair, Mrs. Woodby. The ringing of the telephone. We received six calls from prospective clients this morning, bringing us to a total of eight. There are two fresh cinnamon rolls in the bread box. I took the rest to Mrs. Snyder."

Now I had to compete with Mrs. Snyder and her infant for baked goods?

"Now, then, let us review our case," Berta said, pulling out her detecting notebook.

Ten minutes later, I had devoured the cinnamon rolls and we had refined our to-do list. Well, Berta called it our "list of hot leads," but to me it seemed lukewarm at best. It looked like this:

Visit Glenn Monroe's apartment, search for clues about his private life and possible interest in treasure.

Dig for more details about Isobel Bradford's impostor at Carter's Menswear in Mystic, and in Carvington.

Ask Theo why he was at New York City Hall last month.

Research Miss Murden's new motorcar—funds linked to Carvington Fish Co.?

"The trouble is that Theo Wainwright and Miss Murden are surely spending most of their time at Montgomery Hall," Berta said, "and we have been banned from the premises. How are we to interview them?"

"I can't imagine either of them agreeing to speak with us on the telephone. We'll think of something."

After I dressed, I pulled on a coat and my late husband's rubber overshoes, and promenaded Cedric up and down puddle-bogged Longfellow Street. The trees were nearly bare, and the leaves that had so romantically fallen now clogged the gutters.

As Cedric and I walked back to Number 9, I noticed Ralph's Chalmers at the curb in front of my steps.

My blood began to simmer. I quickened my pace and, seeing him sitting behind the wheel, I rapped on his window.

He leaned over and lowered it. "Morning, kid. Nice stompers." He was chewing something and holding a newspaper.

"You have some nerve, persisting in this ridiculous ruse."

"It's not a ruse, it's my bread and butter. And why would I stop? Mr. Wainwright hired me to tail you until you wrapped your case, and by the looks of it, that isn't going to happen anytime soon."

"You're wrong. We're this close"—I held up a pinched thumb and forefinger—"to cracking this thing. I'm warning you, Mr. Oliver, you stay out of our way."

Ralph was studying our second-story windows. "Say, what did Mrs. Lundgren make for breakfast?"

"You're impossible." I spun around, clumped up the steps in the rubber overshoes, and shoved inside.

Upstairs, I told Berta we had company in the form of a ginky gumshoe.

"Has Mr. Oliver had breakfast?" Berta asked. "You did not eat both cinnamon rolls, did you, Mrs. Woodby?"

"Yes," I said, "I did. And don't feed him, for Pete's sake!"

Berta and I packed our suitcases. I waited as Berta badgered Mrs. Snyder one last time, and then we set forth in the Duesy with

Ralph tailing my bumper. Berta had nestled the Eastman Kodak Brownie, our collapsing hobbyist's camera, in her handbag.

"I spooled in a fresh roll of film," Berta told me as I zipped uptown.

"You know, we never really agreed on what to do about Lem Fitzpatrick's demand for those photographs. You simply steamrolled ahead and told Lem that we'd—"

"We must take those pictures. Lem has the diamonds. How else could we possibly retrieve them without risking life and limb?"

"Do you really wish to horse-trade with a gangster?"

"The prospect is more appealing than that of women's prison."

I didn't doubt for a moment that Theo would have the police arrest us for theft. Would a court of law convict us? The fact that Berta had a sometime gangster beau certainly wouldn't impress a judge and jury. So even if there was only a slim possibility that Lem Fitzpatrick would honor his word and return the diamonds, well, as much as I hated the idea, we had to take a stab at it.

"All right." I sighed. "We'll take the photographs."

"I knew you would see reason, Mrs. Woodby."

"I wouldn't call the plan *reasonable*," I said.

20

························

The first stop was Glenn Monroe's home, the address of which Jillie Harris had supplied last night, 412 at the Branson Building, Central Park West. This was a monstrous chunk of a late-Victorian luxury apartment block. Pointy, steep roofs, gargoyles, tiers of bow windows, encrustations of wrought iron—the works.

I parked across the street. Ralph rolled up behind me, and I shot him a dark look in the rearview mirror. He winked, and shook out his newspaper. He wasn't coming in, then. Good.

Berta, Cedric, and I swanned past the Branson Building's doorman without incident. The concierge inside the lobby was another matter.

"Excuse me," he called in a stony voice from behind his desk. "May I be of assistance?"

"Allow me to do the talking," Berta whispered to me out of the side of her mouth.

"All yours," I whispered back.

We approached the concierge.

"Good afternoon," Berta said. "I am here to interview for the position of assistant cook in the kitchen."

"Oh?" the concierge said. "I was not aware that a position had been advertised."

"It has not been advertised," Berta said. "You see, my cousin used to work in the household of the Gregorys of Henderson Place, and it was there that she met the son-in-law—a chauffeur, you see—of the former assistant to the head cook of the Branson Building."

The concierge's eyes were glazing over. "Quite. And who is this?" He looked at me accusingly.

"My deaf-mute niece. I was forced to bring her along for the day, as her mother is having a kidney operation."

"But I saw her speaking to you."

"We both are able to read lips. A most nifty skill."

"Very well. You will find the stairs down to the kitchen beyond the elevators."

"Thank you," Berta said.

A minute later, Berta and I descended into a hallway outside a clattering, steamy kitchen.

"Now what?" I said. "No one down here will believe your outrageous tales."

"Perhaps not," Berta said, "but there are always the dumbwaiters."

"How do you know they're dumb?" I said indignantly.

"You misunderstand, Mrs. Woodby. Look."

I followed Berta's pointed finger to a long row of metal dumbwaiter doors, all surmounted by brass plaques indicating the apartment numbers to which they led.

"Ah, there is 412," Berta said.

"Oh no," I said. "No, no, *no*."

"It is spacious," Berta said in lulling tones. "Not at all like those horrible little dumbwaiters that hold nothing more than a tea tray.

Your hips are smaller than mine, Mrs. Woodby, so I am afraid you must go up."

For the first time in my life, I wished my hips were bigger. "Oh, fine." I pushed Cedric's leash into Berta's right hand, dumped my handbag in her left, made certain the coast was clear, slid open the dumbwaiter door, and climbed in. I had to remove my hat and scrunch myself over like a pill bug, but I fit.

"Good luck," Berta whispered, and slapped the door shut.

Blackness, and the aroma of ham wafting from another dumbwaiter. Then, a shudder and the groan of cables. Up, up I went at a pace just slow enough to foster horrific visions of plummeting to my death (weren't the cables groaning a little too vociferously?) or else being somehow sandwiched at the top.

The dumbwaiter stopped, and here was another sliding door with light shining through the crack. I pried my fingernails into the crack and slid the door open.

I tumbled out onto a tiled kitchen floor. I got up, dusted myself off, and looked around. The kitchen appeared to be utterly unused except for a half-full bottle of gin and a few dirty dishes on the draining board. I tiptoed through the apartment, heart thumping, and took stock.

Sitting room: Masculine leathers and glossy wood. Grand piano. Tall windows overlooking the park. Whopping framed photograph of Glenn in a white dinner jacket over the fireplace. Large selection of cowboy novels and typed radio scripts on the bookshelf. Nothing hinting at treasure. Rolltop desk holding tidy piles of bills and receipts (restaurants, tailors, hatmakers, hairdresser, manicurist, masseuse), bankbook (robust balance, strictly biweekly deposits, and no large, blackmail-payment-like deductions).

Bathroom: Medicine cabinet stocked with Alkacine and French aftershave lotions and balms. Downy Turkish bath towels.

Bedroom: As tidy and impersonal as a hotel room. Two large closets stuffed with exquisite suits, shirts, coats, shoes, and silk ties. No diary. No love letters. No treasure maps. No photograph albums. No address book. No guns.

Long story short, everything in the apartment was as bland as Cream of Wheat, except for one thing: the large puppet in a straw hat, sitting on the chest of drawers in the bedroom. Its painted wooden head was hinged open in a permanent grimace, its red curly hair looked genuinely human, its soft limbs were attired in denim overalls and a plaid shirt, and a wheat stalk protruded from its bucked wooden teeth. It was the sort of thing you hope not to see when you're, say, waking up at midnight in a hayloft.

I slunk by the farmer puppet without making eye contact, battling the absurd notion it was looking at me. Glenn must have kept the puppet as a memento of some theatrical production he'd been in. But what a thing to have looming over your bed.

I stuffed myself back in the dumbwaiter, pushed the button, shut the door, and sank back to kitchen level.

Berta thwacked the sliding door open. "Well?"

I half tumbled out, wincing as a nerve in my back twanged. "Nothing of interest—unless you count a nightmarish puppet. It's very much the pad of a well-to-do bachelor who doesn't spend much time at home. The police may have already removed important clues—there was barely anything of a personal nature up there." I took my hat, handbag, and dog off Berta's hands. "Let's get out of here."

The drive up the coast to Carvington was damp and miserable. Rainwater seeped in from the top of my window, the windshield kept fogging up, and my tires, balding and due for a replacement I couldn't afford, skidded on the road. Ralph drove steadily behind us, never more than one motorcar back. Try as I might, I couldn't stop sneaking peeks at him in the mirror. With every glimpse of his square shoulders and tilted hat, my heart wrung itself. Why, oh, why couldn't he leave me in peace to patch up my broken heart?

We stopped in Mystic before motoring the last miles to Carvington, going once again to Carter's Menswear. Ralph stayed inside his motorcar at the curb. He was eating something out of a paper sack.

Inside, a lumbering, messy-haired fellow was folding a stack of denim overalls at the counter. He frowned at us as we approached. I smiled, and asked him if the lady shopkeeper was in.

"Willa told me about two nosy ladies in high heels, prying about our customers." He gave Berta and me a scornful top-to-toe, and then regarded Cedric as though he'd like to convert him into a Russian hat. I assumed that Willa was the lady shopkeeper to whom we'd spoken yesterday and this fellow was, perhaps, the husband she'd mentioned.

"That was indeed us," I said. "And we were hoping we might be able to speak a bit more—is she in?"

"Nope. Visiting the dentist."

"Poor thing," Berta said with a sympathetic tongue cluck. "I don't suppose *you* could tell us about the customer in question, the wealthy-looking lady—fur coat, pearls—who purchased a hat, rain slicker, and a pair of men's trousers?"

"I could," the shopkeeper said. "But I won't. We respect our customers here at Carter's."

"Oh good," I said. I went to a garment rack and selected two yellow fisherman's raincoats and hats—the subtler colors were sold out—and carried them back to the counter. "I'll take these, please."

The shopkeeper's eyes went narrow and glittery, but he rang up the items and wrapped them in brown paper. I took the packages and my change and said, "Now, then. The customer in the fur coat and pearls? . . ."

He scowled.

I beamed.

"She purchased a fisherman's raincoat and hat, said something about being on holiday in a cottage and needing rain attire for her walks on the beach—although why anyone would walk on the beach in November—"

"Wait—Willa didn't tell us the bit about the holiday cottage," I said.

Berta said, "Where might one find a seaside holiday cottage to let in, say, Carvington?"

"Carvington? Only a few of them there, all in a row on the waterfront."

Whoopee!

"Who owns the cottages?" I asked.

"Oh, one of the old Carvington families. Not sure which."

Berta and I thanked the shopkeeper and went outside.

"I think we've found where our Isobel Bradford impostor is hiding out," I said. "Now all we must do is go to her cottage and corner her. She just might be our murderer."

"She also may have seen or heard something the afternoon of Rudy's death."

Next, we stopped into Rexall Drugs. Ralph watched our movements from behind his windshield. I haughtily pretended not to notice.

Amid the posters cluttering Rexall Drugs' doorway windows was one advertising Menchen's Manikins, just like the one I'd seen in the New London train station. I paused. Glenn's farmer puppet . . . could there possibly be a link? Surely not. The world is, alas, full of puppets.

I went inside and purchased three Milky Way chocolate bars and a box of Marie Antoinette pearlized face powder. Berta purchased the latest *Spectral Stories*, the cover of which depicted a ghost looming over a séance.

Obviously, Berta had not once been disturbed by the supposed ghost at Montgomery Hall. I myself was off *Spectral Stories* for good.

Last, we stopped at a bakery and purchased a white paper sack filled with sugar cookies. Provisions, you understand.

By the time we stepped out of the bakery, Ralph's Chalmers was nowhere in sight.

I frowned up and down the bustling street. "Where has that pill gone?"

"I would have thought you would be pleased that we have shed him," Berta said.

"No." I shook my head. "He's up to something."

The rain was splattering harder by the time I parked the Duesy on Church Street in Carvington. The Old Whaler's Inn was a cumbersome clapboard building with dark blue shutters and lace curtains in every window. A sign cut in the shape of a spouting whale hung over the door.

"It will be drafty and mildewy," Berta said.

I switched off the engine. "We'll be able to smell George Washington's morning breath in there."

"Alas, we have no alternative."

"Why don't we ever have alternatives?"

"That is a very good question, Mrs. Woodby."

"Look. There is Ralph's motorcar, parked across the street. You didn't tell him we meant to stay at this inn, did you?"

"No. He must have deduced it. Mr. Oliver is remarkably clever."

"Conniving is more like it."

We gathered up our suitcases and parcels and battered into the lobby of the Old Whaler's Inn, which was really only an entry hall with a long, steep spill of stairs, wilted wallpaper, and a reception desk.

The unwholesome-looking young man behind the reception desk informed us in a monotone that rooms were available. He was lanky and wan, with a too-small suit jacket that revealed his knobby wrists, and greasy dark hair combed straight down from his hairline.

We booked ourselves into "deluxe" accommodations, which meant we'd have private bathrooms. Gorgeous! You see? November need not be utterly dismal. I'd have a hot bubble bath at first opportunity, with a French clay face pack and some chocolate—

"Hot-water boiler is broken," Knobby Wrists said.

Of course.

"Did a man by the name of Mr. Oliver check in quite recently?" I asked.

"Why, yes. Only ten minutes ago. But he has already gone out. He asked me for walking directions to Carvington College. He said he was interested in the fine architecture on campus."

Architecture, my foot. He was off to see Theo Wainwright. And coincidentally, I wished to speak with Theo, too.

Berta had read my mind. "We meant to go for a walk to the campus, too," she said. "We do so adore architecture." She bugged her eyes meaningfully at me. "Shall we, Mrs. Woodby?"

"Lovely! But first, I must make a telephone call." I had promised Eustace I would telephone as soon as I booked into the inn. I turned to Knobby Wrists. "Is there a public telephone on the premises?"

He pointed through an open pair of pocket doors. "In the parlor. Ten cents per call."

"Highway robbery," Berta muttered.

The parlor was decorated with slack floral sofas, Colonial-style cabinets, and a coal fire gasping its last in the stone fireplace. I found the telephone on the wall beside a framed print of the Pilgrims' first Thanksgiving.

Miss Murden answered the telephone at Montgomery Hall and gruffly agreed to fetch Lord Sudley. Theo must have decided to allow her to keep her job, then. If Rudy had really meant to fire her, she had benefited from his death. Would someone really murder a man just to keep their job? It was a bit extreme. Then there was the matter of Miss Murden's fancy new motorcar, and the Carvington Fish Co.'s oyster operations Lem Fitzpatrick had mentioned—

"Lola, my dear." Eustace was on the line. "Have you returned to Connecticut?"

"Yes, and we have a new lead." I glanced over my shoulder to confirm the parlor was still empty, and lowered my voice. "I think we might have pinpointed the Isobel Bradford impostor's hideout."

"Great Scott! Where?"

"In a rented holiday cottage on the waterfront, here in Carvington. We're going to investigate in—" I glanced at my wristwatch. "—in about an hour or so." I wished to allow enough time for Berta and me to speak with Theo Wainwright at the college.

"Allow me to come along," Eustace said.

Berta would hate that. "I don't know. . . ."

"As your client, I insist. And as the man who adores you, Lola, well, you could be placing yourself in danger."

"All right." It's awful; I just can't say no to sweet talk. "Meet us here at the Old Whaler's Inn at six o'clock."

"Right-ho, my dear."

Just before Eustace rang off, I was certain I heard an extra click on the line.

Someone at Montgomery Hall had eavesdropped on our chat.

When I returned to the lobby, Knobby Wrists had gone upstairs with our suitcases and parcels. I clipped on Cedric's leash, and Berta, Cedric, and I set off for the college.

Carvington College was just the sort of morose, ivy-clad cluster of buildings you'd expect from a notable New England school. Berta,

Cedric, and I passed between two grand brick pillars and into a network of brick paths and boggy lawns.

College boys toting books, satchels, and umbrellas crisscrossed the paths. Victorian-looking streetlamps shone in the dusk. We stopped a pimply boy and asked him for directions to the history building.

"Fisk Hall?" he said. "In the quadrangle."

We wandered around some more and found Fisk Hall. HISTORY was carved in Gothic letters in the stone lintel. Inside, parquet floors creaked and antique dust tickled my nose. We found a directory board.

"Theo is studying a Colonial Connecticut war, remember?" I said. "So we must want the American History department, which is . . . third floor."

Berta sighed. She disliked stair-climbing and I couldn't blame her, since the boots she always wore gave me hammertoes just from looking at them.

On the third floor, gold letters on frosted-glass door windows advertised the occupants: PROFESSOR DUDSWORTH; PROFESSOR GAZAM; GRADUATE STUDENT OFFICES.

"This must be it." I rapped on GRADUATE STUDENT OFFICES.

"It's unlocked," a male voice called. "Give the knob a jiggle."

I jiggled and then pushed the door open halfway. Five or six wooden desks heaped with papers and books filled a small room that smelled of stale coffee and moist socks. Theo sat at one of the desks, a typewriter in front of him, a pile of books beside him, and a bemused-yet-icy expression on his face.

"Oh, looky here," he said to Berta and me. "Humpty and Dumpty. We were just discussing you pair."

We?

I pushed the door wider. Cedric whimpered and bounded forward so suddenly, his leash was ripped from my hand.

21

....

Ralph lounged in a chair across from Theo, and he gave me a crooked grin before bending over to pet Cedric, who was gyrating like Josephine Baker.

Theo said, "Shouldn't you pair begin searching for my father's diamonds before it's too late? You've got about, oh, thirty-odd hours left before I ring up Carvington's boys in blue. So far, it doesn't seem like you've made very good use of your time. My detective here, Mr. Oliver—"

"Ladies," Ralph said with a nod, as though he didn't know us. I guessed he hadn't filled Theo in on the finer points of his relationship with the Discreet Retrieval Agency.

"—has just been apprising me of your movements during the past two days, and we've been having quite the laugh. Bakeries and bathroom stops seem to factor in most prominently."

Sounded as though Ralph had withheld the important things. He wasn't an utter blister, then.

"What are you doing here on campus, Mr. Wainwright," Berta

said, "when you now have a perfectly nice study in your new mansion?"

"I require peace and quiet, and Coral is driving me off my trolley. She's in drunken hysterics about Glenn Monroe being poisoned. Swears up and down that the ghost did it. Little fool."

"Why not cast her out?" I said. "You aren't obliged to give your late father's girlfriend room and board, are you?"

"She has no place to go. No family. No job. Besides which, she's squizzed around the clock. If I sent her packing, she'd probably be hit by the first bus."

It didn't seem like Theo to act the gallant. Coral must hold some sway over him. Jillie Harris had hinted that Glenn Monroe might've been keen on a cute fellow up in Connecticut. . . . *That* would certainly give Coral some sway.

"We have learned a curious little tidbit about you, Mr. Wainwright," I said. "Someone saw you going up the steps of New York City Hall last month."

Theo scratched the tip of his nose. "Fascinating."

"What business had you at City Hall?" I asked.

From the corner of my eye, I noticed Ralph shifting in his chair. That dratted jelly bean was enjoying the show.

"I read a bit more about you two in the newspapers in the college library," Theo said. "You're a sort of case study for a psychiatrist. Mrs. Woodby here used to be rich, but now she's poor. That's a dangerous type, I'd think. She has a taste for the finer things in life, but she hasn't the funds for them. So of course she'd steal diamonds. And then there is Mrs. Lundgren, the poor Swedish village girl who found herself working for the fat cats on the Gold Coast. It must've been awful being surrounded by all that finery you couldn't afford."

"I would think, Mr. Wainwright, that *you* would be a dangerous type," I said. "A man who has always been poor, always scraped and scrimped and who now finds himself both fabulously wealthy and the owner of an estate upon which, as legend has it, treasure is buried. A coincidence? Perhaps not."

"You two are pests. You think you're very clever, but really all you are is two dumplings who printed up some fancy business cards."

"I'm sorry, Mr. Wainwright," I said, "but flattery isn't going to work."

Ralph stifled a chuckle.

"Tell us what you were doing at New York City Hall that day in October," I said, "and then we'll be on our way."

"I have work to do," Theo said, "so if you don't leave now, I'll telephone the police. How would you like that? There is a telephone just downstairs."

Desperate, I glanced at Berta.

"Mr. Wainwright," she said in her most grandmotherly voice, "if you do not tell us what you were doing at New York City Hall, we will be forced to tell the police that you knew you stood to inherit your father's estate well in advance of his death."

Berta was bluffing—we had no proof of this, although the idea had been in the background ever since we found out that Theo had conveniently inherited all from Papa Rudy.

His cheeks went putty-colored. "What proof have you?"

"Do not worry your handsome little head over such details. Now, what were you doing at New York City Hall?"

"You're making a fuss about a minor coincidence," Theo said. "Yes, I was at City Hall that day and I did happen to run into Glenn Monroe and some insipid blonde—I suppose she's who told you about seeing me there, or was it Glenn, before he—" Theo swallowed heavily. "I only knew Glenn by sight, but he was always coming up for the weekend to get crocked with Coral. That day, I was in the city to visit the bookshops and purchase a new pair of shoes. When Glenn and the blonde saw me, I was merely riding the subway—the Lexington Avenue line—from Brooklyn up to Hunter College, where I meant to visit a good friend of mine, a graduate student. The Lexington Avenue line is the only one that'll take you to the Upper East Side, you do realize."

"Oh yes," I said. "I know. But I also know that Hunter College is a ladies' college, and I have such a difficult time, Mr. Wainwright, believing that you have a lady student friend. I seem to recall you saying something to the effect that ladies should stick to stenography courses."

"I do make exceptions, provided the lady is clever enough." Now Theo was toying with a pencil. Tapping the eraser on the desk, rolling it between his fingertips.

"What about City Hall?" Berta asked. "That is a great distance from Hunter College."

"Yes, well, you haven't allowed me to get to that. I get queasy on the subway, and, well, quite frankly, by the time the train reached the City Hall stop, I was afraid I was going to be sick, so I got out and went up. There is the park there, but I wasn't about to be sick in the garbage bin or the fountain, so, seeing the steps to City Hall just nearby, I decided to go inside and look for a public washroom. That's when I saw Glenn and his blonde."

"I see." Jillie did say that Theo had behaved in a rushed and awkward fashion. If he'd been about to sick up, he would have seemed rushed and awkward.

"Satisfied?" Theo asked.

I glanced at Berta. She nodded.

"Yes, thanks," I said to Theo. "Have a delightful evening, boys!" I picked up the end of Cedric's leash and tugged him out of the office.

"Theo knew in advance that he stood to inherit," I said to Berta once we were back outside on the quadrangle. The rain had let up, and the crisp evening air was smoky with the scents of autumn. "Marvelous bluffing, Berta."

"Thank you."

"And I didn't buy his line about the lady graduate-student friend at Hunter College. Hunter College ladies are bona fide bluestockings. If he even mentioned stenography courses to one of them, they'd throw their coffee in his face."

Back at the Old Whaler's Inn, I parted ways with Berta in the upstairs corridor. I still hadn't told her that I'd invited Eustace along to spy on the holiday cottages on the waterfront. I just couldn't bring myself to do it, even though I fully realized that this was just as unpartnerlike as I had accused her of being.

I found my small room. Although stale with mildew, slope-ceilinged, and furnished with dumpy antiques, it was indeed equipped with its own tiny bathroom as well as an electric fire. I changed into thick woolen layers, reapplied my lipstick, and, inspired, added my new fisherman's raincoat and hat. I'd purchased them to make that shopkeeper sing, but I decided I may as well put them to good use. Then I wondered what to do with Cedric. I couldn't leave him in my room, because he had a bad cushion-chewing habit. Nor did I wish to entrust him to Knobby Wrists. I'd probably find Cedric's bangs greased and down-combed upon my return.

"You may leave the dog with Mother," Knobby Wrists said when I explained that I needed to venture forth—for exercise—in the rain and did not wish to subject my dog to the ill weather. "She enjoys dogs. You will find her in the kitchen." He pointed past the staircase, where light leaked from a cracked door.

"Thank you," I said, and with Cedric in my arms, I went with trepidation to the kitchen.

It turned out that cadaverous, monotone clerks sometimes have old dears for their mothers. Mrs. Lancaster—that was her name, she told me—stood over a pot of something bubbling and delicious-smelling, and agreed to look after Cedric. "I'll feed him, too, if you like."

"All right, but his eyes are bigger than his stomach."

"His stomach looks plenty big to me."

Berta, with her handbag slung over her arm, was speaking with Knobby Wrists at the front desk when I returned. She, too, had taken the practical step of donning her new yellow raincoat and hat, and she resembled an enormous rubber ducky. She turned to me with a victorious glitter in her eye. "Mr. Lancaster tells me that a lady matching the description of *our friend* has been letting the cottage with the blue door, just down the path from the Carvington Fish Company warehouse."

The front door opened and Eustace strode in with a baffle of wet wind. "Good heavens, is that you, Lola?" he said to Berta.

"No." Berta flipped up the brim of her hat.

"Oh. I beg your pardon, Mrs. Lundgren." Eustace turned to me. He wore a posh-looking oiled canvas coat, tall hunting boots, and a tweed hat with the brim turned down. "Hello, Lola. So nice to see you again. Heavens, you do look rather sweet in that getup."

"These old things?" I smoothed my rubbery cuff.

Berta gave a ladylike snort.

"Well, then, shall we be off?" Eustace said.

Berta started, and then sent me a frown. This was the first she was hearing of Eustace accompanying us. I shrugged, which only made her frown deepen.

"And how are things at Montgomery Hall, Lord Sudley?" she asked.

"A bit tense, truthfully. I get the distinct impression Theo would like me to leave posthaste."

"Is Mr. Eccles still there?" Berta's face was cherubically blank.

"Oh yes. Still sorting out reams of papers and so forth, and he's urging Theo to write out a will of his own."

My scalp prickled. In the opulent world I'd inhabited for the duration of my adult life, new wills always spelled *ill* will. Sometimes they even spelled malice.

"What about Coral?" I asked.

"Still loafing about. I can't think why Theo hasn't tossed her out. She really seems to give him the pip. I suppose it's because she's so dashed pretty."

"I gathered that Miss Murden has been kept on," I said. I thought of the extra click on the line earlier.

"Yes, Theo agreed he requires a housekeeper and, well, Miss Murden is already ensconced. Shall we be off?"

Approximately ten minutes later, Eustace and I were lurking in the dark beneath a tree across from the waterfront buildings. Berta had toddled away with the camera to the Carvington Fish Co. warehouse, where she intended to take some photographs provided she could locate the light switch.

What had happened to Ralph? I hadn't seen him since we left Theo's office at Fisk Hall. Had he given up on tailing us? He wasn't the type to throw in the towel.

"It's the cottage with the blue door," I whispered to Eustace over the swish of salty wind. "No lights on. Our impostor must not be at home. Let's go." I couldn't wait to find out who this woman truly was.

"Do you mean to . . . break in?"

"I do it all the time," I said. "Is that troubling?"

"No, actually, it's rather . . . stimulating."

We crossed the road and Eustace tried the doorknob.

"Dash it all," he said. "It's locked."

I wiggled the sash window nearest the front door. "It's not latched, but it's a little swollen from all this rain—ah—there we go." I got the window mostly open, slung a leg over the sill, and ducked inside. Eustace followed and closed the window behind him.

The darkened cottage was furnished with humble furniture, faded quilts, hooked rugs, and driftwood bric-a-brac. In the little kitchen, food-crusted pots and pans littered the stove, and an unlit kerosene lantern sat on the table.

"That must be the lantern she was carrying in the woods the night before last," I whispered. "That was her!"

"Lola," Eustace murmured behind me.

I turned. "What is it?"

His dark eyes glittered, and the thin blue light from the window made his features more Mr. Rochester–like than ever. He was leaning slowly toward me with the very specific look of focus men get when they've got One Thing on the brain. He murmured, "Good God, you're so deuced alluring when you're playing at detective."

"I'm not *playing*," I said, drawing back with a frown. "If there is nothing else here in the kitchen, let's check the bedroom." As an afterthought, I peered into the icebox. A bottle of milk and two eggs.

We went up the creaky staircase to the single loft bedroom. A suitcase sprawled open on the floor, and a few books sat on the nightstand. I went to the nightstand and Eustace went to the suitcase.

The topmost book was a ten-cent romance titled *Lady Clarissa's Fall*. Underneath lay a well-worn copy of *Lost Treasures of the United States*, by Mordecai Kennington III. "Good golly!" I said. "This is the book Berta saw in Glenn Monroe's valise—not the same copy, of course. This one's much more worn. The impostor is a treasure hunter! I knew it."

Eustace came over and looked over my shoulder. I flipped *Lost Treasures of the United States* open to the bookmark—a grimy joker playing card—to a chapter titled "Treasures of the Nautical Northeast." A passage had been underlined in pencil:

This local legend is all the more piquant for having a ghost story wrapped up in its threads. The old sages of Carvington swear that a spectral woman in white guards the treasure buried on the estate. Whether she is the widow of whaler Captain Montgomery, a colonial dame, or perhaps some tragic Pequot maiden, no one is able to agree. The sages do agree, however, that whoever draws too near the hidden treasure will be haunted by the woman in white. It was even reported to me that in 1881, a young woman visiting from Maine was pushed to her death on the Montgomery mansion's stairs by the ghost. Another account tells of the ghost walking for eternity back and forth along the old colonists' farm wall, now deep in the trees of the estate, while yet another account claims that in 1902, a history professor from the nearby college was attacked with a large stone by the specter near the old Indian oyster-fishing place, and that he languished for weeks before dying. What these anecdotes suggest about the location of the lost treasure is up to the reader to decide.

Goose bumps tingled my arms. "If I believed in ghosts, I'd say that the treasure was either hidden in the house—near the stairs, perhaps—buried along this stone wall, or else buried at this old Indian oyster-fishing spot. I saw that stone wall. But where could the oyster-fishing spot be?"

"Well, oysters grow in shallow, protected waters," Eustace said. "Coves and bays and so forth."

Mental note: Tell Berta about the real estate preferences of oysters.

I returned the book to the nightstand. "Was there anything interesting in the suitcase?"

"Only clothing. Oh—and a small theatrical makeup kit."

"Theatrical makeup?" Greasepaint. That scrap of golden paper I'd found outside the conservatory yesterday . . .

"Mm. I suspect our impostor is an actress."

Downstairs, the front door banged shut.

"Oh dear," Eustace murmured.

I looked around desperately. No closets, no wardrobe, and no way my womanly bulges would compress enough to fit under that bed.

"What does a professional detective do in this sort of circumstance?" Eustace asked me.

"Run." I dashed to the windows and looked out. The porch roof was right there, and not too steep. I unlatched the window, wiggled up the sash, and squeezed through. "Hurry!"

Out came Eustace's big boot. He made it out and we were both clinging to the windowsill, standing on the slippery porch roof. Eustace edged to the drainpipe, grabbed it, and slowly slid down. I slid down next. I'd made it halfway when the drainpipe groaned and split off from the side of the house. I clung like a bug, legs kicking into nothingness, as the drainpipe slowly bent to a right angle and deposited me neatly on the wet ground.

We ran across the dark road to the tree. We were both panting when we stopped, and when we looked at each other, we burst out laughing.

"Oh, Lola Woodby, I am perishingly fond of you," Eustace murmured, and drawing me close, he kissed me silly. My knees wobbled, my breath quickened, and various things tingled and fluttered because, well, Eustace was an awfully good kisser. His hands on my shoulders were firm and comforting, and he smelled wonderful, too, like shaving balm from Selfridges and peppermints from Harvey Nichols and, faintly, the sort of saddle soap reserved for the tack of prizewinning Arabian horses.

My heart alone was unresponsive. It sat in my chest, beating placidly, refusing to join in the festivities. Which was perfectly fine with me. My heart had done nothing but hurt me.

My eyes happened to rove past Eustace's shoulder. A man-shaped silhouette assembled itself in the grainy shadows beside the impostor's cottage.

Ralph.

He dissolved back into the darkness. He'd seen me in Eustace's arms.

Well, super. It was best that he knew I had no intention of going stale on the shelf.

22

Eustace and I kissed a little longer, although I couldn't seem to keep my mind on it anymore.

"Look," I said, pulling away. "I see a woman through the cottage windows."

We watched as a figure moved to and fro in the main-floor rooms. She wore a dark fisherman's raincoat, but her gray, frizzy head was bare. She was, without question, the woman who had claimed to be Isobel Bradford the day Rudy was shot. She'd been here all along, a mere mile from Montgomery Hall. She could have shot Rudy. Surely she could have stolen into the house and poisoned Glenn's Alkacine, too, or maybe she had even done that before she left the house the first time.

She could be our killer.

"I have a good mind to march right in there and demand an explanation," Eustace said.

"No. Look—she's going out again. Let's follow her. If we confront her, she'll probably lie, but if we catch her in the act of treasure hunting, even take some photographs . . ." I squinted toward the fishing warehouse. "Berta should be done by now. I wonder what's keeping her."

"Well, you haven't the time to wonder," Eustace whispered, "because there goes your quarry."

The impostor stepped out of the cottage, carrying a shovel and the unlit kerosene lantern. She peered up and down the road, and then headed toward the Montgomery estate.

Eustace and I waited until she was on the path leading up the slope toward the forest. Then we followed. At the top of the path, I looked down at the moonlit sea. Wind buffeted up off the water, stinging my cheeks and filling my ears. Just past the breakers, a small boat was sailing west.

"I wonder why that boat doesn't have any lights on," I said.

"Mm. Seems a bit foolhardy."

We plunged into the dark trees, and our pace lagged as we strained to make out the path. Wind shuffled the branches overhead, and racing clouds made the moonlight flicker like a movie projector.

"There she is," I whispered to Eustace, pointing. "She's keeping to the path."

"Walking with a good bit of purpose, too, as though she's already decided where she'll dig this evening."

On and on the impostor walked, keeping to the trail that followed the tumbling stone wall. I developed a blister on my right pinky toe. Perhaps T-straps had not been the wisest choice.

As we approached the field that extended to the house—I could see its lights winking between the trees—a woman's voice somewhere behind me said, *"Lolaaaaaaaaaaaaaaaa."*

For crying out loud.

I spun around in time to see—oh golly—a white form flit behind a tree trunk.

"Eustace!" I whispered. He was hiking ahead, oblivious. Why

hadn't he heard the voice? Was it because of the wind? Why hadn't he noticed me stopping? *"Eustace!"* I whispered, more loudly.

Still, he kept going. I hesitated for a split second. I could yell for Eustace or run after him—two methods that would alert the Isobel Bradford impostor to our presence—or go to the tree behind which the white form had disappeared and sort things out. Alone.

I went to the tree. Forced myself to the tree, even though it felt as though the air had grown frigid and honey-thick.

Wait. Wasn't that what the air always did in *Spectral Stories?*

I reached the tree. Slowly, very slowly, I tiptoed around it, sticks and leaves crunching underfoot in the darkness. On the other side was—nothing.

WHACK! Something hit the back of my head with pitiless force. Stars exploded, and I was falling forward.

I broke my fall with my hands, my right wrist trilling with pain. Panting, I lifted my head. I caught the briefest glimpse of that wicked white form before it disappeared behind another tree trunk.

I scrambled to my feet, woozy and flooded with pain. I staggered through the underbrush in the direction the form had gone, screaming "EUSTACE! EUSTACE!"

"Lola?" I heard him shout in the middle distance. "Lola! Where are you?"

"Over here!" I cried. "Come quickly!"

I reached the second tree behind which the apparition had disappeared, circled around. Again, nothing.

Except—pounding footsteps coming closer, closer—

A bulky shape in a raincoat with a shovel and a swinging, unlit lantern stampeded past.

The Isobel Bradford impostor. She'd heard Eustace and me yelling, and she was running back to her rented cottage.

Oh no. She would not get away this time.

"Hold it right there!" I shouted.

I suppose my tone was not sufficiently masterful, because she continued to run.

I started after her, but immediately tripped on a tree root.

"Allow me to handle this," Eustace said, appearing out of the shadows pushing, of all things, a bicycle. "And look what I've found. I'll just—"

"No!" I yelled. "This is my investigation and my suspect—rats, she's going to get away." I ripped the bicycle handlebars from Eustace, threw my leg over, and, despite the wobbling front wheel and my throbbing wrist and head, pedaled furiously in the direction the impostor had fled.

"Lola!" Eustace called after me.

The going was bumpy, and wet branches raked and stung my cheeks, but soon the jogging silhouette of the impostor was once more within view. I dug deep into the pedals, closer, closer—when she glanced back, I saw the whites of her eyes—

My front wheel hit a rock. I pitched over the handlebars and felled the impostor like a lioness upon a gazelle. Or perhaps a rhinoceros upon another rhinoceros.

She struggled beneath me in a tangle of raincoats, crying, "Get off!"

I pinned her shoulders with all my strength. We were both breathing hard. "The police are on the way," I lied, "but maybe I'll let you go if you tell me what you're doing out here." She could've been the murderer, of course, but I had no other way to coerce her.

"Promise?"

"Sure." I sat back heavily, and the impostor struggled upright.

"Why are you following me?" She stood. Her frizzled gray hair was a cloud around her face. Her eyes gleamed like black buttons.

"I'm a detective," I said, getting to my feet. "Who are you, and why did you steal that invitation from Isobel Bradford's brownstone in Boston?"

"You figured that out? Perhaps you aren't as dumb as you look."

"I don't look dumb!"

"Who wears high heels in the woods? And what kind of detective wears a bright yellow raincoat?"

"Just answer the question."

"My name is Clementine Brezka and I live in New Jersey. I was doing a little work up in Boston—"

"What sort of work?"

"Let's just say I make it my business to relieve rich fools of their excess booty."

"You're a con artist."

"Call it what you wish. It's a time-honored profession. I was making a canvass of Marlborough Street, saying I was collecting funds for the Museum of Fine Arts—all the rich Boston ladies go in for that—and while the butler left me waiting in the foyer, I perused the mail. The invitation hadn't been opened yet, but I took a peek. And the funny thing was, Montgomery Hall rang a bell. I'd read about it in a book, you see."

"*Lost Treasures of the United States?*"

"You've read it?"

"Um. Yes."

"I recognized Montgomery Hall as the location of a legendary buried treasure, so I swiped the invitation, thinking that it might be my ticket to search for the treasure. And it was."

"How did you know Rudy Montgomery had never seen Mrs. Bradford before?"

"He'd written a personal note in the invitation, saying he hoped that they would finally meet."

"Lucky for you."

"I've always been lucky." A siren wailed in the distance—someone *had* telephoned the police—and I heard Eustace crashing around in the underbrush. He must not have been able to find us in the dark.

I didn't shout for him; I didn't wish to stem Clementine's confession. "I've done nothing but make an honest stab at finding the treasure."

"You've impersonated, scammed, and trespassed," I said.

"Something tells me you do the same sorts of things on a regular basis."

"It's my job."

"Well, then it looks like there isn't much difference between a gumshoe and a con artist." Clementine snickered. "I'd wager that you and I aren't much different, Lola. Was your husband an alkie, too?"

"Womanizer."

"Ugh. Dead?"

"Yes."

"Mine, too. And I suppose you had a rough-and-tumble childhood like mine, and perhaps you went on the stage at a tender age?"

"What? No."

"Oh. I suppose all the mascara threw me off."

Clementine was backing away, and I didn't try to stop her, because suddenly, strangely, I was rooting for her. From the start, she had been a doozy of a murder suspect. Yet several minutes earlier, she had come running through the woods from an entirely different direction from that white flitting form. Clementine wasn't the "ghost." She wasn't the one who had hit me on the back of the head, or pushed me at the top of the stairs, or tried to frighten me off the case with all that moaning business. And more and more, my gut told me that the murderer and the ghost were one and the same, which made Clementine . . . innocent. Or, innocent of murder, at least.

Clementine was several paces way, and about to turn.

"Did you murder Rudy Montgomery and Glenn Monroe?" I blurted. The sirens were louder.

"Of course not, dear. Why would I? All I want is the treasure. That's all I've ever wanted."

Men's shouts and flashing lights advanced through the trees. Clementine slipped away into the shadows.

"Lola," Eustace cried somewhere behind me. I turned to see him striding forth. "Lola, are you quite all right?"

"Yes," I said, suddenly going limp, "although I wouldn't say no to an aspirin." I told Eustace how I'd heard that ghost voice and seen a figure flitting amid the tree trunks, and how I'd been hit in the head. I also told him I'd tackled Clementine, how she'd confessed to being a con artist and gotten away.

"How ghastly," Eustace said when I finished. "About the ghost, I mean to say. Someone is quite intent on drawing out that macabre prank."

Prank seemed a little mild, according to the throbbing bump at the base of my skull. "Where did you find that bicycle?" It was still crumpled on the ground nearby.

"It was leaning against a tree farther up the path."

"I think it might belong to Theo. I saw him riding a similar bicycle."

Eustace chuckled. "Do you suppose Theo is your ghost, then?"

"Why not? Theo isn't a large man, and his voice is on the reedy side. Why are you looking at me like that, Eustace? It's only a few bumps and scrapes—What are you—? Oh." Oh no: Eustace had taken both my hands in his and gone down on bended knee.

"Lola, you are simply magnificent." He reached into his jacket and withdrew something small—it was difficult to make out in the poor light—oh yes, a little box. A box too small for, say, a handgun. Too small for much of anything but a few shelled peas or—

The box popped open. Nestled inside, a large canary diamond pierced the darkness.

"Lola, would you do me the great honor of becoming Lady Sudley at the soonest possible juncture?"

I tore my eyes from the ring. I was seeing stars again. Sparkling, canary yellow stars. I tried to speak, but instead my tongue made a sound like peeling cellophane.

Eustace's voice grew husky. "I know it's premature, but I simply cannot help myself. I have never felt this way about a woman before. I am mad about you, Lola. I cannot eat, I cannot sleep . . . no, don't reply—I see you're uncertain. This is a rotten moment, isn't it? Don't give your answer now. Think it over. Tell me later—but soon."

I swallowed. "All right." A pause. "Where did you get that ring?"

Eustace stood, snapped the ring box shut, and it vanished into his pocket. "It belonged to my aunt Iphigenia. I telephoned her— she lives in New York City—and asked if she had anything she'd be willing to part with to aid her lovesick favorite nephew. She sent it up by courier on the afternoon train."

"Hey!" a man yelled. "Who's over there?"

"Lord Sudley," Eustace called. "And a lady."

Eustace curled a protective arm around me, and soon the woods were alive with two tromping policemen and swinging flashlight beams. I'd have to wait until later to examine how I felt about Eustace's offer.

The policemen said they had received a telephone call from Montgomery Hall, describing suspicious lights and shouting in the forest. Eustace smoothly explained that he and I had been taking a romantic moonlit stroll when we came upon a woman digging beneath a tree.

"Who was it?" one of the officers asked.

"I'm not entirely sure." I wouldn't throw Clementine to the wolves. "But she went that way." I pointed west, the opposite direction than Clementine had fled.

"I suspect she's dangerous," Eustace told the officer. "She has been using an assumed identity, and as far as I can make out, she has been trespassing regularly on this estate."

After the police had finished questioning us, Eustace led me through to Montgomery Hall's garage, helped me into his motorcar, and gave me a lift back to the Old Whaler's Inn.

"I hope Berta is all right." I scanned the blackness beside the road as we drove. "Once she went off to take those photographs, she simply disappeared."

"I meant to ask—for what earthly reason could you possibly require photographs of that warehouse?"

"Oh, nothing."

"Ah. Well, your Berta is a tough nut. I shouldn't worry too much about her."

23

At the inn, Eustace escorted me upstairs and we went straight to Berta's door. She flung it open after one knock. Cedric yapped and squiggled on her bed.

"Thank goodness you are all right, Mrs. Woodby!" Berta still wore her boots and dress. "When I heard those sirens—"

"Thank goodness *you're* all right." Despite Berta's unpartnerlike habits, I would be shattered if something befell her. I turned to Eustace. "Thank you for your help."

"You haven't forgotten what I asked?"

"No," I said gently. "Please allow me a bit of time to get my head on straight."

"Of course, my dear. I do hope you feel better. Good night."

I closed Berta's door, went to her simmering orange electric fire, and flopped onto the rug in front of it with a moan. "Oh golly, my wrist and my head. Berta, have you any aspirin?"

"Only a flask of gin, I am afraid, and even that is somewhat depleted."

I peered up at her, my assorted pains momentarily forgotten. "Depleted? What's the occasion?"

"I will get to that."

"Why must you always be so mysterious? Gin will do." I stuck my hand in the air.

"What did Lord Sudley ask you?"

"Nothing important."

"Wives are not required to testify against their husbands in courts of law, you know."

"Exactly what are you implying, Berta?"

"I think you know perfectly well what I am implying."

"Is it so very difficult to picture me as Lady Sudley? Never mind! Don't answer."

"You would live in England, I suppose?"

"Of course not. Not most of the time, anyway."

"Oh dear. Then there are the stewed tomatoes at breakfast to consider. And quite a lot of tweed would be required as well, Mrs. Woodby. I am aware of your feelings about tweed."

"I could work around that."

"Croquet?"

"Absolutely manageable."

"What about foxhunting?—"

I gasped and looked at Cedric.

"—or any hunting, for that matter? You do not like guns."

"All minor details."

Berta stuck an unstoppered flask in my hand.

"Thanks." I took a long gurgle of gin.

"I will only add that Lord Sudley is very persistent, Mrs. Woodby, but you must not mistake persistence for seduction."

"Persistence means he cares."

"But if he must be so tenacious, it suggests that *you* do *not* care."

I fluttered dismissive fingers. I wasn't in the mood for a Sigmund

Freud session starring Berta. There were too many other things flap-
ping in the wind.

Once the pains in my wrist and head had receded to a dull roar,
I told Berta everything, culminating in my capture of Clementine
Brezka. The one bit I glossed over was how I had allowed Clementine to slip away. That seemed like a private matter. A private matter
that Berta would condemn.

Berta said, "Lord Sudley proposed marriage to you moments after
you told him you had made headway in the murder investigation?
How very distracting of him."

"You're missing the point," I said. "I unmasked a con artist, and
if my gut is telling the truth, I've eliminated one of our suspects."

"Your gut is telling you that Clementine is not the murderer?"

"Yes. What about you?" I rolled over to toast my B-side before the
electric fire. "Did you get the photographs?"

"Indeed I did. I began by snapping several shots of the warehouse
interior, which will come out a treat due to the electric light—we
must get them developed and mail them to Lem Fitzpatrick without
delay. No sooner had I finished than I heard the sound of a motor. I
slipped out of the warehouse and went down to the beach to have a
stealthy look. It was a powerboat, proceeding slowly up the coast just
past the breakers, without a single light on."

"Yes, I saw that boat."

"Suspecting the boat might be of interest to Lem Fitzpatrick—
although realizing that in the darkness I had no chance of snapping
a good photograph—I stole up the beach, following the boat's progress."

"You must've been going at a good trot," I said, taking another
sip of gin. A warm snuggly feeling was spreading through me. Perhaps, however, that was because Cedric had descended from Berta's
bed to curl up on my liver.

"I was going like a pig to market, Mrs. Woodby. Granted, the boat was traveling at a remarkably slow pace. All of its lights were unlit, so I strongly suspected that the sailors wished to avoid detection. It passed the beach in front of Montgomery Hall, rounded the point upon which the lighthouse sits, and disappeared from view. By the time I was able to see around the point—"

"Golly, you must've trudged a mile."

"I am exhausted. As I was saying, by the time I was able to see around the lighthouse point, the powerboat had begun to make slow passes back and forth across the water."

"Where?"

"In that cove—you know, the one that lies just around the light-house point."

Cove. *Cove.* Now, why was that making my weary mind go ding-a-ling?

"But what was the powerboat doing?"

"I do not know. I assume that that cove belongs to the Montgomery family—to Theo, I mean to say—but as it turned out, I was prevented from further investigation." Berta's eyes flashed.

"Oho," I said. "Now we're getting to the part that made you slosh down half of this gin." I gave the flask a shake.

"Surely I did not drink half."

"But it's almost gone."

Berta sniffed. "As I traversed the beach, I presently became aware of a flashlight beam swinging about behind me and someone calling my name. I turned and, to my relief, saw that it was none other than Mr. Eccles, the lawyer."

"I *see.*"

"You see nothing, Mrs. Woodby, although I saw a bit more than I wished to, considering that Mr. Eccles wore only his nightshirt and shoes beneath his coat. When you see a man's bare calves, it so often alters your opinion of him."

"Were Mr. Eccles's calves so unsightly?"

"No, no, it is not that. I do not mind men with robust calves. It is that I saw him in all his vulnerability, you see, and it became clear to me that Mr. Eccles—no matter how dashing a figure he cuts in his Madison Avenue suits—is really only a trained sea lion. He forbade me from continuing my reconnaissance mission."

"The bossy buttons! On what grounds?"

"That I was trespassing on his client Theo Wainwright's property. Well. I allowed Mr. Eccles to escort me back to Montgomery Hall, and I accepted a ride from him back here to the inn. But I assure you that I turned down his invitation to dinner. If there is one thing I cannot abide, it is an officious person."

"You prefer fellows who aren't afraid to break the rules for your sake." I slid her a glance. "Fellows like Jimmy the Ant."

Berta patted her bun. "Theoretically, yes."

"Was Mr. Eccles the one who telephoned the police?"

"Of course. He grew alarmed, he said, when he saw lights and heard shouts in the forest."

Deeper and deeper. Weirder and weirder. If I were a wimp, I'd hang it up on the Rudy and Glenn murders, head back to New York, and get busy on whatever cushy retrieval jobs were piling up on Mrs. Snyder's telephone memorandum pad. But I'm not a wimp. I blame my mother.

"I need to go to bed," I said. "I'll tell you the rest in the morning."

"I think that is a fine idea," Berta said, "because the electric fire is beginning to make your raincoat smoke."

When Berta and I entered the Red Rooster the next morning, the locals weren't precisely staring, but I couldn't ignore their sneaky-eyed whispers. News of the debacle in the Montgomery woods last night had made the rounds.

But I had bigger fish to fry. Number one, my aching head. (I hadn't yet decided whether it was the lump at the base of my skull or my gin hangover that hurt more.) Number two, Eustace's proposal of marriage. I had tossed and turned all night without reaching any sort of conclusion. I didn't know him very well, but thirty-one-year-old widows don't turn down offers from landed gentry. At least, that's what my mother would say.

The snag was   Ralph. If I married Eustace, propriety would demand that I never saw Ralph again. Was I up for that?

Once we were seated at a corner table, Berta unfolded one of the newspapers we'd purchased at Wolcott Tobacco & Stationery on the walk from the inn. I picked up yesterday's *New York Evening Observer* and flipped through.

There it was, Glenn Monroe's obituary. He was born and raised in Portland, Oregon, where he performed alongside the rest of his family first on the vaudeville stage and then in some sort of itinerant theatrical production. As a young man he tried his hand at "serious theater," eventually winding up in New York, but since his knack for vocal impersonations and sound effects was wasted there, he entered the new field of radio broadcasting. The rest was history. The piece ended, "Mr. Monroe is survived by one sister, Undine French of Corvallis, Oregon."

I passed it over to Berta.

Where had that farmer puppet in Glenn's apartment come from? The vaudeville stage?

The gossipy blond waitress, Judith, poured our coffee and then hovered, wiping her free hand on her apron. "Now that my boss isn't watching," she whispered, "did you hear what the ghost did up in the woods last night? Clobbered some treasure hunters over the head with rocks?"

My skull throbbed. "Actually, that was—" Berta stopped me with a kick under the table.

"What else?" Berta asked.

"Well, Al and Gert—those are the policemen here in town—they chased some lady in a Chevrolet clear to Rhode Island before they lost her."

"Judith!" the man behind the counter bellowed.

She scurried away.

"Clementine Brezka is on the lam, then," I said.

"Why are you pleased?" Berta demanded.

"I'm not!"

"You are smiling."

"Only because I've been pining for coffee. Although . . ." I explained to Berta how Clementine couldn't have been the "ghost," and thus that I no longer considered her a murder suspect.

"Why must the murderer and the ghost be one and the same?" Berta asked.

"Well, the ghost could be someone who believes that the woman-in-white ruse will keep people away from the treasure. But the ghost has been trying to harm *me,* and I'm not looking for the treasure. I'm looking for the murderer. So it stands to reason that the so-called ghost and the murderer are one and the same."

"That does sound logical. Although . . . you are unwilling to entertain the possibility that you have seen and heard . . . an authentic ghost?"

"Don't be dippy!" *Was* I unwilling? Was Berta? Her face was serene and pinkly scrubbed. Her round blue eyes glinted with intelligence. Pulp consumption or no, surely she didn't go in for spooks. "If it's truly the case that the ghost and the murderer are one and the same, Berta, then we're down to only two suspects. Theo Wainwright. Miss Murden. Neither has an alibi and they both have an excellent motive, so what we must do is push the murderer into making a mistake, or else we must dig up some kind of foolproof evidence of the murderer's guilt."

"If only we could quiz persons at Montgomery Hall without fear of arrest," Berta said.

"If only we could search their closets for bloody shovels and white gowns."

"We could enter the estate in disguise."

I suppressed a snort. "Spies must blend into the scenery. Blending isn't really our strong point."

Berta unclasped her handbag, which sat on the chair beside her, pulled something out, and placed it on the oilcloth. It was the latest issue of *Spectral Stories*, the one with the ghost looming over the séance. She said, "I have an idea."

I looked blankly at the magazine. "I can't even begin to guess."

Berta leaned forward. "If we cannot go to Montgomery Hall to question our two suspects, then we will bring them to us." She nudged *Spectral Stories* an inch closer to me. "We will conduct a séance."

Coffee went down the wrong pipe. I coughed. "You're joshing."

"Indeed I am not. I have read so many stories about séances, I could play a medium in my sleep. What is more, I recently read a story that explained the proper technique for producing raps beneath a séance table. One need only affix a bit of metal to one's bootheel and strike it on the chair leg. I have already asked the clerk at the Old Whaler's Inn if we might use the parlor for such an event, and he said yes, provided we pay a small fee—"

"Stop." I held up a hand. "Do you truly believe Theo Wainwright and Miss Murden will accept our invitation to a *séance?*"

"Yes. If, that is, the invitation is sufficiently threatening."

"What sort of threat?" I thought of the Colt .25 I knew to be nested in Berta's handbag.

"The murderer has surely grown anxious. They have killed twice, and if the invitations suggest that we know who the guilty party is, they will attend the séance if only to learn where they stand with us and our investigation."

"Sounds . . . dangerous."

"Nothing ventured, nothing gained."

I sipped coffee, considering. It was a loopy ruse. Imprudent. Preposterous. "Okay," I said. "I'm game."

24

After breakfast, I took Cedric to pay his respects to a gatepost, while Berta visited the powder room in the Old Whaler's Inn. Then we motored to Mystic to develop and mail our photographs. No Ralph in sight. Was he so hurt by seeing me lollygagging with Eustace that he'd quit the case? Or was he simply blending seamlessly into the backdrop?

And why did the entire topic make my stomach clench?

I parked on Main Street in front of Grady and Sons Camera. Cameras, boxes of film, a display case of camera accessories, bottles, and sheets of film crammed the little shop from floor to ceiling. The air smelled tartly of developing chemicals. The man behind the counter told us it would be an hour to develop the film, so we said we'd return.

"It'll be seventy-five cents," he added.

"In New York it costs only fifty cents to develop a roll," Berta said with a huff.

The man merely shrugged.

Next, we found a stationer's shop, where we purchased a box of blank cards and envelopes. We spent an hour in a coffee shop, writing out the invitations to our séance. We used up several before we got the wording just right. In my best finishing school penmanship they read,

The Great Madame Bergen, renowned spiritualist, requests your attendance at a private séance during which she will summon the spirit of the Lady in White and enjoin her to reveal ALL SHE KNOWS.

This afternoon, 13 November, 1923, 4:00 pm.
The Old Whaler's Inn
Carvington, Connecticut

This sounded, Berta and I agreed, sufficiently threatening.

"I can't help thinking Miss Murden and Theo will simply laugh and toss these into the wastebin." I licked an envelope seal. Writing the invitations reminded me of how I had neglected to hire the caterer and mail the invitations for my sister's wedding. Guilt zinged through me.

We collected and paid for our photographs at the camera store. The snaps Berta had taken inside the Carvington Fish Co. warehouse were bright and clear. The others were grainy and dark, although one photograph of the boat going up the coastline was more or less decipherable.

"Wait," I said, squinting, "it was a *powerboat*?"

"I told you it was a powerboat, Mrs. Woodby. I wish you would li—"

"Was there a powerboat inside the warehouse last night?"

"Why, no."

"Don't you remember how Abe Murden covered up that powerboat with a tarp when we spoke to him in the warehouse a few days ago?"

Berta tipped her head. "No. Wait—yes. Yes, I do recall that. He seemed a bit edgy about the entire business, almost as though he wished to hide the boat. Why would he wish to hide a powerboat?"

"I'm not sure, but considering he's Miss Murden's brother, and considering it was likely he sailing that powerboat in the cove last night, I think we ought to find out."

We went to the post office and mailed the photographs express to Felix the Cat at Caffè Agostini on Macdougal Street.

The postal clerk looked at us a little funny, but the photographs were on their way. They would reach New York by midday tomorrow. I clung to a slender hope that Lem Fitzpatrick would hold up his end of the bargain and return the diamonds.

The only trouble was, even if he did, Theo wanted his diamonds back *tonight*.

We motored back to Carvington and, belatedly realizing that all potential courier boys were in school at that hour, hired Nat at the grocer's to deliver the invitations to Theo and Miss Murden. We told him to try Montgomery Hall first and, if he did not find Theo there, go to Fisk Hall on campus. We had to pay Nat triple what a child would have charged, much to Berta's chagrin. On the flip side, Nat had his own motorcar, so the invitations would be dispatched at the speed of diesel.

Then, we waited.

After lunch at the Red Rooster, we returned to Flintock's Groceries. Nat told us that he had successfully hand-delivered the invitations to both Miss Murden and Theo at Montgomery Hall. After that, Berta said she needed to rest if she was to put on a convincing show as Madame Bergen. As soon as she said *nap*, I went all drowsy myself.

I plugged in my electric fire in my room and was just about to unbuckle my T-straps when there was a rap at my door. Cedric ignored it and curled up in the armchair.

I opened the door. It was Knobby Wrists.

"Telephone call for you in the parlor, madam," he said.

"Lola?" Eustace said when I picked up the receiver. "What's this about a séance at the inn? I assume those outlandish invitations are your doing?"

"Yes." I explained how Berta and I hoped to draw out the murderer.

"Far-fetched, I must say," Eustace said.

"Perhaps. But it just might work."

"May I come?"

"Of course."

A pause. "And . . . may I expect an answer from you this evening?"

I couldn't keep him waiting around forever, could I? "Yes. Yes, you may." I rang off.

In the lobby, I paused at the front desk. "Pardon me," I said to Knobby Wrists, "but do you know much about the oyster trade?"

He looked up from his accounting book. "Oh yes. My uncle was an oysterman, and my grandfather before him. That was when there were still oysters to be had along this coast. They're scarce now. No one managed the harvesting and seeding properly. As a child, however, I recall dredging oysters with Uncle Harold. How I hated it. I always grew seasick. Even now I feel sick whenever Mother fries oysters. In fact—" He sniffed the air. "—I believe she's frying some now."

I did smell salty oil on the air, and clattering sounds came from the kitchen. "Is there any reason, if a person happened to be harvesting oysters, why they might wish to keep their powerboat concealed?"

"A *power*boat, you say?"

"Yes."

"It is illegal to use a powerboat in the harvesting of wild oysters, at least here in Connecticut. And dredges may weigh no more than thirty pounds."

"Illegal?"

"Yes. Oystermen may use them in their own cultivated beds, but there are none of those hereabouts. No public wild beds either." Knobby Wrists peered at me. "Who has been dredging oysters with a powerboat?"

"Oh, no one," I said. "Thank you."

I went upstairs, itching to tell Berta what I'd just learned, but trying to wake her from a nap was as worthwhile as trying to wake a hibernating groundhog. I lay down in my own room, but rest was out of the question with all these churning thoughts. Miss Murden's costly new shoes and motorcar. Her brother Abe's powerboat sneaking along the dark coast. Lem Fitzpatrick's suggestion that Carvington Fish Co. was selling oysters at below-market prices . . .

Miss Murden already had a solid reason to have bopped off Rudy: to keep from losing her lifelong housekeeping post—and her home— at Montgomery Hall. But it was also beginning to look as though the Murdens were operating some sort of shady oyster scheme. What if Rudy had been involved somehow, and as a result, the Murdens rubbed him out of the picture?

The question was, would someone really murder for . . . *mollusks*?

At four o'clock that afternoon, all the preparations for our séance were complete. Berta and I had dragged three sofas to the edges of the parlor to make way for a round table covered with a fringed velvet cloth. Upon the table sat a tarnished candelabra with unlit candles, a box of matches, a bowl of corn chowder, and a slice of Boston cream pie. Berta had explained to me and Mrs. Lawrence that spirits required sustenance, so any medium worth her salt presented food to boodle the spirits into communicating.

"You know we aren't *really* going to communicate with a spirit," I whispered to Berta when Mrs. Lawrence was out of earshot. We hadn't had a second to converse privately, so I'd have to wait to tell her about how powerboats were illegal for oyster dredging. We hadn't had a moment to eat anything, either, and as it was pressing on toward evening, I admit that I fleetingly considered stealing the ghost's slice of Boston cream pie. "We're only trying to spook the murderer into a misstep."

"You never know," Berta whispered back, rearranging the bowl of soup. "In any case, we must create an occult setting if we wish to unnerve the killer."

Motion outside the parlor windows caught my eye, and I hurried over to see a gleaming black motorcar roll to a stop on Church Street. Mwinyi, tall and nimble in a blue wool overcoat and chauffeur's cap, got out and opened the back door.

Not Theo, but Coral emerged, in a cream-colored coat with a white fur collar, a cream wool cloche, and displeasure written all over her elfin face.

Why was she here?

Then Theo emerged from the motorcar. He was bundled in a houndstooth wool coat that was too large for him—could it have been Rudy's?—and he glanced up and down Church Street. Then he and Coral went side by side toward the inn's front door.

I was about to turn away from the window when another luxe black motorcar drew up. Eustace's Duesenberg.

Voices in the lobby made me turn away from the window. I went out to find Berta greeting Theo and Coral.

"I knew it would be you pair," Theo said with a smirk. "Madame Bergen! What nonsense. And I can't say I much appreciate the threatening tone of the invitation. You two are really audacious, do you know that?"

"Yes, we do," I said. "Please take a seat at the table in the parlor, just through here."

Coral was removing her hat. "I *adore* the head scarf, Mrs. Lundgren. Very gypsy. When Theo and Eustace mentioned there was to be a séance, I simply *couldn't* stay away. What fun! I wonder if we could badger Rudy's spirit into communicating with us. *He* could tell us what happened, and we'd be done with this. Where should I put my coat?"

"You may place it on one of the sofas in the parlor," Berta said.

"Peachy."

Coral and Theo went into the parlor

"I saw Lord Sudley outside," I whispered to Berta, "but what about Miss Murden? Should we wait for her?"

Coral swung around. "Oh, Miss Murden is coming. She told me so at lunch. I don't think she'd miss this for the world."

Eustace was the next to step through the front door.

"Lola," he said, wearing a guarded expression. "You look lovely. Hello, Mrs. Lundgren. Lola, might I have a word?" He glanced around the lobby. "In private?"

Here we went. He wished to know whether it was thumbs-up or thumbs-down re me becoming Lady Sudley. And I hadn't yet decided on my answer. "All right," I said with forced cheeriness. "We're still waiting on Miss Murden, so I suppose we have a few moments."

Berta looked disapproving. "I shall make the final preparations for the séance."

"Why don't we go back to the kitchen?" I said to Eustace. "We may speak privately there. The innkeeper said she was going out for the afternoon. She wants no part in occult activities."

Eustace chuckled. "I can't fault her for that." He followed me back to the kitchen and shut the door behind us. He looked down at me, twisting his hat in his hands. "Well, then. Here we are."

"Yes." My eyes strayed to the Boston cream pie on the kitchen table. Good golly, a slice would be nice.

"I've got some news," Eustace said.

"Oh?"

"I'm booked on the *Queen Mary* to Liverpool in a few days' time. I've purchased two first-class stateroom fares."

"You're returning to England? What about the murder investigation?"

"What of it, my dear girl? You and your Swedish sidekick have been blundering about for a week now, with absolutely nothing to show for it—"

"Not *nothing*."

"—and I have my estate to run. I received word that Sudley House's roof has sprung a leak, and you've no idea what a headache it is to manage the construction of a new roof on one of these old places. Requires a military mind and a bottomless bank account. At any rate, I must return home. I don't think we'll ever get to the bottom of Rudy's death—or Glenn's, either, although I suspect his death was really something to do with the radio station and all the petty jealousies among those actor types. I'd put my money on whoever has gotten the job as *The Filmore Vacuette Hour*'s new host."

"But—"

"I shall pay you and Mrs. Lundgren for your time. She'll need the money, of course, and you will probably enjoy having a little something of your own to spend until we're wed, won't you, my proud little pigeon? After that, everything that is mine will be yours. It will be pleasant to see you dressed as a lady at last—we must do something about that before we board the ship, actually, because I always run into people I know shipboard and we can't have you looking like a sad little shopgirl, now, can we?"

My fingernails nipped into my palms. "Eustace, we never did discuss where we would live if we were to be wed. In order for me to keep up my detective agency, I really must live in New York City—unless, of course, I could convince Berta to move to England and set up shop there, but she has the lowest opinion of stewed tomatoes for breakfast—"

"Keep up your detective agency? While you're married to me? Lady Sudley, private eye? You must be joking, my dear."

"I'm not."

"But that would not do at all. Why, it's—it's patently absurd! What can you be thinking? You'll have charities to run, village fetes at which to appear, not to mention keeping up with all my social circle."

"You wish me to be a hostess and nothing else?"

"How can that possibly come as a surprise?"

I had no idea. Perhaps I was mad. Or merely a numskull. Either way, I finally had my answer. "Eustace, I think you're an absolute peach and a prince among men and all that, but I'm afraid there is no way I can become your wife."

"You'd rather be an impoverished gumshoe, flirting with danger and subsisting on tinned beans?"

"Berta would never allow a tin of beans to pass her threshold—but, yes. Yes, I suppose I would."

"But, my dear, you require someone to look after you."

"Actually, I think I manage quite well looking after myself."

Eustace hung there for a moment, speechless. Then he moved to the table, dragged out a chair, and sank into it.

I got out some plates and forks from the hutch, sat down across from him, and cut us each a slice of pie. "Here," I said. "Eating will make you feel better."

Eustace grimaced down at the pie. "I don't enjoy pastry."

Chewing pie, I poked around the kitchen and found a covered dish of fried oysters. "What about these?"

"Oh, very well." Eustace took three oysters and set them on his plate. I turned and replaced the dish beside the stove. Hopefully Mrs. Lawrence wouldn't mind me helping myself. I sat down again.

"These oysters are delicious," Eustace said. He pushed his plate toward me. "Try one."

I didn't really want a fried oyster. I wanted more pie. But I dutifully ate one. "Scrumptious."

"You're lying." Eustace's lips stretched into a nasty line. "You do realize that I hired you to look into Rudy's death only because I thought you were beautiful, don't you?"

I blinked. "But you hired us to retrieve your rhinoceros trophy before we had ever met."

"Oh yes, that was a legitimate case. A simple matter easily handled by bumbling women. But Rudy's death? I never believed for a moment that he was murdered. I only suggested it so I could spend more time with you and, quite frankly, so I could enjoy watching you flounder about, trying to detect. It's dashed cute, you know."

"But—"

"Rudy committed suicide, Lola. There never was a murder."

"What about Glenn Monroe?"

"I told you, someone at the radio station must have killed Glenn."

Suddenly, eating was the very last thing I wished to do. I set down my fork. My mind dizzily raced through all that Berta and I had learned. Could we truly have imagined all those suspicious words, possible motives, evasive behaviors? Was it all merely *Lurid Tales* and *Spectral Stories* clouding our common sense?

No. No, no, no.

Eustace said, "I'll pop a check in the post for you and Mrs. Lundgren, since I think you ought to be paid for your time, even if it was only for my amusement. Now, I really don't have the heart to watch your little séance charade, so I'll be off. Good-bye, Lola. Don't feel too badly. You really are marvelously pretty." He stood, lifted his hat, and pushed out of the kitchen.

I sat there at the kitchen table for a few ticks, too stunned to move.

The thing was, I no longer trusted *anything* Eustace had told me.

25

When I went into the lobby, Berta popped her head out of the parlor. "Are you quite ready, Mrs. Woodby? We have been waiting for you for an age. Miss Murden arrived and we are ready to begin."

There was no time to tell Berta about Eustace's lying. That, just like my discovery about how powerboats aren't legal for oyster dredging, would have to wait. "Coming," I said.

"Everyone must hold hands," Berta said once I had taken my place at the séance table. The pocket doors were shut, the electric lights were off, and in the candelabra, four weak candle flames shuddered. The parlor seemed without margins, the ceiling and walls receding in velvety shadow. There were five of us: Berta, I on her right, then Miss Murden, Coral, and lastly Theo.

We joined hands. Miss Murden's hand was small, sturdy, calloused, and cold. She was still a little breathless from her walk. On the other side of the candles, Coral's fair face seemed to float, disembodied, and Theo was slouched back into half darkness.

"Goodness, Lola," Coral said, "what kind of face powder have you been using? You're shining like a specter in this candlelight."

Dratted Marie Antoinette Pearlized Complexion Powder.

"We will begin," Berta said. She chanted, "Spirit of the Lady in White, we summon you tonight—"

"It's not precisely night yet, you know," Theo interrupted.

"Must you always spoil the fun, Theo?" Coral snapped.

"Don't you two sound just like an old married couple," Miss Murden said, smirking.

"What's that supposed to mean, you creepy old trout?" Coral said.

Berta continued, "—Reveal to us your secrets of yore, of diamonds bright or golden ore."

"I thought we were going to ask about Rudy's death," Miss Murden said. "I don't care about that treasure bunkum."

"First things first," Berta said. She rearranged her face and closed her eyes. "Spirit, we bring you offerings and, trusting that you enjoy pie, entreat you to reveal the secrets of the Other Side. I will ask questions, O spirit. Rap once for yes, twice for no."

Was it just me, or was the parlor's temperature dropping? Maybe it was only a draft coming through the chimney flue.

"O spirit, tell us," Berta said, "is there truly a Montgomery treasure?"

RAP.

"Is it diamonds?"

RAP RAP.

"Is it gold?"

RAP RAP.

"Is it . . . money?"

RAP.

"Is the treasure buried on the Montgomery estate?"

RAP.

"This is a waste of time," Miss Murden said. "Let's speak to

Mr. Montgomery now." She raised her voice. "Mr. Montgomery, this is your loyal servant, Esther Murden. Tell us, sir, were you murdered?"

Coral gasped. Theo scoffed. Then we all waited.

Silence unfurled in the dark. Miss Murden's hand perspired.

RAP.

We waited. No second rap. However, a strange gurgling sound emanated from one of the parlor's murky corners.

"He *was* murdered!" Miss Murden cried. "Oh, I don't believe it!"

"Wow, this is fun," Coral said. "Say, Rudy, while we've got you on the line, tell us, is anyone else going to die?"

Again, the strange gurgling, followed by a muffled hoggish snort.

RAP.

"Oh my dear Lord," Miss Murden whispered, shrinking back. Her hand in mine was now shaking and slippery with sweat. Theo was looking twitchy, and even Coral's eyes flicked from face to face around the table.

I cleared my throat. "Mr. Montgomery, is your killer sitting at this table now?"

RAP. Pause. *RAP.*

No? What was Berta up to?

I sent her a look, and she twitched her nose.

She hadn't made that last rap. Someone was interfering!

"Mr. Montgomery," I called, "is your death linked to Miss Murden's newfound wealth?"

Miss Murden yanked her hand from mine. "How dare you?" she snarled.

RAP RAP.

"Is Theo truly your son?" I asked.

RAP.

"Does his visit to New York City Hall have any bearing on your murder?" I asked.

"Who have you been speaking to?" Theo lunged forward so hard, he hit the edge of the table and sent the candelabra wobbling.

"Don't let these old girls get under your skin, Theo," Coral said. "They're bluffing. Bluffing about everything. I suppose one of them is a whiz at playing the castanets with her feet, or—"

Miss Murden let rip an eardrum-splintering scream. She shot to her feet, pointing at something at the margin of the quivering candlelight.

A blobby apparition in white swayed. Then, to my horror, it lurched toward us.

Wait—was that Coral's cream-colored coat? Yes, it was, and there was Theo's houndstooth number. The coats slid off and we were all staring, speechless, at Jimmy the Ant in a striped suit.

"Gollygeebejabbers, why didn't anyone wake me up?" he said, rubbing his eyes. "I've been snoozing on that sofa for hours. What's going on here, anyway? Is that Boston cream pie? Boy oh boy, somebody gimme a fork."

Someone—Theo—snapped the overhead lights on.

"Lovely séance, girls," Coral said, getting to her feet.

"For God's sake," Theo said, snatching the coats off the floor. "I've had it with your nonsense. Absolutely had it!" He helped Coral into her coat. "I'm warning you for the last time, if I don't have my diamonds back by midnight tonight, I'm going to the police."

Coral and Theo left, and Miss Murden clumped after them seconds later.

"Jimmy!" Berta cried. "What are you doing here?"

"Came ta see you, tomato." He grinned, his glass eye lolling, and slipped a thin arm around her waist.

She wiggled from his grasp. "You have a great deal of explaining to do."

"Sure do. Hows about I do it up in your room?"

Berta looked at me, flushing.

"*We* have a few things to discuss, too," I said. "Those raps, to begin with—which ones didn't you make?"

"As soon as you began asking the questions, Mrs. Woodby, I made no more raps."

"Who do you suppose it was?"

"The murderer, of course."

A chill slithered along my spine. "We didn't force the murderer into a confession with our séance. We've only stirred up more trouble. And there are a few other things I have learned. . . ."

Jimmy was covertly caressing Berta's hand, and she wasn't really listening to me.

Far be it from me to halt other ladies' romantic reunions.

"Why don't you and Mr. Ant talk things over," I said, "and then we really must discuss what to do next."

Berta and Jimmy left in a hurry. They were halfway up the stairs when I heard them whispering and giggling.

By the time I had straightened up the parlor, put away the pie, and washed the corn chowder bowl in the kitchen, I was sweaty and a bit sick in the pit of my stomach. I chalked it up to disillusionment. After all, my earl in shining armor had turned out to be nothing but an ass in a tin can.

I'd just go upstairs, have a little lie-down, and allow my stomach to settle before talking over this mess with Berta. . . .

When I woke, I was more queasy than before. I checked my wristwatch. After eight o'clock! I'd been asleep for hours.

I coaxed myself out of bed, plodded to Berta's door, and knocked.

"Is that you, Mrs. Woodby?" came the muffled reply. There was a thump, padding footsteps, and then the door swung open and Berta's face appeared in the crack. I caught a glimpse of Jimmy the Ant sitting up in bed in a Henley undershirt.

"A most exciting development has occurred," Berta said.

"I see that."

She edged the door shut a few inches. "Mr. Ant is merely, ah, his gout—"

"You need not explain a thing to me. But we *do* need to—"

"Jimmy has brought the diamonds."

"He has?" I squealed.

"Shush. Yes. He secretly procured them from one of Lem Fitzpatrick's safes."

"He knew the combination?"

"He blasted it open with nitroglycerin," Berta said in the same tone a mother uses when bragging about her child's spelling bee victory.

"Lem will have his head!"

"Not if he doesn't find out. Jimmy replaced the entire safe with an identical one, and put pebbles inside. With any luck, Lem will decide the diamonds were truly pebbles all along."

"We've got to take them to Theo."

"First thing in the morning, Mrs. Woodby."

"No, now. Theo was explicit about the midnight deadline." We were saved! Perhaps. We had to get a move on. I'd tell Berta about the oyster dredging and Eustace's lies as soon as we delivered those diamonds to Theo . . . and as soon as my digestive tract stopped its contortionist feats.

Berta sighed. "Oh, very well. I suppose I will sleep more soundly tonight with those diamonds out of my hair. Give me a few minutes to ready myself."

26

Ten minutes later, Berta, Jimmy, Cedric, and I stepped out of the Old Whaler's Inn and into a boundless misty night. My queasiness had progressed to a bona fide stomachache, and despite the chill in the air, perspiration dewed my upper lip.

Was it that Boston cream pie I'd eaten? Or perhaps the fried oyster Eustace had urged upon me . . . Had I eaten a bad oyster? Shucks.

"Come on, Mrs. Woodby," Berta called from the passenger seat of Jimmy's Buick. Jimmy revved the engine. "Why are you dawdling?"

"Sorry." I climbed into the backseat and settled Cedric beside me. "I don't feel so hot."

"Lovesick?" Jimmy asked in his grinding-gears voice.

"No. Ordinary sick. I might've eaten some bad shellfish."

Berta swung around to face me. "Did you turn down Lord Sudley's offer?"

"Yes."

"Did you leave your food unattended with Lord Sudley?"

"What are you suggesting?" I gulped bile.

"Simply answer the question."

"No." *Yes*—I had turned my back on Eustace and my pie while fetching the fried oysters.

"You *did* leave your food unattended! Mr. Ant, please drive directly to the hospital. Mrs. Woodby may have been poisoned."

"Don't be ridiculous. Mr. Ant, please take us to Montgomery Hall."

Jimmy angled the Buick away from the curb. "Gonna need directions either way."

"We're going to Montgomery Hall," I said.

"Hospital!" Berta yelled.

"If I still feel ill after we deliver the diamonds, I'll go to the hospital," I lied.

"You're as stubborn as a mule, Mrs. Woodby."

"Thank you."

Berta rattled off the directions for Montgomery Hall to Jimmy, and we were off.

"Is Mr. Ant not a superb driver?" Berta said over the seat as we barreled along Church Street.

"Swell." I clawed my fingernails into the upholstery.

"He does not lurch and swerve as you do, Mrs. Woodby. Oh dear. Someone has drawn up very close behind us."

It was true: the interior of the Buick was flooded with the light of another motorcar's headlamps.

Jimmy stepped harder on the gas.

The other motorcar sped up.

"Maybe they wish to pass," Berta said.

"Okay, I'll let 'em pass, then." Jimmy swung onto a side street.

Tires screeched as the other motorcar turned, too.

"Oh dear," Berta said. "Oh dear oh dear oh dear."

"Don't you worry about a thing, tomato," Jimmy said, gunning

another turn. We were on a street of modest clapboard houses leading toward Carvington College.

"They are gaining on us," Berta said. She fumbled with her
handbag, pulled out her Colt .25, and began to crank her window
down.

"What are you doing?" I cried.

"I shall extinguish their headlamps and force them to stop."

"Naw, sit back, tomato. What's this up here? Some kinda school?"

"The college," Berta said, "but you are not supposed to—"

Jimmy bumped the Buick up the curb, through the brick archway, and we sailed flat out across the grass. "Goin' kitty-corner," he
said.

Our headlamps bounced off the buildings, people shouted, and
we dinged one of the streetlamps before we passed through another
brick archway, flew off the curb, and joggled onto the street.

A tooth-rattling smash behind us. I corkscrewed around to see
that the other motorcar had hit a brick pillar.

"Lost 'em," Jimmy said. "Heh-heh-heh." He floored the gas.

Vomit. Vomiting would be pleasant. As we rumbled along the
main road, I wondered in a distant, sweaty way if it could be Eustace
pursuing us. Miss Murden and Theo had spiffy motorcars. Clementine had a motorcar, too. Maybe she wasn't really gone.

"The gates to Montgomery Hall are just up here on the right,"
Berta said.

"Gotcha."

"Here. Slow down—stop! The gates are closed!"

Jimmy rammed the Buick through the gates, and we were zoom-
ing up the dark wet driveway beneath arched black trees.

Then, the growl of an engine behind us, and a single headlamp
appeared in the rearview mirror.

"For the lova peach cobbler," Jimmy muttered, and pitched off the
driveway so suddenly, Cedric and I were tossed to the opposite side

of the backseat. We swerved through the forest, branches screeching along the Buick's sides and rocks clanging on the chassis.

"Where are you going?" Berta cried.

"Dunno," Jimmy said. "What's out this way?"

"THE SEA!"

The other motorcar had somehow gained on us—I woozily figured that it must've come down to more cylinders—and then—*holy cow!*—a gunshot popped and a bullet dinged off the Buick.

"That is *it*," Berta said. She checked her Colt's chambers, twisted herself out of the window, and aimed—

Just as Jimmy hit a rock. We jounced, and Berta's gun flew out the window into the night.

"Drat!" she cried.

Why hadn't I brought my handbag? I could've vomited into my handbag. What about my hat? It was a favorite, a navy felt cloche, but under the circumstances—

We burst out of the trees. Out to the right, the lighthouse flashed rhythmically into the abyss. Oh, and straight ahead?

A long stretch of dock, golden in the headlamps, and beyond that the maroon-black sea.

"*Stooooooop!*" Berta wailed as we catapulted onto the dock. The boards under our tires made a hollow *thunkety-thunkety-thunkety*.

Jimmy braked, but the dock was slick with rain. We skidded along, soared into the darkness, and with a jarring smack that made me hit my head on the ceiling, we splashed into the water.

"I cannot swim!" Berta wailed.

"I'll save ya, tomato." Grunting, Jimmy shoved open his door.

The Buick wasn't, for some reason, sinking, but I grabbed Cedric and climbed out the window. I lost my balance and dunked into the freezing water, holding Cedric tight to my chest.

And oh, thank sweet baby bejeezuz, my feet touched the bottom. Well, sort of touched—I was wearing pumps, and the bottom of the sea was lumpy and jagged underfoot. I scrambled and sloshed to stay upright, finding that the water, though choppy, was only up to my waist. We might turn into ice cubes, but no one was going to drown.

Wait. These sharp lumpy things underfoot . . .

"Oysters," I said. "Sewant Cove is full of *oysters*. Remember that file in Rudy's study, the one that said 'Oyster Preserves'? It referred to this. This is a wild oyster preserve! The Murdens must be poaching here."

Berta was preoccupied with rattling her door handle.

Then it dawned on me that the other motorcar had crashed nose-down on the rocky seawall beside the dock. Two men were clambering out. One was tall and gangly; one was puny. They were peering out at us, and I saw the metal glint of handguns.

Not Eustace. Not Theo.

The gangsters from the *Merchants Limited* train.

"Um, Berta?" I whispered.

She didn't hear; she was still stuck inside the motorcar, bumping her weight against the door, and when Jimmy yanked it open, she poured out into the water. "Aghh!" she cried.

"Don't worry 'bout a thing, tomato," Jimmy said, attempting to slither his arms around her.

"Not that!" Berta cried. "I've dropped the diamonds in the water!"

"Berta!" I whispered, louder this time.

Jimmy and Berta looked up and for the first time noticed the men peering out at us from the seawall.

"Oh dear," Berta murmured. "Jimmy, can you save us?"

Jimmy scratched his cheek.

"Hey!" the gangly thug yelled. "Get over here now, and bring them diamonds! And you, Jimmy, you're gonna be in real hot water with Boss. He said he was gonna string you up like a duck in Chinatown!"

"Jimmy," Berta whispered, "why do you consort with such persons?"

"Gotta make a living, queen bee."

"Get a move on!" Gangly brandished his gun. "Put your hands up, and nothing funny or you're Swiss cheese!"

Jimmy and Berta raised their hands, I raised my hand that wasn't hugging Cedric, and we waded toward shore.

"Any ideas?" I whispered to Berta.

"No. Jimmy?"

"Thinkin' on it."

"Think harder!" I whispered.

We stumbled and crunched on the underwater oysters, and emerged on the narrow strip of beach below the seawall—the tide must've been out—dripping, quaking, teeth chattering.

"Does the pooch bite?" Gangly asked me, gesturing down to Cedric.

"Only if you're a bratwurst," I said.

"We got a real wiseacre here, Danny," Gangly said to the puny one—who was wearing the same enormous glasses he'd worn on the train. "Come on up here. We're takin' the three of you back to the city to see Boss."

"Still no ideas?" I whispered to Jimmy.

Jimmy shrugged limply.

Berta was correct: Jimmy wasn't really gangster material. Good gravy.

Once we'd clambered to the top of the seawall, Gangly keep his gun drawn while Danny approached Jimmy, ordered him to put his hands up, and commenced patting him down. In his sopping suit, Jimmy looked like a drowned weasel.

I tried to swallow my queasy panic. "If you don't mind me asking," I said, "how are you going to take us back to the city if your motorcar is stuck on those rocks?"

The thugs glanced at their motorcar and then at each other.

"We'll steal another motorcar, I guess," Danny said. He finished patting Jimmy down, and then went to Berta.

"If you touch me, you'll regret it," she said coldly.

"Just doin' my job, lady."

"We do not have the diamonds."

"Sure you do. We saw Jimmy take 'em outa the safe, followed him all the way up here   "

"You mean you saw Jimmy blow them out of the safe," Berta said. "With nitroglycerin."

"That what he told you? Haw-haw! And then we saw him give 'em to you."

Berta scowled. "You were spying through my bedroom window at the inn?"

"Well, Gus here was. Gus is the one who does the squirreling up the drainpipes bit. I just gave him a boost."

Berta was practically vibrating with fury. Danny patted her sides as gingerly as one would a soufflé.

"Nothin'," Danny said to Gus.

"I told you," Berta said, "they sank to the bottom of the cove."

"The doll with the pooch must have 'em," Gus said to Danny. "Frisk her."

Danny came at me, all handsy. Cedric growled and lurched in my arms. I struggled to keep him contained and squeezed my eyes shut as Danny patted me down and up again.

"Nothin'," Danny said, mystified.

"We *told* you," I said. "They're in the water. So why don't you let us go?"

"No chance. Boss wants Jimmy here's neck like nobody's business. All righty, get in line. We'll walk over to the big house I saw back there and take a motorcar from their garage. Bet they got some real fancy ones. C'mon, march."

A figure strolled out of the trees. I saw him first, but Gus saw him a split second later. "Hold it!" Gus shouted, and trained his gun on the figure.

The figure strolled closer, and I knew that smooth-jointed gait. "Wowie, you folks sure look like you're having some motorcar trouble. Need a hand?"

It was Ralph, in a wool sailor's coat, tall rubber boots, and a knitted cap. Berta and Jimmy kept their traps shut about recognizing him. So did I, although my knees were weak with relief . . . or maybe Jell-O knees were only the latest symptom of my hideous stomach complaint.

"Who are you?" Danny called.

"Ebeneezer North. Call me Eb. I tend the lighthouse just over there." Ralph offered a hand.

Neither Danny nor Gus shook his hand, but they both relaxed slightly. "You got a tow cable?" Danny asked.

"*We can just steal a new motorcar,*" Gus whispered to him.

Danny whispered back, "*And leave Boss's car here to rot—and for the fuzz to find it?*"

"Sure I've got a tow cable," Ralph said. "It's in my motorcar. I'll go and get it."

"All right," Danny said. "But we're in a kinda hurry."

Ralph loped away—he never loped, so this was part of the act— and we waited for a few awkward minutes. Presently he returned behind the wheel of his Chalmers. He backed up so his rear fender was lined up with that of the thugs' tipped motorcar, switched off his engine, hopped out, and produced a coiled metal cable and a flashlight from the backseat.

Why the heck did he have a tow cable on hand?

"All righty," Ralph said, uncoiling the cable. It had a hefty metal hook on each end. "You fellas come over here—I need one of you to hold the flashlight and one of you to hold the hook in place—that's right, come on over." Danny and Gus met Ralph at the Chalmers's rear bumper. Ralph passed Danny the flashlight and handed one of the hooks to Gus. "Just hook that right under the fender there—see that little ridge?"

Danny and Gus crouched, bending their heads to see underneath the fender. With the other metal hook, Ralph neatly clocked each of them in the back of the head. They went down like dominoes.

Ralph began to coil the tow cable up again. "Get in the car," he said to Jimmy, Berta, and me. "These two are out cold but who knows for how long."

We all piled into the Chalmers, and we were off.

In the front passenger seat, I was shaking-wet, and so queasy and achy, I couldn't speak, although my mind was stammering, *Thank you, thank you, thank you, Ralph. And I'm sorry, I think. And . . . I still love you. Phooey.*

Cedric climbed out of my arms to boost his front paws on Ralph's lap. I lay my head on the door, shut my eyes, and prayed I would not vomit in front of the love of my life.

Berta said, "Mr. Oliver, would you kindly motor us directly to the hospital in Mystic? Mrs. Woodby may have been poisoned by Lord Sudley."

"Jiminy Christmas," Ralph muttered, and he hit the gas hard.

We somehow made it to the hospital—it was all a twisty, churning blur during which I somehow managed to tell Berta how Eustace had been lying to us about, well, everything, and how powerboats are illegal in the oyster trade, and how Abe Murden must be poaching the Montgomery oyster preserves in Sewant Cove. Then Ralph and Berta were guiding me into the emergency room, speaking as rapidly as radio broadcasters to doctors and nurses while I lay on a wheeled bed, squeezing my eyes shut against the surface-of-the-sun lights.

Someone made me sit up—I don't know who because I still

couldn't open my eyes—and I was being told to drink down two tablespoonsful of syrup of ipecac, which would have been sickeningly sweet if I hadn't already been around the bend, followed by a full glass of water.

Everyone stepped back. A nurse nestled a metal pan in the bed beside me. Several minutes passed during which I rode the roller coaster inside my skull.

I bolted upright in bed and was sick in the metal pan.

"Thank heavens," I heard Berta say.

"Gollygeebejabbers," Jimmy muttered.

Ralph said, "Whew."

I pried my eyes open and yelled, "Get out of here, all of you!" Then I was sick again.

And again and again, and even when there was nothing left, my innards continued to wrench themselves. Finally that stopped, too, and the nurse switched off the overhead light, and I slept.

27

....

I woke. For a moment I had no notion where I was, with these pale yellow walls and the too-tight sheets forcing my feet sideways, and there was someone sitting beside my bed, legs crossed, reading a newspaper.

The newspaper lowered to reveal shining agate gray eyes, ginger stubble, and smiling lips with heartrending little parentheses at their corners.

"Ralph," I croaked.

"You pulled through, kid."

I struggled upright, realized I was in a clinging hospital gown, and drew the covers up to my chin. "Where is Cedric?"

"Mrs. Lundgren took him for the night."

"Do you have the time?"

Ralph smiled. "Depends on what you had in mind."

"Why are you here?"

"Let me think." He folded the newspaper. "Because you could've died last night and I didn't feel right about going back to the inn for a refreshing snooze?"

"It was only a bad oyster," I said.

"You sure about that?" Ralph's eyes lost a little of their sparkle.

"No, actually. I'm not. Lord Sudley lied to me. Lied and lied. I'm not sure what to think."

We shared a long, searching gaze. Was there hurt in Ralph's eyes? Yes. Jealousy? None that I could make out. Love? Well, yes.

"Nurse," he called as someone passed by the open door.

A nurse stopped in the doorway. "Yes?"

"See to it that Mrs. Woodby here gets some breakfast. Coffee, eggs, pancakes, the works. Oh—and she likes bacon."

"Yes, sir." After giving Ralph an appreciative once-over, the nurse hurried off.

I said, "Mind if I ask how you happened to be on the Montgomery estate last night just in the nick of time—thanks for that, by the way—"

"My pleasure."

"—opportunely wearing a salty dog disguise? Oh—and with a tow cable in your motorcar?"

"I always have a tow cable in my motorcar because you might have noticed it's a heap of junk and I have to get it towed pretty regularly. The disguise, well, that was just so I could blend in around town, you know."

"How did you wind up in the right place at the right time, though?"

"I was sitting at a window table at the Red Rooster, eating dinner and minding my own business, when I happened to see you and Berta tearing down the street in that skinny little gangster's motorcar. I didn't like the looks of it one bit, especially when I saw a second motorcar take off after you. So I got in my own motorcar, and followed."

"Oh." I swallowed. "Thanks. Thanks for . . . taking care of me."

"I'll tell you, Lola, my heart just about stopped when I saw that idiot drive his motorcar into the sea. I was running down to help you when I saw you stand up. After that, I hung back. I didn't want those two thugs to see me. I wanted to figure out how to finesse the situation."

I smiled a little. "You certainly did finesse it."

"And Lola. About that thing we were talking about. The, uh, the domestic thing. The . . . forever thing."

I sat quite still in that bed. The scent of starch rose up from the tight sheets, and the clock on the wall ticked louder. I looked at Ralph with his forearms braced on his knees, his weathered skin, and that white divot of a shrapnel scar, all laid bare in the thin morning light. And his eyes. They weren't cool, ironic, keen, or laughing this time. They were open wide with a bruised-looking vulnerability.

Understanding dawned.

Ralph needed someone to take care of *him*. He would never admit it in a million years, but he did. I'd been so selfish, childish, thinking only of my own desires and plots and expectations. He was the wounded one—or, at least, he had been just as wounded by life as I had.

I took a deep breath. "I—"

"Let me start," he said.

"Oh. All right."

"I wanted to tell you," he said, weaving his fingers together, "that I've been thinking, and I was a little too . . . too harsh, I guess the word is. I'm going to stay open to your ideas. The domestic thing. And forever. But just . . . just give me a little time, okay?" He looked at me, naked hope written all over his face.

"All right," I said. I blinked away the moisture in my eyelashes. I'd give him all the time in the world, and to Halifax with what Mother would say.

Ralph was bending over me, bracing a hand on my head-board—

Berta burst in carrying Cedric, with two handbags swinging from her elbow. She shut the door behind her. "Quickly, Mrs. Woodby! The police are here, speaking with a nurse!"

Ralph straightened.

"What?" I said. "Police?"

"Theo must have sent them to arrest us for stealing the diamonds. Do not dillydally!" She thrust Cedric into Ralph's arms, hurried to the window, and gave it a jiggle. "Thank goodness we are on the main floor."

No kissing Ralph, then. Although probably for the best, since I needed a toothbrush like anything.

I whipped off the bedclothes and went to the window. Air wafted up beneath my flimsy hospital gown, and my feet were bare.

The men's voices grew louder, with the nurse's annoyed voice woven through.

"I'll stall them," Ralph said. "And I'll take the pooch. Scram— and be careful." With Cedric in his arms, he slid out the door and shut it.

Berta passed me one of the handbags she was carrying. It was mine. "Here," she said. "I brought this from the inn. I know you have great quantities of makeup in there, and we will need it."

"Really?" I said. "Why?"

"No time to explain now." Berta hoisted her leg, and was out the window. She thumped onto the ground below.

I climbed out, too. As I did so, a little voice in the back of my mind said, *The open window. The* OPEN WINDOW, *you nitwit!*

But, not having had a drop of coffee, I ignored it.

"I feel like an escaped mental patient," I whispered to Berta. We hurried alongside the building. "My brother-in-law, Chisholm, would say my whole life has been leading up to a moment such as this."

"Do not spleen so, Mrs. Woodby. We are close to cracking this case like a peanut."

"Really? How—?"

"First things first—we must flee." Berta stopped at the corner of the hospital and peered around. She pulled back. "Drat. There is another policeman loitering about by your motorcar, which I drove from the inn."

"I'm standing here barefoot in a giant paper serviette, holding my handbag, and it's November and—"

"*Do not spleen*. Wait here. I shall return."

"What are you going to do?"

"Have faith, Mrs. Woodby."

"Oh, fine." I huddled in the shrubbery and watched Berta toddle away and out of sight.

I didn't wait long. An engine roared up in front of my hiding place.

"Mrs. Woodby!" Berta cried. "For heaven's sake, get in."

I poked my head through the branches. Berta sat behind the wheel of a large, dirty truck with FREDERICK BROS. GUTTER CLEANING painted on the side and a ladder tied to the roof. I scrambled over, climbed in, and Berta pressed the gas pedal before I'd even slammed the door.

"Where did you get this rig?" I called over the chugging engine.

"I borrowed it from the hospital parking lot."

"Borrowed?"

"We will return it as soon as we are able."

"The keys were left in the ignition?"

"No. Jimmy taught me how to hot-wire motorcars once."

"On a date?"

"Going to the movie palace eventually grows tiresome."

Truly? Ralph and I had never seen more than a few minutes of any motion picture; too busy canoodling.

Berta swung the truck out of the parking lot and onto the street.

"Where are we going?" I asked.

"That depends. What sort of makeup do you have in your hand-bag?"

Too dazed to argue, I unclasped my handbag and rummaged. "Only a lipstick and Maybelline cake mascara."

"Then our first stop is Rexall Drugs to purchase items to complete our disguises."

"Disguises?"

"We are on the lam, Mrs. Woodby, and if we are to conclude our investigation before the police arrest us for stealing Theo's diamonds—"

"We could simply produce the diamonds. We know where they are."

"If those thugs did not extract them from the cove already. I do not wish to take any risks."

"Right," I said. "And about our investigation—you mentioned something about cracking it like a peanut?" My temples pulsated a demand for coffee, and my belly growled. How could I detect while running on empty? I rummaged through my handbag again, but came up with nothing but a crumpled chocolate bar wrapper.

"Indeed. I had a most elucidating conversation with Mwinyi this morning."

"Mwinyi? Why Mwinyi?"

"I was exceedingly distraught by the possibility that Lord Sudley had attempted to poison you, Mrs. Woodby, and that, taken in combination with the revelation that he lied to us about so many things, well, at the crack of dawn, I telephoned Montgomery Hall with the intent to demand answers from him. However, Mwinyi answered the telephone and told me that Lord Sudley had already left for the city."

"He's sailing for England, he said."

"Fishy, is it not? Now, do you recall how Lord Sudley claimed

Mwinyi accidentally fired that first gunshot we heard the afternoon
Rudy died? I pressed Mwinyi upon that point, and he told me that
Lord Sudley lied to us about that, too. That first gunshot was fired
by Lord Sudley."

I sat there for a long, blank moment, jouncing on the truck seat.

We'd been thoroughly duped. Lord Sudley had abetted Miss Murden, Theo, or Clementine in killing Rudy and, most likely, Glenn.

To think I'd been tempted to marry him! He might've been planning to murder *me.*

"What about the second gunshot?" I asked.

"I do not know. In fact, I am not entirely certain which gunshot
was which. . . ."

I sat up straighter. "We must speak with Coral."

"Coral?"

"About *the open window* in Rudy's bedroom. Why didn't we ever
ask her about it? That open window was the one out-of-place thing
in that room. That open window might have been the killer's one
mistake! We're supposed to be professional detectives, but we may
as well be a couple of caged parakeets for all the—"

"Calm down, Mrs. Woodby."

"I'm calm!" I cried. "Now, drive me to the nearest telephone!"

"We will go to Rexall Drugs first," Berta said, serenely stepping
on the gas.

Twenty-ish minutes later, I dialed 0 from a coin-operated telephone
in the lobby of Mystic's movie theater, and asked to be put through
to Montgomery Hall.

I wore corduroy trousers tucked into muddy rubber boots, a smelly
wool coat, and a wool hat, all of which I had found in the back of
the truck. My complexion had been muddied by a liberal applica-
tion of Tahitian Princess face powder from Rexall Drugs, and my

upper lip sported a small, smarmy mustache in the style of motion picture villains. This I had painted on with cake mascara and a brush wet with my tongue.

Hovering close to me—or, rather, close to the telephone earpiece—was Berta, disguised more or less in the same fashion as I, although her mustache was fuller.

Mwinyi answered the telephone and then, after a few more minutes, Coral was on the line.

"I'm so glad you rang," she said.

"Oh?"

"I heard you might have kicked the bucket last night."

"I didn't know you cared. Speaking of kicking buckets, I wonder if I might ask you a question or two about the murder investigation."

"Still flogging that dead horse?" Coral laughed. "Lord Sudley told me he hired you to look into Rudy's suicide because he thought you were cute. There's simply no accounting for taste, is there?"

Not for the first time, I wished Coral didn't have a bulletproof alibi for the time of Rudy's death. Heck, she didn't even have a good motive, since Rudy's death had left her high and dry. "There are oodles of loose ends," I said, "and Mrs. Lundgren and I aren't quite ready to throw in the towel."

"You'll have to throw it in soon, sweetie, because Theo sent the police out to arrest you."

"Listen, Coral. I must ask you about how Rudy's window was open when his body was discovered—"

"Rudy's window? You really are grasping at straws, aren't you?"

"Please."

Silence. "Oh, all right. But not over the telephone. Why don't you come up to Montgomery Hall—"

"And risk being trapped by Theo?"

"Fine—what about in the country somewhere?"

Berta shook her head. *"Too exposed,"* she whispered to me.

I said to Coral, "What about . . . What about in Carvington? On the village green, perhaps?" There were usually enough people milling around Carvington for us to be inconspicuous there.

"Oh, all right. See you there in thirty minutes or so?"

"Swell—oh, and we'll be in disguise." I hung up.

"What if this is a trap?" Berta said. "What if Coral brings the police along?"

"That's a risk we're going to have to take," I said.

28

....

In Carvington, parked motorcars lined Church Street. I'd forgotten that today was the day of the Menchen's Manikins puppet performance for which we'd seen advertisements.

"All for the best," I said as Berta parallel parked the truck to the accompaniment of shouts and honks. "We'll blend in with all these people around."

We got out, and crossed the street to the village green. There, a puppet theater crouched on the muddy grass. This was a red wagon whose side had been hinged and propped open to reveal a red-and-white striped curtain. Children frolicked around a sandwich board reading MENCHEN'S MANIKINS SHOW AT with a removable wooden piece stuck on crookedly reading *12:00*.

We hung back from the crowd, beside a large tree. Sure, we wore disguises, but I didn't think for a second that they'd hold up to scrutiny. Berta's mascara mustache was already smudged.

A teenaged girl was wandering through the crowd with a wooden tray holstered around her neck, upon which doughnuts were piled. "Apple cider doughnuts," she called. "Two for five cents!"

I could smell the cinnamon from several feet away. I hadn't had breakfast yet. I had left my handbag in the truck, naturally, but I'd had the prudence to bring my coin purse along. I pulled it from my coat pocket and popped it open.

There, twinkling amid pennies, quarters, nickels, and dimes, was the golden curl of paper I'd found outside Montgomery Hall's conservatory. I'd forgotten all about it. Probably meant nothing. I dug out a nickel, and when the doughnut girl came by, I purchased two doughnuts.

Still warm, too. *Bliss.* I bit into one just as tinkly music began, and the crowd hushed. The striped puppet theater curtains opened to reveal a painted forest backdrop.

A fox puppet popped up, bounced around, and pawed at its whiskers. A trumpet blatted inside the puppet theater, and a theatrical British-accented voice said, "Tally-ho and view halloo!" The fox puppet jostled up and down, and the backdrop behind it moved to give the impression of countryside passing by. Then a foxhound puppet appeared, to the delighted shrieks of the audience, followed by an English gentleman hunter on horseback, his dangling legs quivering. The fox bounced, the foxhound and hunter pursued, and then suddenly the fox twirled around, clacked its little wooden teeth, produced a blunderbuss, and—*BANG! BANG!*—shot the foxhound and hunter. Shiny red ribbons tumbled from their breasts, miming blood, and they collapsed.

"To the underdog!" the ventriloquist cried as the fox's jaws moved.

The crowd roared with laughter and the curtains swung shut.

I polished off the first doughnut and started on the second.

Bang, bang.

My brain, thrilled by sugar, began to whirr smoothly. Memories surfaced. Dots connected. The open window. The golden curl of paper.

Bang, bang.

"I know what that golden scrap of paper is," I whispered to Berta.

"You do?" she bleated.

"Shh! And here comes Coral. Just follow my lead." I stuffed the remaining chunk of doughnut into my mouth.

Coral sidled up to us in her cream-colored coat and cloche hat. "My, my. Don't you two look a treat in your ickle disguises," she said. "Say, Lola, you've got sugar or something on your mustache." She glanced at the puppet theater, which had launched into what appeared to be a rendition of "The Three Little Pigs." "Ugh," she muttered. "I didn't know there was a puppet show. I just hate puppets. Why don't we go and talk somewhere else?"

"I think puppets are rather charming," I said, watching her closely. *I was correct. I had to be correct.*

"Macaroni! They're creepy. Cut to the chase, girls. I don't have all day and, let's be frank, neither do you. Fact is, I saw a paddy wagon on my way here—pointed in this direction."

Uh-oh.

"Why was Rudy's bedroom window open that afternoon?" I asked, keeping my voice down although it was probably unnecessary, since everyone was engrossed in the three pigs. "That's how we heard your argument so clearly, you know."

"Oh. That. That was because I'd been smoking in the bedroom earlier and it always made Rudy absolutely ratty. He hates—hated—the smell."

"Except . . . I've never seen you smoking a cigarette," I said.

"What did you say?"

"You frequently mention a hankering for a cigarette," I said, "and I've seen you with a certain gold lighter in your hand, but I have never actually seen you smoking."

Coral's beautiful elfin face hardened, her lips thinning to a knife's edge. "Well, you don't really know me very well, do you? I shouldn't have come here to meet you. You girls are cuckoo." She spun on her heel and strode away across the green.

Berta and I followed.

"What is this about cigarettes and lighters?" Berta asked me, breathless.

"You'll see."

Coral crossed Church Street and glided along the sidewalk, forcing everyone in her path to veer away. We lost sight of her as a motorcar rumbled past. When it had gone, she was nowhere to be seen.

"Where is she?" I said.

"Perhaps she went into the Old Whaler's Inn."

"No—look. There she is. She's going into the alleyway beside Flintock's Groceries."

We crossed the street, hurried along the sidewalk, and turned into the narrow cobbled alleyway. Coral was almost at the end, where it opened out onto another street.

"I know how you killed Rudy," I called after her. My voice echoed off the silver-shingled buildings.

Coral's shoulders hunched. She stopped, and turned. "I haven't the foggiest what you're getting at, sweetie," she called back.

"You're a ventriloquist."

"Ah!" Berta murmured. "A *ventriloquist.*"

Coral's face pinched, but she didn't run.

"You and Glenn Monroe grew up together, didn't you?" I said. Berta and I were five paces off, then four, then three. We stopped. "Your families worked in vaudeville and puppet theater—something a lot like Menchen's Manikins, I'm guessing? What luck that we happened to see them today—it has made everything snap into place for me. Both you and Glenn learned how to produce sound effects and to expertly imitate voices. Glenn was your oldest friend—your *only* friend, as far as I can make out. He knew too much, didn't he? He knew what you'd done to Rudy, or he was close to figuring it out, so you poisoned his Alkacine. Your heart must be icy indeed to have been able to kill your only friend."

Berta said, "Perhaps, Mrs. Woodby, we should save the philosophizing for a different time. Regarding the cigarettes—"

"Mrs. Lundgren and I found a fragment of golden paper outside the conservatory," I said, "and we believed it to be the discarded wrapping of either stick greasepaint or artist's oil pastels. No. It was from a *firecracker*."

Berta and Coral both gasped.

"An awfully basic theatrical sound effect," I said, "one that we should've caught on to much earlier."

Coral stood frozen.

"But why don't we start at the beginning," I said. "When you caused Rudy to leave the hunting party and return to the house when he realized—perhaps you pointed it out!—that he did not have his lucky rabbit's foot with him. He hurried back to the house and you followed, claiming that he'd need help finding it. You followed him up to his room and shot him in the head. Everyone in the house heard the shot, but we all thought it was something else. A meat mallet or a champagne cork or a different gunshot from the hunting party in the field. Then, as Rudy lay dead, you employed your ventriloquist's skills to feign an argument with Rudy. *You* played both parts, Coral. Then you set up Rudy's suicide note, placed a door key on the floor just by the door, left the room, and locked it from the outside with a second key. When the police broke down the door, they assumed it was locked from the inside and that they knocked the key to the floor. Once again, misdirection. You're awfully clever at misdirection, Coral. So clever, we never even considered the possibility that you could be the killer."

"Oh shut up, you thick-ankled little meddler," Coral snarled.

"After that, you went down the back stairs and into the conservatory, lit a firecracker with that gold lighter of yours—the firecracker must have had a very long and slow-burning fuse, to buy you a minute or so to get away and establish your alibi before the explosion. You hurried to the drawing room—unknowingly passing Glenn in the study on the way—and encountered Mrs. Lundgren and me there. Very soon after that, we heard what we believed to be the fatal gunshot."

"And," Berta said, eyes agleam with comprehension, "since Clementine Brezka happened to open one of the drawing room windows a few minutes earlier, we also smelled gunpowder, which we mistakenly attributed to the fact that Rudy's bedroom window, just above us, had also been open."

"Then there's the treasure," I said. "You capitalized on the legend of the Montgomery treasure to distract us even further from the truth. More misdirection. You planted that book, *Lost Treasures of the United States,* in Glenn Monroe's valise, knowing that it would be found after he died, and that people might begin to wonder if his death—and Rudy's—was really to do with the treasure. And I admit, Mrs. Lundgren and I bought it. At least for a time. You were the ghost, too. You did all that theatrical moaning and groaning, you pushed me at the top of the stairs, and *you* hit me on the head with the rock out in the forest. You overheard Lord Sudley arranging to meet me to spy on the Isobel Bradford impostor at her holiday cottage, and you followed us. Were you wearing that smashing cream-colored coat last night, too? But here's the bit I haven't completely worked out yet. You had an accomplice—you *must* have had. Someone who fired that first shot, out with the hunting party, to disguise the one that actually killed Rudy. It was Lord Sudley, wasn't it, Coral? Rudy's bedroom window must have been open so that you could signal to each other, time the gunshots precisely. The one thing I can't understand is your motive, though. You didn't seem to gain much from killing Rudy. You weren't even in his will. Was it jealousy on Lord Sudley's part, and revenge on your side?"

The purr of an engine drew all our eyes to the far end of the alleyway. An ink-black motorcar—was that a Duesenberg or a Rolls-Royce?—rolled to a stop.

"Someone's here to get you," I said to Coral.

"Wrong. Someone's here to get *you*." Coral whipped a pistol from her handbag and pressed it to Berta's cheek.

29

I'm just like a lioness, sweeties," Coral said. "I go for the weakling in the herd." She smiled at Berta. "And that's you, old lady. Now, you're going to get into that motorcar, or you're toast. Go on. March!"

Berta shuffled toward the motorcar.

"You, too!" Coral barked at me.

I followed Berta, with Coral just behind us.

It was a Rolls-Royce. I couldn't see who was behind the wheel. Lord Sudley? Miss Murden? Theo? Clementine?

"Go on," Coral said. "Get in, or I'll shoot."

"Murder in broad daylight?" I said. "That isn't really your style."

"There won't be any witnesses. Every last yokel in town is watching that puppet show."

Berta opened the door and climbed in. Coral nudged me inside, too, the snout of her gun on my neck.

No one else was in the backseat. And behind the wheel was . . .

"Mwinyi?" I gasped.

Of course. Mwinyi. He *had* fired that shot, after all. Eustace was innocent.

Doughnuts churned in my stomach. I may have cracked the case, but Berta and I had played right into these villains' hands! First, Berta must've given Mwinyi the idea to lie about Lord Sudley firing that gunshot, during their telephone conversation this morning. And then when I'd telephoned Coral, I cemented her suspicions that we knew too much.

That we had to be eliminated.

Mwinyi was popping open the glove box, taking out . . .

Another gun.

Beside me, Berta was rigid with fright. I didn't feel precisely happy-go-lucky myself.

Coral climbed in beside me and slammed the door. "Only the old one," she said to Mwinyi. "I don't want to have to drag both of them around."

What did *that* mean?

Mwinyi leaned over the seat and thumped Berta across the temple with his gun. She uttered *"ouff,"* and sagged against the window.

"You monsters!" I cried. "Berta!" I shook her. *"Berta!"*

No answer. Her eyes were shut, and blood trickled from her hairline. But she was breathing. Still breathing.

"Drive," Coral said without inflection.

The motorcar rolled forward.

"Help!" I screamed. "HELP!" But the streets of Carvington were deserted; everyone was on the village green, and—

"Shut up," Coral said. "And if you try to make a break for it, I'm killing the old bird."

"Where are you taking us?"

"That's a good question, sweetie." To Mwinyi, she said, "Let's go to Theo's mud pit out in the woods. The one he's finished with." She leaned back on the seat. "Those stupid mud pits could hold a dozen bodies each."

"There is something the matter with you," I said. "You're missing something."

"Yeah, it's called a heart, honey. I was only about three years old when my mother told me I was born without one. You know what? It suits me just fine. I look around at all you other women with your sniveling noses and bleeding hearts, and I think, *whew*, lucky me. 'Cause without a heart, there's nothing that can stop me from getting to the top. I've always used men to get what I want—you oughta try it sometime, Lola. It's easier than plugging away yourself. Make them do the grunt work, that's what I say. They're all a bunch of lunkheads who think girls are like game—hunt 'em down, bag 'em, and move on to the next. So I thought, heck, I'll beat them at their little sport. *I'll* hunt *them*."

I watched Mwinyi's rigid shoulders, the back of his curly head with the chauffeur's cap as he motored swiftly along the main road. He was aiding and abetting a murderess—and, quite frankly, a crackpot. Why?

Coral seemed to read my thoughts. "It wasn't until Rudy hired Mwinyi last spring that I found a man who's my equal, a man who is also willing to do whatever it takes to get to the top. I had been thinking of trying to get my claws into Rudy, matrimonially speaking, even though it seemed like a lost cause. But then, once we were all in Africa, I started dreaming really big. Why not have a sheik like Mwinyi, a pile of raw diamonds—Mwinyi stole those from a fellow in Africa—*and* the Montgomery fortune? Shouldn't the spoils go to the girl who's clever enough to figure out how to take it all?"

Winslow Bradford must have known something about those stolen diamonds—hence his deathbed remorse—but he must also have believed his friend Rudy was behind the smuggling. That's why he never told anyone the truth—to protect his friend.

Coral went on, "Rudy told me he had a bastard son in Carvington, a wimpish college guy, and that he meant to leave everything to this wimp when he died. *Bingo,* I thought. Wimpy, brainy types are sitting ducks for girls like me. They've got no experience. We got married at City Hall in Manhattan—"

"*Married,*" I muttered. "*Of course.*" Hadn't Miss Murden said Coral and Theo were bickering like an old married couple at the séance?

"—and kept it hush-hush. I told him I had to let his dad down easy and everything, to give me some time."

The Rolls-Royce was turning, and we went through the gates of Montgomery Hall and started up the drive.

Coral said, "Anyway, I returned to America as Rudy's bit of cake. Mwinyi came, too, of course, and so did our scrumptious diamonds, sealed up in that rhinoceros trophy. We thought we'd just keep them in there. Save them for a rainy day, you know, or at least until after we figured out how to sell them."

"You must have panicked when Berta and I found the diamonds," I said. "And when we lost them."

"I was simply out of my mind, sweetie, but I had to keep my cool, didn't I? I just made sure Theo pushed for their return. I understand they're in the cove now. Maybe I'll make Theo get in there with a diver's helmet and fish them out." She laughed.

"Theo is your puppet," I said.

"Yeah." Coral smiled. "I guess he is."

"You made Theo hire Ralph Oliver to tail us."

"That's right. I heard you arguing with some fellow on the telephone and after you left, had the operator reconnect me. I figured if I stirred your man troubles into the mix, it would make things that much stickier for you. Now I realize I should've bumped you off first thing."

"Does Theo know you killed his father?"

"I think he's getting suspicious. It's been tough for me to be sweet to him this past week—my nerves are like electrical wires. And he's always had his suspicions about Mwinyi—hasn't he, my darling? So I'm gonna have to get rid of Theo sooner than I thought. But—first things first."

Mwinyi had turned off the drive and was bumping across the wet grassy field, toward the line of bare trees.

For the first time, real fear zinged through me. That blank, bunny rabbit kind of fear. The fear of prey.

No. I would *not* allow these frosty-hearted villains to do away with Berta and me. Yet . . . they held the guns.

We were in the soup again, and it was coming to a boil. How to get out? Think, Lola, think!

We rumbled closer to the trees. Closer.

Think.

Well, everyone has a fatal flaw. I'd begin there. All right. Coral was vain, heartless, and cruel. But she had done everything, not for lust or pride or revenge, but out of basic greed.

Greed.

I slid my fingers inside my coat pocket and felt for my coin purse. Coral, frowning out the windshield, didn't notice.

Mwinyi rolled into the trees, parked, and switched off the ignition. Leaving the key in the panel, he got out and circled around to open Coral's door.

Droplets from branches overhead splatted on the motorcar's roof. A tendril of exhaust drifted, phantomlike, away into the misty tree trunks.

"Get out," Coral said, nudging me with her gun barrel.

I got out. That big dark muddy hole was *right there*, yawning wide, smelling of worms and rot. There was the pile of excavated dirt, on which leaned a mud-caked shovel. Theo must have forgotten it.

Coral and Mwinyi stood side by side, both guns aimed at my noggin.

"There's been quite a lot of talk about the Montgomery treasure," I said, struggling to speak calmly. "I wonder if Theo's been digging for treasure all this while."

"Don't be stupid. He's digging for his vile old artifacts."

"Everyone knows the treasure is money," I said, "but no one knows what kind. But I heard that pirates used to stop along this coast, and—I have this on good authority—the treasure is gold bullion. Thousands'—perhaps *millions'*—worth of gold bullion."

"Shut up and get down in that hole," Coral said to me. "Hop to it."

"Not really my idea of a good time, but all right," I said. I leaned over the hole a little, and discreetly dropped in the curl of firecracker paper. It fluttered to the bottom and—hallelujah—landed gold-side up. "Goodness! What's that?"

"What're you yakking about?" Coral said.

"Down in the hole—why—is it—! What a coincidence! Could it possibly be . . . *gold?*"

Coral and Mwinyi locked eyes.

"Gold?" Coral's tongue darted out to wet her lips. "Where?" She and Mwinyi, still with guns cocked, stepped over and bent to peer into the hole.

"It is gold," Coral breathed. "Mwinyi! *Gold!*"

Meanwhile, I had slipped over to the dirt pile, hefted the shovel—

Coral was halfway down into the hole, mud smeared across the back of her creamy wool coat, when I whacked the back of her head with the shovel. She crumpled into the pit. Mwinyi swung around to face me, gun poised, just as I wound up again. *Clang.* I got him in the side of the head. He fell on top of Coral.

I dropped the shovel, ran to the motorcar, and switched on the ignition. "Don't worry, Berta!" I babbled. "We're on our way to the hospital!"

Mwinyi was climbing out of the hole, still with that bally gun at the ready, as I zigzagged away into the trees. As I careened onto the drive, a blue police car roared into view. I parked, got out, put up my hands, and, breathing hard, I waited.

The journey back to Manhattan that night was a blur. Ralph drove my motorcar, and I sat with Cedric on my lap in the passenger seat. Berta slept in the backseat the entire way, white gauze looped around her head like a tiara. The doctor had sewn two stitches just at the hairline, and she had taken aspirins washed down (*not* per the doctor's orders) with gin.

I'll back up. There were the Carvington police herding Coral and Mwinyi into a paddy wagon, my ambulance ride with Berta to the hospital, and police questionings at the station. It turned out that Nat from Flintock's Groceries had telephoned the police after seeing Berta and me being stuffed at gunpoint into the late Rudy Montgomery's Rolls-Royce. Then Ralph, who had been searching frantically for us, had showed up with Cedric at the police station. There was the hasty packing of Berta's and my suitcases at the Old Whaler's Inn and settling our bill with Knobby Wrists.

I was fine. Nervy, exhausted, but also elated at having cracked the case. My only regret was not having figured things out sooner. Perhaps Glenn Monroe would be alive still.

"I heard that sigh," Ralph said, glancing over at me in the passenger seat. "You did your best, kid, and you did one heck of a job. It'll be in all the papers tomorrow. Brace yourself."

"I *am* bracing myself," I said, "but not for that. We must still face Lem Fitzpatrick about those diamonds." Jimmy the Ant had vanished—Berta had mumbled something about Canada—and Theo knew the diamonds were in the bottom of his cove. The diamonds weren't Theo's, of course, but the little cockroach would keep them since we had no way of tracking down their original owner in Africa. "Lem is going to be sore with Jimmy for stealing the diamonds from his safe, but he's also going to be sore at *us* for thwarting his two thugs—I don't even know if they've gotten out of the Carvington jail yet." They had been found wandering the estate early that morning and arrested for trespassing. "On the other hand, we did mail the photographs he requested, so perhaps he'll decide we're square." I rubbed my forehead. "It's all a mess. And I really don't wish to be in a mess with a top-brass gangster."

"We'll think of something," Ralph said. "Don't worry about it."

I didn't miss the flex of his jaw.

We motored on and on along the dark, twisty coastal road. Just two days ago, the drive up, with the squeaking windshield wipers, gusts of rain, and the slip of the Duesy's balding tires, had felt dismal and precarious. Now, those very same things—even the balding tires— seemed to carry a whiff of adventure. I could take care of myself. I knew that I could. And I could, in my own secret ways, also take care of Ralph. But *this* was something else, this sense that if Ralph and I were side by side, not only were the grimmest circumstances tolerable, but the big wide world would offer up all its freshness and potential. Maybe that feeling was love. Maybe it was hope. Maybe it was friendship. Maybe it was all of the above.

"What about the Montgomery treasure?" Ralph asked presently.

"I'm not sure." I stroked Cedric's neck fuzz. He was out stone cold. "Perhaps it's only a legend—the stories are certainly vague enough. But . . . I wonder. Did you ever notice Coral's jewelry, all those white beads?"

"Sure. Necklaces and bracelets and earrings. Somehow didn't seem flashy enough for that kind of girl."

"That was wampum. Shell beads. I remember it from a history book I read in high school. The Indians used wampum as a sort of currency, and then when the English colonists arrived, *they* used it for currency, too. It was money, you see. And guess what wampum is made of?"

"Oyster shells?"

"Bingo. And there are oysters galore buried underwater in Sewant Cove." I shrugged. "Or maybe it's pirate's bullion or deeds to tracts of royally owned land in Maine or, who knows, a sack of wooden nickels. In a way, it's nice to know there are some things we can't figure out. As long as those things aren't harming anyone, I mean."

"Yeah." Ralph kept his eyes on the road. "A little mystery and magic never hurt anyone."

30

I woke to ringing. Dratted ringing. Ugh. I rolled over on the sofa and snuggled up to Cedric's fluff on my pillow.

More ringing.

I struggled upright and staggered through my apartment to the telephone.

"Ngh?" I mumbled, my eyes still glued shut.

"Lola? Lola, are you drunk? It is eight o'clock in the morning! Do not tell me that you have been out all night in one of those illegal liquor establishments!"

"Hello, Mother." Oh, golly. *No.* Mother had returned from Paris. "How was the journey? Refreshing?"

"Of course not, Lola. You know I cannot abide those staterooms. They make one feel as though one were in prison, I don't care how many gold tassels they sew to the cushions. But Lillian's wedding gown is complete—we brought it back with us, and I hope she quits the cream cakes or she won't fit into it; the wedding is still six months away, long enough for her to simply explode—and her trousseau is being sewn this very instant by a fleet of Paris's finest seam-stresses, although I was disappointed to learn that half of them were actually from Spain. I thought I was paying for *French* seam-stresses. Now, then. You have addressed and mailed the invitations?"

"Of course." I regarded the box of invitations and dust bunnies at my feet.

"And the caterer. Did you select and reserve the services of a caterer?"

"Yes."

"Which one?"

"Oh. Um, it'll be a surprise. When I see you."

"I don't know why you insist upon surprises and intrigue and hugger-muggery, Lola, I really don't, although I strongly suspect it has to do with the oceans of rubbishy fiction you have been devouring since your adolescence. Very well. Come to see me at home at seven o'clock this evening. We'll have dinner—I'll tell Marguerite to make clear broth and a vegetable terrine, since Lillian and, most likely, you, could benefit from a light repast."

"Sounds positively scrumdiddly, Mother. Good-bye." I slung the receiver in its cradle.

Oh dear. Time to snap to it.

Sometime in the past twelve hours, a mad plan had taken root in my mind. It was a long shot, riddled with problems and, perhaps, a touch of risk.

I ran it by Berta, who was preparing to go out.

"It is indeed mad," she said, buttoning her coat. "Although I can-not think of any alternatives. We must attempt it. Now, I am off to the printer's to have new business cards done up. I will ask them to change our motto to 'No job too tricky,' if you approve."

"Sure."

"And then I am going to market for more bacon and eggs. When I return, we must get to work. Mrs. Snyder has compiled a list of fourteen potential clients whom we must ring back without delay." Berta stooped to gather up the mail that the postman had jammed through the slot earlier. "Please sort this. We must become more systematic."

She left, and I perused the mail while drinking coffee at the kitchen table. Bills, mostly, but also a letter from Eustace, Lord Sudley.

Funny. I hadn't seen him since the day of the séance, when he'd left the Old Whaler's Inn in a snit. I had swung from suspecting he had poisoned me, to thinking he was Coral's accomplice, to not knowing *what* to think of him.

I tore open the envelope. There was a plump bank check, and a handwritten note.

Dear Lola,

It has taken me a day of reflection to come to the conclusion that I treated you in a rather beastly fashion. When you turned down my proposal of marriage, you see, my pride was wounded to the quick. That is the Achilles' heel of men, I daresay: pride as soft as tallow. I wish you to know that I really believed myself to be in love with you, although now I see that I may have been simply too caught up in the glamour of it all—American gumshoes, murder, and all that—to really see straight. I do believe you are a queen among women, and I will always think of you with a bit of a sigh. However, today at my hotel I happened to meet a most fascinating American heiress who is also embarking for Liverpool tomorrow, and I think she will help me to forget you.

I fancy I also owe you an explanation about my motives for having enlisted your help in retrieving my rhinoceros trophy—which is already stowed safely in a crate of straw in the ship's hold. The trouble is, I am an absolutely beastly shot. Oh, I went on hunting trips with Rudy and Winslow, but that was because

I enjoyed the camaraderie and the great starry skies of the out-
back. But it was a rare occasion when I hit anything. Now it has
come to pass that I've been nominated for the very select Mount
Olympus Club in London. This is a gentlemen's club that holds,
arguably, more social status than any other of its kind in, per-
haps, the world. Far be it from me to turn the nomination
down. Unfortunately, one requirement for admission is to pres-
ent to the selection committee a hunting trophy of great merit, a
trophy that one has killed oneself. You can probably guess that
the one and only meritorious animal I ever killed was that rhi-
noceros, and that was by sheer luck. And as I am a gentleman
and therefore a man of honor, I could never pass off as my own a
trophy that someone else bagged. There, then, is the reason I so
urgently required the rhinoceros trophy, and I thank you and
Mrs. Lundgren for retrieving it for me and, of course, for bringing
poor old Rudy's murderer to justice.

Sincerely,
Eustace, Lord Sudley

Well, what do you know?

At one o'clock, Berta and I clambered out of a taxicab in front
of Ambrose's Confectionery-Caterer on Forty-fourth Street. Ralph
was waiting for us on the sidewalk, fedora dipped, hands in overcoat
pockets, shoulders lifted against the wind.

Cedric bobbed up and down on Ralph's shins, and Ralph bent to
give him a scratch. "Ready to go in?"

Berta nodded.

Honestly, I was a bit frazzled, and it wasn't only because of the
Mad Plan. I had managed to get all Lillian's wedding invitations
mailed off, but there was a chance that one of our séance invitations had been mailed by mistake to Society Matron Catherine Von
Trappen.

"Ready," I said.

Ambrose's put Delguzzo's to shame. The tables were daintier, the upholstery more marshmallowy, the chandeliers more migraine-inducing, and the ladies-of-leisure clientele wore fashions so new, they hadn't yet been pictured in *Vogue*.

Berta led the way toward the back. I followed with Cedric in my arms, and Ralph was just behind me.

Every last lady-of-leisure watched Ralph as he went. Every last pair of lady lungs ceased to breathe.

And then it was *my* turn to stop breathing, because we had arrived at Lem Fitzpatrick's table. He hunched at the tiny table alone, smoking moodily, making his expensive suit look cheap.

"Well, if it isn't dollface and her circus troupe," he said.

Berta, Ralph, and I sat.

"So," Lem said, blowing smoke, "you said on the telephone you had a business proposition for me?"

"That is correct," Berta said. She had made the telephone call earlier, somehow managing to get Lem on the line after calling all three branches of Ambrose's. "You tell him, Mrs. Woodby," she whispered.

I took a big breath. I explained how Jimmy the Ant had brought us the diamonds and fled for parts unknown—

"It was a gesture of love," Berta said.

"Uh-huh," Lem said.

—and how, as the result of a motorcar chase with Lem's own henchpersons, the diamonds were underwater. "It's a shallow cove," I said, "but it would be difficult, if not impossible, to retrieve those diamonds in a discreet fashion, particularly since the owner of the cove, Theo Wainwright, has surely launched his own retrieval effort. Which is why we have come to you with an alternative proposition."

Lem flicked ash into a sugar bowl. "A booby prize, huh?"

I plowed forward. "My sister, Mr. Fitzpatrick, is to be married this spring in what is being spoken of as the society event of the season. My parents—Mr. and Mrs. Virgil DuFey of Park Avenue—are spending an appalling sum on the nuptials, and they naturally require a caterer. A caterer of great distinction and style that is able to roll out wave after wave of savories and dainties for a party of five hundred or so. A caterer who not only stands to earn a great deal from the proceeds, but who stands to rise to the very tippy-top of New York City's society caterer gold-star list." On my lap, hidden beneath the table, I crossed my fingers.

Lem didn't answer for two full drags and exhalations of his gasper. Finally, he said. "Okay—"

I could breathe again.

"—'cause I like the photographs you sent down. They didn't come out too nice, but getting those shots took guts. I like dames with guts. And I guess your crazy detective work shut down that oyster-poaching operation up in Carvington, so I'm back on top of the oyster biz here in New York. I like that, too. So, okay. You're on for the catering deal."

"Thanks awfully, Mr. Fitzpatrick," I said, unclasping my handbag. I filled out the blank deposit check my father had given me ages ago, and slid it over. It was as crumpled as a hankie, but Lem didn't comment on that, and the four of us sealed the deal by clinking teacups of gin. "You won't regret it," I said.

A schoolmarmish little voice in the back of my head said, *He won't regret it, but you probably will.*

Back outside, the clouds had sunk lower. Berta went to the curb to hail a taxicab.

"Want to go out after you have dinner with your mother?" Ralph asked me. "I'll take you dancing. Help you forget all the bad stuff."

Frigid wind whipped down Fifth Avenue, slicing through my coat.

I shivered. "You know, I think tonight's a night for cuddling with one's sweetie in front of a crackling fire. Not dancing."

Ralph brushed the backs of his knuckles across my cold cheek. "Crackling fire? Cuddling? Okay. I think I can handle that."

As Berta waved for a taxi, as Cedric tangled his leash around our ankles and snagged my last good pair of silk stockings, Ralph and I kissed. Nope, it wasn't picture-perfect. A moth had fluttered out of my fur collar, and we had motorcar honks and the scent of roasting frankfurters for ambience. But Ralph was in my arms again, the Discreet Retrieval Agency's future was rosy, and I held out hope that my mother would never know that her younger daughter's society wedding of the year was to be catered by a gangster.

It wasn't perfect, but it was all mine.